PRIDE OF
THE BIMBOS

PRIDE OF
THE BIMBOS

John Sayles

An Atlantic Monthly Press Book
Little, Brown and Company — Boston – Toronto

SECOND PRINTING

T 07/75

ATLANTIC–LITTLE, BROWN BOOKS
ARE PUBLISHED BY
LITTLE, BROWN AND COMPANY
IN ASSOCIATION WITH
THE ATLANTIC MONTHLY PRESS

LIBRARY OF CONGRESS CATALOGING IN PUBLICATION DATA

Sayles, John, 1950–
    Pride of the Bimbos.

    "An Atlantic-Monthly Press book."
    I. Title.
PZ4.S27534Pr   [PS3569.A95]   813'.5'4   74-34177
ISBN 0-316-77230-5

Designed by Susan Windheim

Published simultaneously in Canada
by Little, Brown & Company (Canada) Limited

PRINTED IN THE UNITED STATES OF AMERICA

Tuesday

1

The morning haze came alive with gold as the sun promised to appear behind the Ferris wheel. Color crept across the carnival grounds, gaudily blinking from the booths and trailers, glinting off the frozen rides. A small man in a three-piece suit and a red-haired boy walked before it. They skirted a baseball diamond stamped in green and dark blood red and headed down a slope to a tangle of pine. The small man stopped several times to bend and flick the grass dew from his shoes with the side of his hand. He and the boy were the same height.

"Listen kid," he said, "couldn't you just tell what it is first?"

"Then it wouldn't be a suprazz," said the boy.

"What kind of surprise is it that I have to carry my piece at seven in the morning?"

"You'll see."

They reached the woods and the boy poked around till he found a marked footpath. They could hear a stream running up ahead.

"Seven in the morning and the kid takes me on a safari."

"It's not far."

They went in deeper, leaves and needles dripping, the stream sound growing louder, then hooked abruptly round a bend. They were met by a towering figure half-hidden in the shade of a pine. The boy started to speak but the man pushed him down into the brush at the side of the path and leaped in after. He jammed his back against a tree trunk, pinning the boy flat on the ground with his leg, and fumbled in his jacket till he unsnagged a gun.

"Hold it!" said the boy, trying to squirm free, "That's it! That's the suprazz!"

"What?" The man was frantically working an ammunition clip into the gun.

"The suprazz. It's a target."

"A target." The man's breath shuddered out of him.

"I put it there. Nailed it up."

The man turned and slowly peeked from behind the trunk. The figure was motionless in the pine's shadow. The man stepped out into the path and came cautiously forward, gun thrust ahead of him, using both hands to keep it steady. He entered the shadow. A long thin cardboard cutout of a man was nailed to the tree. SAMMY "STILT-MAN" SLIGH said the faded banner painted on its chest. The face was decomposed to a dark gray.

"Shit!"

There was a crack, the gun hopped and a gouge of white wood appeared in Sammy's belly.

"I didn't mean to spook you." The boy had come out on the path behind him.

"You shouldn't pounce things on a guy."

"I'm sorry."

"There's some surprises a guy doesn't need."

"You mad at me?"

The man took a deep breath and lowered the gun to his side. "Nah. You just got this innocent tree plugged with lead is all."

"Found it in the shed under the roller coaster. I meant it for target practice. So you be good an ready if he should catch up to you."

4

The man snorted a laugh. "Thanks kid, but I don't need it. I shoot just fine."

"But you never practice."

"You seen too many tales of the Old West. That crack shot stuff is a lot of malarkey. It's not a question of shooting straight. It's who sees who first. That's why I asked you to keep your eyes open for me."

"Is he that tall?" The boy nodded to the cutout.

"Almost. Taller than your daddy anyways."

"Is he that dark?"

"Darker. Black as a coal shaft at midnight."

"An he's quiet."

"Comes like a cat."

"Cept his eyes don't shine."

"You got him. That's the man."

"You think he'll really come for you?"

"He might. You can't be too careful."

"Then whah won't you let me tell the others?"

"Make them too jumpy. And if Mr. Bob didn't like the idea there goes my job. It's better this way. Just you and me."

"Yuh."

The man snapped the ammunition clip from the gun and handed both to the boy. "Now you run these back up to the van and stick them in my trunk. Then meet me up by the road. We want to catch that ride and get in and out before the stores get crowded."

"Okay."

"And hey —"

"Huh?"

"No more surprises. Save a lot of wear and tear on the woods."

The boy held the gun out away from his body, his thin arm straining a little with the weight of it, and disappeared back up the path.

The man turned to the cutout. "Well, Cardboard," he said fingering the hole in its stomach, "at least you know I'm for real. You and the kid."

5

2

Small black children warred about the pumps, hurling clumps of redclay at each other. As in any war the civilians got the worst of it, chickens fled in terror from careless feet and bursting clods. The pumps were the only cover in the yard, they bore no marking but for redclay wounds. Whatever brand of gas they had once advertised was long since faded. A large black woman in a sleeveless T-shirt looked out through the window of the unpainted store.

There was an abrupt cease-fire. A purply-red car came rolling in, a big, new-looking car. The kind of car you might see in magazine pictures. It hummed quietly and then stopped. A man got out, a man half again as tall as a man should be. He was dressed head to toe in purply and purply-red clothes and his skin, too, was the dark, dark shade that local people called purple. It was that black. The man's eyes were steady but slightly red, like he hadn't been to sleep in a long time.

The large woman came from the store, frowning and crossing her arms over her chest. She seemed to take forever, as if she were on a morning stroll and hadn't seen the man. She stopped a few yards away.

"Hep you?"

"I need some gas."

6

"Got no gas."

"What's in the pumps then?"

"Nuffin. They stop the gas three-fo year ago."

The purply man sighed. The children and the chickens, growing brave, surrounded the car. The children watched the man from the corners of their eyes, ready to bolt away if threatened. They stood shyly, one bare foot covering the other, peeping through the tinted window and maybe fingering a quick line in the film of morning dew that had begun to evaporate from the car. The chickens were bolder, testing the tires for air and walking underneath to check the suspension.

"What do you sell here?"

"Nuffin. Useta be a store. Jus lives here now."

"I need to know," said the tall man, "if there was a carnival through here lately."

"Carnibal?" The woman frowned more deeply, suspicious.

"Like a circus. With rides and games and exhibitions and all that. Did one come through here a while back?"

"We never had nothin like that round here. Nothin like that." The man reminded her of the way her daddy had once described a hustlin man. Only this one wasn't high-yellow and his hair wasn't greased back. "You from Atlanter?"

That would explain it. They had all types of things come out of Atlanta.

"No M'am."

"What you name?"

"Dred."

"Draid. Draid who?"

"Dred is enough."

The man turned to his car and the children all backed up a step. "Could you tell me where I can find some gas?"

"Highway," said the woman. "You a singer?"

That would explain it. Singers on the radio made all kinds of money and didn't know what to do with it, got theirselfs famous and didn't know how to act.

"No M'am."

7

The children clustered around a sharp-faced little boy and began to whisper, never taking their eyes off the tall man. They nudged at the boy but he wouldn't step forward.

"Could you tell me how to get back to the highway?"

"Go the way you goin. You get there."

The man thanked her and went to his car and all the children and chickens scattered but for the sharp-faced little boy. The man scrunched himself into the seat and started the motor humming. The boy stood back as he closed the door. The boy knocked timidly on the window, then flinched back from the sound it made as it slid down.

The man looked at him, waiting.

"Mista," he said, but his voice broke. He tried again.

"Mista," he said, "you a Affican?"

The muscles about the man's lips bunched as if he were going to smile. "You got it child," he said. "That's just what I am." And was gone.

That explained it.

3

Bryce Culpepper squatted on his fitting stool, knees and shoulders almost touching, pants cuffs ridden up to reveal a garter of hairless flesh over each sock. He craned his neck to work the air conditioning out of it. He was alone in the Junior Booterie, knowing how painful and useless it would be to unwind his lanky self with the afternoon rush of bats and brats yet to come. It was better to stay cramped, to scuttle along like a baseball catcher until he absolutely had to straighten to pluck a box from the shelves or work the cash register. Some job. Of course there were fringe benefits. There was the chance to flirt with the young mothers, the chance to look up their summer dresses while fitting the little ones' shoes. They knew, thought Bryce, they knew and they wanted it. Bryce sat on his stool and thought about women. His hands dangled to the floor between his thighs and he seemed to be searching the bottom row for something, though his eyes were closed.

The entrance bell jangled him awake. Two kids, unescorted, a skinny and a fatty. Supermarket tennis shoes with tape wound to keep the soles from flapping and sixty-dollar wingtips. Wingtips?

The fatty also had a business suit and a cigarette hanging from his lip. He was no kid but a little man. A midget.

My, my, thought Bryce Culpepper, nothin like a little sideshow before the main event.

He could tell that the skinny one, the boy, was trash, sand and sawgrass from heel to toe. But the midget was a Jew-looking little customer, from New York or at least Atlanta.

"Can I hep you ginnlemin?"

"Shoes," said the midget, "for the kid here."

New York, the voice was definitely New York. To Bryce everything north of Valdosta was either New York or Atlanta and he prided himself on his ability to tell the difference. "Inny special style?"

The midget hooked his thumbs in his belt and cocked his head to the boy. "Denzel?"

The boy shrugged. "Just like these I got are fine. You know, sneakers."

Atlanta, thought Bryce, how'd these two ever get together? The boy pretended to look around the store but the midget looked right through Bryce. Tough-looking little monkey. Face was almost familiar although it wasn't a famous-looking face. "Whynch you sit down here, sonny, and we'll have a looksee what your footsize is."

"Seven and a half narrow," said the midget before Bryce could find the slide measure. The boy sat and began to undo his laces, scattering little bits of dried redclay on the carpet. Bryce scooted over to the tennis shoes on his stool and pulled a box from the second shelf. The boy's feet were as bad as Bryce had expected them to be.

"Just slip these on and I'll lace them up for you."

"I can lace."

Damn kids acted like they were doing you a big favor with their old stinky feet.

The midget was staring himself down in the mirror. He stood with feet planted apart, thumbs in belt, head tilted to the left and cigarette ash lengthening toward the floor. He carried his eyeballs low in their pouches, tobacco-stained eyeballs spider-cracked with red. A tough little monkey. He snorted a laugh through his nose, then turned abruptly to catch Bryce sharing his reflection. If looks were bullets, thought Bryce, I'm a splatter on the back wall. He jerked his eyes to the boy who was getting the laces uneven like they always did when they tied their own. And god*dam* if that midget didn't get more familiar looking every second.

"Tie em good and tight now. Atsa boy. Now whynch you take a little walk, see how they feel?"

The boy stood and thrust his hands into his pockets and strode off in the parody of a walk people use to test the fitness of new shoes. Bryce turned to the little man with his most congenial of shoe-clerk smiles and asked had he met him someplace before?

"Nope," said the little man, "You haven't."

"I'd just swear I seen your face before." Not to mention your stubby little body.

"Nope. I don't know you. Never seen your face. Faces used to be my game." The midget came closer and looked down coolly. If faces had flies, thought Bryce, mine is hanging open. "Nope, Junior, we never met before."

Junior?

The boy came back nodding and making the high shrugging sounds that boys made if their new shoes didn't hurt enough to bother complaining about. Bryce idly squashed the quarter-inch of vacant toe space with his thumb and let one eye wander to the midget. Junior my ass.

"What you mean by 'faces was your game'?"

"I was a private dick," said the midget. "Frisco."

Oh well, New York, San Francisco, same difference. "Detectives get to know faces pretty good?"

"Either you learn faces or you trade your suede shoes for cement ones. Sometimes your memory is the only thing between you and the bottom of the Bay. Like I said before, Junior, your face doesn't ring any bells."

The fella had a nice little style about him but he needed a good whittling down. Just a wee bit too big for his San Francisco britches. But Bryce hated to have to stand up before it was absolutely necessary.

"So! How do they seem to fit?"

"Okay. I'll take em."

"Would you like me to wrap them up or do you want to wear them?"

"Wrap em, I guess. They're kind of new looking to wear."

The boy beat him to the laces. The midget pulled a wallet from its coat pocket. *Damn* if that wasn't somebody's face.

"Listen, maybe I've seen you but you've never seen me. I mean, well" — and here Bryce produced a small, sly grin — "the circus has been through Valdosta a couple times since I moved in, and maybe —"

The midget tore the cigarette from his lips and erased Bryce's head with smoke. "Circus?"

"Yeah, well —"

"What makes you think I ever been with any circus? What do circuses want with a detective?"

The midget stared a few inches from his face. Bryce shivered a little and realized perspiration was freezing on him. The air conditioner, waiting for an answer, said hmmmmmmmmmmmm?

"Oh, right. I forgot. You're a private eye."

"Was."

"Yeah, was."

"Now I'm a ballplayer."

"Right."

Ballplayer?

He wrapped the shoes and felt eyes still glaring at him. Okay you little prick, the time is come to separate the gallons from the half-pints. Bryce Culpepper slapped the boxtop over the sneakers, clapped his hands together, said that'll be siven niney-eight and rose to his full six feet and three inches barely noticing the needles in his back. The midget didn't look up. It burned its low-pouched eyes straight into Bryce's crotch, peeled off a twenty and said take it from this, Junior. Bryce didn't like being stared at down there, he took the money and got himself behind the register.

"Pogo?" said the boy, "I thought you wanted to get yourself something too."

The midget snorted. "Kid, you can tell a man by what he sticks on his feet. You see Mickey Mouse shoes, it's a good bet there's a Mickey Mouse guy inside of them. You don't catch Pogo Burns buying shoes from anybody named Junior Booterie. You wouldn't catch me dead in what they sell here." He pocketed the change that Bryce laid in his hand. "You got those on yet? Let's blow."

When Bryce said bye now the boy grunted yuh and the midget grumbled something the bell jangled over as he flicked his cigarette butt on the pavement and heeled it to a smudge. Bryce waited a moment and then went out front to watch them disappear down the walk, the boy hopping every fourth step with the joy of having his trusted sneakers back on and the midget rolling bowlegged, a little business-suited bear. Pogo Burns, huh? Wouldn't be caught dead in our shoes.

Bryce turned and was stopped by the midget grinning up at him. Only been looking at it two weeks now. It was wearing a Shirley Temple wig, a sailor dress and bloomers, toting a baseball bat twice its size over its shoulder and standing knee-high to a man in drag who looked to have a couple inches on Bryce. Thurs. thru Tues. said the flier, Appearing at the Lowndes County Fairgrounds, The Brooklyn Bimbos in an Exhibition Softball Game. Featuring the Side-Splitting Antics of "Big Bertha" Burns.

Ballplayer my ass thought Bryce Culpepper as the air conditioning turned his armpits to ice.

4

Mr. Bob was pleased to hear his warning cough ricochet back from the tacky center field billboards. He had had to run the kid in charge of the sound system over the coals yesterday. So far during this booking he had put heat on the advance man, the concession leech, the boy who took the tickets and even the carny promoter. Mr. Bob thought of himself as a quiet soul but knew the business value of an occasional ruckus. God made sheep and God made shepherds and sometimes only a little loud barking made it clear which was which. Mr. Bob was a red-faced man to begin with but when he set his blood to boiling he was a fearsome thing to see.

Okay yokels, thought Mr. Bob, siddown cause the show's starting.

"Ladies and gentlemen, may I have your attention please." Mr. Bob's voice was milk and honey over the box. "At this time — it is our pleasure to present — di-rect from their successful tour of the Far East — concluding with this exhibition their special and limited engagement in the *great* state of Georgia — which they have accepted only as a gesture of appreciation to their many loyal fans in this area — the *Dar*lings of the Diamond — those comical cuties — baseball's most bee*you*teeful bonus babies — the world renowed Ba*rooook*lyn *Bimmmmm*boooos!"

Mr. Bob blew a whoopee siren into the mike. The team had worked its way south from its birthplace in Birmingham, hopscotching the carnivals and county fairs, and would remain in Georgia for a while. Mr. Bob looked to the dugout as the hoots and rebel yells died down. Denzel appeared and signaled that the men were ready.

"Opposing our gals today will be the champions of the Greater Valdosta Five-Man Softball League, your own — Sutler Hollow Swamp Rats! Let's hear it for em!"

Confused applause passed like a fart through a crowd. There was neither a Greater Valdosta Five-Man Softball League or a Sutler Hollow (though contributions to maintain the former would be solicited during the fifth inning). The high school boys Mr. Bob had rounded up at two dollars a head took practice swings and acknowledged their following.

"The starting lineup — for the Brooklyn Bimbos — in the outfield — a veteran of countless seasons — this babe has been around, folks — former property of the *Kan*sas City Queens — uh*Long* uhLou*ise!*"

Old reliable Lewis Crawford trotted from the dugout, curtsied to the fans in his Bloomer Girls uniform and headed for center. Lewis Crawford who had hit a steady .235 in the minors, guessing at curveballs and playing flypaper defense for most of his young life. Who touched the big leagues for a cup of coffee in '63, a year the Senators had been desperate enough to need a no-hit outfielder. Crawford who shuttled between Miami and Raleigh, Albany and Chattanooga, Fort Worth and Yuma, where the manager had offered him an equipment man's job or nothing when he got off the train. Who had changed his grip and stance hundreds of times in his career but never learned to predict whether the pitches would dip or tail off, break in or zip straight through, whether he would go up to A ball or down to C, whether the team he was with would fold or stay afloat. Six-five, soft-spoken, face cracking slightly now like an old fielder's mitt, Lewis Craw-

15

ford had swung at air in baseball's tank towns for twenty years and had nothing to show for it but a squirrelly little red-headed kid a waitress in Winston-Salem had tagged him with like a bad rap. The girl had had the good sense to git while the gitting was good, sense that never rubbed off on Lewis. Old reliable Lewis Crawford trotting out in his drag, who took twenty years to give up on his dream, and who still looked at each curveball as if this would be the one that would tell him the secret.

"At first base — a two-year veteran of the game and former utility girl for a house of *ill* repute in New Awlins, Louisiana — Pris*cill*a *Pop*fly! Popfly! And behind the plate — from old Mehico — the sweetheart of Juarez — Car*lit*a del Croutcho!"

Yowls and yoohoos as the two moseyed out together, the first sacker in curlers and the catcher thrusting an enormous air-filled prow before him.

"Now there, folks," said Mr. Bob in his sly-wink voice, "is a chest that *really* needs a protector." The catcher turned and waggled a finger at him in the box.

A. C. Porter and Knox Dickey were a pair of Okies who went for brothers. They had been raised together, ate the same gov. surplus beans, dated the same girls, stole from the same corncribs and shared the same heroes. The heroes were a center fielder from the next county named Mickey Mantle and John Dillinger, a promising young pitcher who had strayed from the basepaths long before their day. The bank robber's legend proved to be the more powerful, perhaps because he died in his prime before the legs started to go, and the two buddies shared a five-year stretch for an ill-conceived gas station boost. They called each other pardner, had half a brain between them as Mr. Bob was fond of saying, and were firm in their resolve to protect each other's back and never trust a woman. That was why Dillinger bought the farm, they would say, he didn't have a pardner he could count on.

"On the mound for the Bimbos today — our rookie sensation — a little number we picked up working as a carhop in *Oke*echobee, Florida — Miss Fastball of 1972 — and be kind fellas cause she's a little new to this kind of work — Miss — *Sally Buns!*"

Out walked the boy they all called Pitcher, just Pitcher, walking with what he thought was cool dignity. But the blond go-go dancer's wig, the cotton-titted peasant blouse and red hotpants, the boy's slim, nearly hairless arms and legs invited a lower, more leering type of call from the crowd. Pitcher with his red-volcanic pimpleface powdered over, his slight build and haughty bearing, was not, from the alcoholic distance of the cheap seats, a bad looking piece of ass. Is he or isn't she? they wondered out loud. It was an ugly reaction, thought Mr. Bob, but it brought a certain element back for more the next day and box office was the name of the game. And Pitcher refused to play it for laughs. Not a bad boy all and all, thought Mr. Bob, but no showman.

"And now — at shortstop — the *star* of the Brooklyn Bimbos — recently banned from Charlotte North Carolina for hustling Little Leaguers for nickels — the *small*est strike zone *east* of the Pecos — the *one* — the *only* — *Big! Bertha! Burns!*"

The people went apeshit as Pogo Burns trundled to his position. Pogo Burns who had appeared to Mr. Bob one night as if an angel of the Lord telling Mary the news. "I hear you're looking for a shortshop," he had said as introduction. "I'm your man." Mr. Bob had actually been scouring Birmingham for a midget, but if this one had its heart set on shortstop it was no skin off Mr. Bob's nose. The crowd roared approval as the shortshop greeted them with his favorite theatrical gesture, the flipped bird.

"Let's have a large hand for the little lady!" A carnival was all circles, thought Mr. Bob, one within the other. The circles of ownership, of leasing and subleasing, the Ferris wheel, the wheels of fortune, the rings of people around each attraction. And at the very center of all the circles, at the soul of the carnival, was the freak. The freak was what everything revolved about. Mr. Bob had himself a team of freaks, not the best or brightest men he had ever had, but at least they were white. Mr. Bob was of an old school.

"And there you have them ladies and gentlemen — the

world-famous Brooklyn Bimbos!" Another blast of the whoopee siren into the mike.

Unannounced, a boy in faded jeans and new sneakers dragged a canvas equipment bag in front of the dugout and sat in the grass. Denzel Ray Crawford, nine years of age, a Texas League blooper no one really wanted responsibility for, veteran batboy of endless summers on the road, a boy too smart for his own good. His only job was to keep the beer out of the sun and do a brief walk-on in the third inning, sneaking behind Pogo on his way to bat and perfectly mimicking the midget's gait, running for cover when Mr. Bob said "Monkey see, monkey do" over the loudspeaker and Pogo gave half-hearted chase.

The lineup completed, Mr. Bob, fight manager, labor camp recruiter, land speculator, dealer in other men's sweat and other men's money, plopped down the needle of the little record player beside him and for the thousandth time it trekked the rugged road of The Star-Spangled Banner. There was an unpatriotic titter when the first baseman removed his wig, curlers and all, and held it over his heart. Mr. Bob settled down to his six innings of snappy patter and sly suggestion. He made a mental note to chew the lot man out for leaving the field in its present state. Mr. Bob did not like to run a sleazy operation.

The showers took a good three minutes to clear the rust from their pipes. They shivered and rattled till aroused enough to vomit something like warmth. Old Lewis had to dip a good deal to get any water over his shoulders. Denzel showered in his daddy's drippings, holding a mushy gob of soap and listening to one of Pogo's detective stories. Pogo would always just walk up and start a story. "Chicago, back in '52 it was," he might say for an opening, or "Frisco, the bad winter of '68," or may be even "Did I ever fill you in on how the pistol they called Mean Matousek finally hung up his spikes?" Head tilted back slightly, the marsh-smelling water slicking his hair straight back, he lathered his chest and drummed his stories out in the staccato of a thirties' movie.

18

There was a little Cagney in the stance, a little Bogart in the voice, a little Robinson in the face, and a little Garfield in the hurt look he turned to the jockstrap-slings and towel-whips that interrupted his monologues. The Bimbos' locker room was a locker room like others, the backslaps a little harder, the jokes a little raunchier, the curses gruffer and more elaborate. They had two hours of geek humor and wolf whistles, two hours of faggotry to scour from their hides. They washed their balls as if grooming a fine steed, soaping and rinsing and weighing them in the palm and soaping again. Denzel wondered at their balls from the corners of his eyes. Even Pogo, who like himself was short for his age, even Pogo was a man down there. He's a ballsy little guy, they would say of the midget from time to time. It was not so bad, thought Denzel, to be a little guy if you were a ballsy one.

A. C. and Knox whooped and hollered like school was out, smacked adhesive tape on anything hairy and drew shaving-cream boobs and bush on the walls. Pitcher wet himself down alone in the corner, remaining aloof and wanting to join in, chewing down the beginnings of a smile. He rubbed his face raw with coarse brown industrial soap, determined that if his acne would not disappear it would at least suffer for staying.

Denzel hid himself casually behind a washcloth till Mr. Bob hollered in that it was high time they put some distance between themselves and Valdosta and Pogo finished his story to the machine-gun chatter of the closed-off pipes. Mr. Bob stood in the archway with fresh towels for his charges, compliments of a dozen different Dixie Motels.

5

"Come back na!"

Fast Freddy sang at the Massachusetts plates as they rode off. They bore left, following the Alternate 17 sign.

"They'll be back awrat," said Harm, sitting in the shade by the soda machine, "less they plan on Parris Islan for their sun 'n' fun. Thas a Masschooses and two Pincilvainyers'll be back. Bet?"

"No bet," said Fast Freddy and scurried into the office.

There was no use betting because Harm would win. Harm always won. Harm made up the games.

Coy Baker pulled through in his pickup and Freddy ran out to give him his dollar's worth.

Coy was a local so he didn't count. Harm had decided that today they would play Cars. Harm never tired of Cars, there did not seem a thing he would rather do than sit in the shade of the gas station at the edge of the Port Royal Swamp and play it. The game drove Fast Freddy out of his skull.

There was no use complaining because Harm wouldn't listen. Harm never listened. Old bastard owned the station.

Hot gas vapor gagged Freddy as he squatted behind the pickup. The hottest part of the day lay ahead. Freddy plucked the single from Coy's hand without looking at it and stood back to let him pass.

The station was a landmark, the big orange shell blazing out in the sky after miles of sullen puddles and Spanish moss. It was an oasis for the North people who came down State 21 through Charlotte and Columbia, heading for Savannah and the Pecan Pass to Florida. Vacation people who stopped nearly out of gas with squirming children in the rear seat and road maps papering the front.

But the maps lied, or maybe it was the roads, because if they were followed the cars would veer off left to the ocean instead of meeting Alternate 17 and continuing to Georgia. The maps had the town of Yemassee smack on a nonexistent road, a combination of 21 and 17 that didn't occur. The two roads crossed at the Shell station, one bearing right and leading through Yemassee to Florida. This was Alternate 17, but it didn't declare itself with road signs till ten miles down at Coosawahatchie. The other, State 21 bearing left, was labeled with a large and official-looking sign that read Alternate Route 17. It was all very confusing.

To play Cars you kept track of the northern plates that bore left and then waited to see if they would be back in a couple hours for directions.

"Passes the time," said Harm, "and is good business." They usually had to buy gas again.

Fast Freddy tried to ignore Harmon's game. He had a tooth, a molar that was killing him. He had pulled the filling out of it the day before eating a ham sandwich, and it would be Monday before he could get it fixed down in Beaufort. He had enough aspirins to last him the day, but he always forgot to take them until the molar started acting up and it was a half hour before the pills took hold. He had to deal with the whole right side of his head throbbing. It had kept him up all night and he was not in a good mood, twitching and itching and mumbling to himself worse than usual.

"Hey Freddy. Fast Freddy."

He stacked oil cans for a display and tried not to hear Harmon.

"Innytom you got to take a leak it's awrat with me."

His hands trembled a little trying to balance cans on the top row. He wouldn't let Harm make him knock the pyramid over. He wouldn't leave himself open for one of Harm's old jokes.

"Aint nothin you can do when Nature calls."

He had to use both hands on the last one to keep it still.

"Yall know where the key is."

"Dammit Harm, I don't have to pee!"

"Then why," said Harm, "are you shakin like a wet mouse on a frosty mornin?" And Harm spit at an oil splotch and slapped his thigh in laughter the way he did, once, twice, three times.

The only way to get it over with was to let him have his way.

Freddy hurried from the pumps into the office and washed down two aspirins with a Dr Pepper, suffering its medicinal taste. He tried to sit and hold his head for a moment but a '69 Plymouth pulled in and rang the hose. New York plates. Freddy went out to it, as Harm never stirred himself unless someone wished to buy a Souvenir of S. Ca. or needed the key to the john. Harm liked to look a prospect over before he opened up his john.

"Fill her with Supershell and check the oil please." The man at the wheel rolled his window up when he finished talking to keep the insects out and the air conditioning in. Freddy decided not to wash the bug squash from the window unless the man asked him. He could feel a throb distantly growing as he squeezed the pump handle. He snuck his tongue into the hole and poked around. He made too much suction and pulled at the nerve, starting things up again in his jaw. He cursed all '69 Plymouths and the people who drove them.

When he went around front he couldn't get the dipstick back in its sheath to check the oil. His hand shook and the point rattled around the opening. He cursed Harmon's fat butt and the chair it rested on. Finally he guided the stick in with his thumb and forefinger, coating them with oil, and left it there. Let him burn his fuckin engine out. He slammed the hood down and told the man it was fine. Freddy bit on his cheeks to make a distracting pain. The window rolled down.

"How do you get to this Alternate 17?"

By dumb luck, thought Freddy. He mumbled something about just following the signs and the window rolled up. The Plymouth turned left to the ocean. Behind him Freddy heard a gob hit the dust and three mirthful slaps. He turned to Harm. The sun pulled Harm's face up around his eyes, pulled his lip up past his gums. It seemed that Harm had every other tooth, his smile a mouthful of Indian corn. The old man's T-shirt stuck to his scrawny chest the way it always did, Freddy knew the outline of the wet spot as well as the shape of the continents he had learned about in Geography. It looked like Australia or New Guinea or someplace. Someplace far away. Freddy started for the pumps, his shoes sticking in the goo of the new-laid asphalt. If you stood in one spot too long on a hot day, Freddy thought, it would suck a hold on your feet and you would be one sorry tarbaby.

"One Masschooses," grinned Harm, "two Pincilvainyers and a N'Yawk. Gonna be a busy day, son."

Most of the vacation people stopped somewheres for lunch around one-thirty or two, as did Freddy and Harm. They pulled the hose back and sat in the office by the fan, rummaging through brown bags. Fast Freddy sat facing the road with Harm behind him. He didn't like to watch Harm eat. There was a cold beef sandwich and some peanut brittle in his lap, untouched. He cursed his mother for packing such rock-hard stuff. He drank a Coke, pouring it directly on the back of his throat, not daring to strain it through his teeth. He watched the bugs attack the screen door. There were mosquitoes who whined and pinged against it, large, clinging millers left dead or dying from the night before and swirls of nearly invisible little aphids that would be drawn into your mouth and nose with a careless breath. The screen sang and twitched with them and Fast Freddy cursed them, individually and as a group. Harm began to suck a chicken neck behind him so he blasted the transistor radio on.

If you get burnt in Greenville
You might's well save your tears.
The sentence there for vagrancy
Is five-to-seven years.

Harm had had the new blacktop laid around the pumps so the North people wouldn't think the station was a hick operation. On hot days, days like this one, the heat coming up through the dust bent the air above it, the road seen from where Freddy sat wobbled and ran like oil.

The boredom's overwhelming,
You never see the sun —

Freddy offered Harm his food and Harm took it. He turned the volume up a little more to compete with the peanut brittle and began to read things off the back counter, reflected in the window he faced.

You'll memorize the ceiling cracks
Before your time is done.

There were boxes of Pennzoil and Bardahl and STP and an ad for AAMCO Transmission Service. A cardboard Cale Yarborough endorsed spark plugs and Firestone pictured its tires getting the checkered flag at Darlington. There was Three-in-One and Universal and Acme and Fischer. The United Methodist Church was holding a bazaar. There was a calendar branded by the Coca-Cola people. They were all familiar to Freddy as the grease he could never manage to clean from his fingernails.

The news flashed on the radio. The news always made Fast Freddy uneasy, it was all about people who did important things, people who went important places, people who were important. People he would never meet. The people who came through the station only wanted to buy a souvenir of S. Ca. and lay on a beach. They were the most excitement, the most outside contact Yemassee ever got and all they were after was a place to sleep in the sun. A burgundy-colored Coupe de Ville glided to a halt by the pumps. Freddy tried to stare it away but it stood its ground patiently. Sun glared at him from the windshield so he couldn't see inside.

"This is good beef," said Harm, "too bad your maw had to put maynaise on it. Don't care for maynaise. Never have. Go make that sale Freddy."

"It's my lunch hour."

"You aint eatin. You just hop on out there. Got to make hay while the sun shine, Freddy, that Interstate be finish pretty soon."

Fast Freddy cut off the news with his thumb, scraped his chair from under himself, and bustled out to the big car.

The Coupe glistened evenly like it was new, the finish seemingly immune to the dust that coated the other cars passing through. There was a buzz and the driver's window lowered.

Fast Freddy looked to where the driver should be and saw only arms and legs roping up around the steering column. He looked to the back seat and there was no back seat, only a battery of speakers covered in thick tawny fleece. Lounged against these was a man with skin so black that his burgundy turtleneck, his royal purple jacket and slacks, his deep burgundy floppy hat were all set off against it. The only thing darker than the skin were his shades, coal-black wraparounds that mirrored back a slightly bent picture of what the man could see — a thin, nervous boy with a peeling nose.

"Ha much?"

The black man's head was fixed straight ahead. When he spoke to Freddy he didn't turn it. "Don't need your gas."

"Oh." Freddy jerked his head toward the hood. "Chick at awl?"

"No oil. I want to know some things."

25

"Uh-huh." Freddy caught himself squirming in the man's glasses and tried to be still.

"Has there been a carnival around here? With a baseball show? A midget?"

Freddy made a thinking face and scratched his head reflectively though he knew the answer right off. "There was a carny through here bout a week ago but I didn't get over to it, see I work after school here on weekdays an all day Sarday and Sunday, and well —"

"Was there a midget?"

"— Sunday they wouldn't let the carny operate so it pulled up roots and —"

"Was there a midget?"

"Mister, I'd guess wherever there's a carnival there is got to be a midget."

"I'm looking for *one*, specific, *mid*get." The black man nodded his head with the words but kept it straight ahead. "Name of Pogo Burns."

Fast Freddy shifted from foot to foot and shrugged his shoulders.

"Have you seen him?"

Freddy shifted and shrugged and shook his head no.

"Have you heard anything about a midget? Have you heard the name Pogo Burns?"

"Nosir."

The man was still for a long moment and Freddy wondered if he should offer to put air in the tires or wash the windshield. But the tires looked fine and the windshield was unblemished.

"This carnival. Where did it go when it left?"

Freddy noticed for the first time how slowly and clearly the man talked, as if he were explaining something to a foreigner.

"South, I guess. Think I heard they be in Savannah next."

There was a buzzing and the window began to rise and the man was going to get away.

"Say Mister! Mister!"

But the window buzzed shut and the burgundy Coupe

glided away from the pumps and drifted left toward the ocean, leaving Fast Freddy with an enormous bug up his behind. Now he would never know.

Just as he would never know if Harm had been the one who put the Alternate 17 sign on the wrong road.

But today he had one on Harm. He had seen something Harm would never see the like of with his fat butt plastered to a chair. And he wouldn't let on, not right away. Let the old bastard stew in it.

Harmon was picking his teeth inside. Harmon could pick his teeth for hours. "Dint pump no gas."

"Didn't want any."

"Dint pour no awl."

"Didn't need any."

"Whud e want?"

"Ask some questions."

Now I got him, thought Fast Freddy, got him hooked.

But Harm only stood and lifted his chair. "California plates," he said, "first this week." And moved to the door as if that were the end to it.

"There was a giant inside," blurted Freddy, "biggest nigger you ever see, with power windows and purple clothes from head to foot. I think he's after that carnival was here. Lookin for a midget, Pogo something. Pogo Burns."

"Boy," said Harm, "your job here is to sell gasline and wap winders. Not to jaw with people and make up stories. You member that n'will get on just fine."

The screen door slammed behind him and lunch hour was over.

Late afternoon Fast Freddy's molar began to ache and the teeth beside and above it joined in sympathy. He took three aspirins but there was already a needle in his eye and an icepick in his ear and no telling when they'd go away. Freddy cursed everything that moved and Harmon, who didn't. One of the Pennsylvania plates from the morning returned and Freddy trotted out to it. It was feeding time for the mosquitoes. Harm passed, heading for the shelter of the office, and Freddy mumbled that it was a wonder the old bastard could still walk.

The man driving sounded hoarse, there was a fat wet wife beside him and cranky children squabbling in the rear. He said all he needed was directions and a quart of oil. His car was great on gas, he said, but it burned oil.

The mosquitoes lit where it was sweaty on the back of Fast Freddy's neck and behind his ears and he slapped one flat on his arm that had pumped a full tankload of his blood. He hunched his shoulders to cover up and fumbled to open the can. He couldn't find the catch to the hood and the man had to tell him where it was. He dropped the funnel down into the engine and the mosquitoes went for the strip of lower back left exposed when he bent to retrieve it. He heard the man rustling and clearing his throat from over his shoulder. He got everything set and watched the oil ease out, flowing and flowing, rolling down the funnel for ages while he battled the hungry bugs with his free hand. When he finally slammed the hood down the man was waiting for him.

The man spread a mutilated road map out on the hood.

"Now," he said. "Here we are."

He pointed to red-circled Yemassee on the map. Freddy nodded. He looked at the Pennsylvania man and the road map as if he had seen neither a man nor a map in all his experience.

"I want to go to Florida," said the man.

"I want to go to Florida. But if you do what they say," he said, his voice growing louder, "if you follow their directions, you end up here!" He jabbed a finger into Port Royal Sound.

The man made a fist and dramatically closed his eyes.

"Now. What I want from you is this. Directions. Show me. Draw a picture if you have to. Where is the road to Savannah?"

Freddy pointed to the untitled road and said that one there, to the right.

The man looked at it for a long time. "Then why in God's name doesn't it say so?" He looked at Freddy accusingly.

Freddy shrugged and waved a cloud of bugs away.
The man paid Freddy in toll-booth change off the dashboard, patted the road map across his wife's lap and drove off to Florida. Freddy was careful not to step in Harm's fresh gob as he went back to the office to ring up the sale.

The afternoon ached on dully. A Rhode Island came through. A Connecticut and a New York. A Vermont came through, and another Pennsylvania, an Ohio and a caravan of four New Jerseys traveling together. Freddy's teeth hurt and his bites itched and his nose stung where it was peeling. He had missed the carnival all right. He seemed to manage to miss it every year. When he was small his daddy was too busy or the car wouldn't work or the preacher railed against going to it in his sermon and Freddy's mother wouldn't let him go. The last two years he had been working. He had to see the carnival second hand, through other lucky eyes, eyes that were more worldly than his for having gone. There was nothing out of the ordinary, ever, about life in town or at the station. For celebrities they had old Stinkfoot Plott, the local legger who had been found a few years back shotgun-splattered at the edge of the swamps, and Bullhead Aylers's little brother Tommy, the envy of small boys for miles around. Tommy could willfully divert his urine into two streams when he pissed, a talent that earned him the nickname of Moses. And that was it. Some celebrities. A dead bootlegger and a kid with a trick pecker, that was the whole boodle. That was the vacuum that a carny filled, that was the attraction of a place where everything was always out of the ordinary, a place on wheels that had been through every town you could name and was headed for all the ones you couldn't. And Fast Freddy had missed it, it passed him by every year.

A New York, a Connecticut, the first Maine of the month. Fast Freddy cursed every state in the Union, starting with Alabama, wolfed down the last of his aspirin, and remembered the rabbit.

It had been California plates that did it. A thump and a

29

yelp from the road in front of the station and Harm remarking it was the first California of the week. Freddy had run out to see what it was.

It was the front half of a rabbit, eyes bugged up at Freddy in fear, still trying to run. Its front legs scrabbled at the black-top in a frantic swimming motion, it seemed to be trying to pull itself out from a bog hole. The rabbit's hind half was a grayish, furry rag, stained with bright red and paved flat into the road. The pattern of a tire tread was stamped on it. Freddy scurried off a few feet and returned with a big rock. He raised it over his head and took aim, wanting to finish it. The rabbit's eyes, huge and liquid, went from the rock to Freddy's face. Freddy dropped the rock and hurried back to the station.

"Will play a game," Harm had said, "see how long e lasts."

Every half hour or so Freddy would say he's dead, he's got to be, and Harm would shake his head no. Freddy would trot out and sure enough the whiskers would still be twitching, probing, as if they alone could drag it up from the earth's pull, the heart would still be racing in its chest, fluttering fast as nervous fingers in a hot engine, and the pain-widened eyes would still be darting, missing nothing. Harm would gob and slap and bust into a smug grin.

It hung on through the morning, half rabbit and half road, hung on through the afternoon watching them all pass over, Chevys and Fords and an occasional Pontiac; Vermont, Massachusetts and Rhode Island, straining to run but bound to the blacktop. The sun cooked it, uninterrupted but for the shadows thrown by cars passing at fifty miles per hour. They didn't hit it but they never stopped coming.

In the early evening, with no sign or warning, Harm said that's it, it's done for. Freddy found nothing but a stain on the road and a few tufts of grayish fur. There you have it, he had thought, Souvenir of S. Ca.

The burgundy Coupe de Ville glided in from the swamp road about five-thirty. Freddy wasn't sure but it seemed as though it wasn't as shiny as before, as if it had grown a very fine layer of dust. But it might just have been the change in the light.

The window was open when Freddy came to a stop by it. As before, the man left the engine humming.

"I told you I was looking for a midget," he said.

"Yessir."

"You let me go out to Parris Island."

Freddy didn't know what to say. He rocked from foot to foot and wrung an oil rag in his hands.

"Do you think he'd be likely to go out there?"

Freddy gave an elaborate shrug. He had no idea what a midget might be likely to do.

"Do you think he went to join the Marines?"

Freddy thought it might be a joke but wasn't sure enough to laugh.

"Do you think," said the black man, his head fixed straight forward through the windshield, "that you could tell me the road to Savannah? Do you? I wouldn't want to have to come back here again."

Freddy thought it might be a threat but was too curious to be scared. "The one to the right, sir. The one that don't have a sign."

"I hope you're right," said the man and the window began to buzz and rise and the man was getting away again.

"Say Mister! Mister!"

The window halted a third of the way up.

"Listen, uh, could I ask, I mean, uhm, what for do you want to find this midget fella? This Pogo Burns?"

The man turned his head slowly, like a sleepy reptile, till it faced Freddy. Freddy saw that there was no more reflection on the shades, no more thin, fidgeting white boy. When he tried to look through to the eyes inside there was only blackness, the black of emptiness. Freddy had a dizzy, falling sensation for a moment, as if he were looking down a bottomless well and had lost balance. He felt a chill.

"I'm going to kill him," said the black man, and almost smiled.

The window buzzed shut and the burgundy car glided

away. Freddy turned to find Harm standing behind him, actually standing and wearing a frown. He had witnessed, thought Fast Freddy, he couldn't wiggle out of this one.

"Did you see im Harm? Did you see? You hear what he said? Lookin for a midget. Lookin to kill him. Did you hear?"

"Ony thing I heard," said Harm turning back to his chair by the soda machine, "was somebody call a nigger 'sir'."

There was no beating the old bastard.

6

The sides of the huge camper were flame red, bearing the sign BROOKLYN BIMBOS BASEBALL CLUB INC./BIRMINGHAM, ALABAMA. Mr. Bob had a fondness for alliteration. Pitcher was up front with his maps and gas money, A. C., Knox, Lewis and Pogo sat inside playing draw poker. Mr. Bob did not approve of gambling and had his books to work on. Denzel stood behind his father, critical of his play. Pogo read the boy's face and never lost a hand to Lewis. If the boy frowned it meant the old man was playing too conservative, if he bit his lip the old man was bluffing, if he stayed calm and watched the pot the old man had a fat hand. The Okies never read the boy, being too intent on playing the countless hunches they felt. Dice rollers in a card game, they almost always drew two or three and complained to the heavens when their ships failed to come in. Lewis seemed to think the cards would change face as he held them and never drew more than one. Pogo usually came out a little ahead, even though it seemed he never, ever had the cards. Skill beats luck, he would say, sitting on a chair and three canvas bases, puffing his cigar, never losing patience with Lewis's slow play and stolid bad guessing, with the stale poker-joking and loud backslapping of the Okies when they lucked into a pot, or with their badly disguised peeking and the potato-chip grease they spread through the deck.

Pogo was quiet tonight. He managed to stay a little ahead all through the game, absentmindedly raking in his nickels and pennies. But there wasn't the usual lecture on the Science of Poker and his studies with its greatest scientists in the Nevada desert. An inch of ash grew on his cigar between puffs and from time to time Denzel caught him rubbing at his legs under the table.

It was nearly eleven when Pitcher found an eating place still open. They got out and stretched and kicked at the gravel and checked it out with a critical eye, though there was no choice. It was the usual corrugated silver-sided diner with a tickling of nightbugs at the screen door and a buzzing neon sign. Ocracoke Annie's.

"We got miles to make," said Mr. Bob. "Let's go."

They filed in and sat at the counter, the Okies between Mr. Bob and Lewis, Pitcher a few stools down and Pogo and Denzel on the end. Lewis managed to get his hair tangled in a pest strip hanging from the ceiling, scattering crispy black insects.

"At thing look like it caught more flies in its time than you have, Lewis," said A. C.

"Well this is one that's getting away." He separated it carefully, then made a face and patted around to see if any had come off in his hair. "I hope the food is better than the atmosphere."

"Hell, Pitcher wouldn't give us a bum steer. Wouldja boy?"

Pitcher studied the breakfast prices on the wall.

A young girl came out from the rear, yawning. The coverup she used for her pimples had blotched and run with sweat. Her hair hung in strings and was stuck to her neck. "I help you boys?"

"You could help me any old time," said A. C., "but you probly not of age yet."

The girl ignored him and passed out menus. Knox flipped through the titles on the countertop juke selector and punched a couple out. He asked Mr. Bob if he was still buying like he promised and he sighed and said yes and ordered beers all around. The men grew interested in the menus.

> *Hey little girl with the wide blue eyes,*
> *You wanna see a big surprise?*
> *I got some lovin I been keepin in the oven*
> *For you,*
> *For you.*

"Say Honey," asked A. C. "what's a 'hambugger'?"

"What?"

"Right here it says," he pointed to a spot on the page and watched her as she bent over to see. "Hambugger de-lux, eighty-five cents."

"Just Annie's spelling. She run off the menus herself. It's a regular hamburger."

"I hope so. The other don't sound any too good. Neither do these 'sordid beverages' you got here. Your Annie dint pay too much attention at school."

"Didn't make it all the way to the eighth grade like some people we know," said Mr. Bob. "Make up your mind and tell the girl your order."

"Aint he a mean old Daddy?" A. C. asked the girl. She scratched at a dried mustard glob on the counter. "What I think I'd like, Mr. Bob, is a date with Sugar here. You ever meet a baseball player before, Sugar?"

"Nope." She turned her eyes to her pad.

"Well don't hold your breath," said Mr. Bob, "cause there's none to be found in this room."

> *Cute little foxy with a fuzzy tail,*
> *My recipe just cannot fail,*
> *You'll be adyin just to start in afryin*
> *With me,*
> *With me.*

The girl went to take Pitcher's order, sneaking a look back at Pogo. She dropped her pencil on the floor and upset a ketchup bottle bending for it.

35

"Aw now look, A. C., you've went and got her all nervoused up. Honey," called Knox, "you nemmine this ol boy here, he just making talk is all."

"I'd be making something else if I got the chance," said A. C., and the two of them began to giggle.

"Hayseeds," muttered Pogo.

"Now what would you do with a little-biddy thing like that, pardner? She aint no biggern a minute."

"Oh, I'd figure something out. You heard the line about big things coming in small packages."

"At vulgarity," said Mr. Bob, "I draw the line."

Hot little honey with your lips so sweet,
I got a dish that can't be beat,
When I'm done abakin it I'll start in amakin it
With you,
With you.

The Okies struggled to keep their faces straight when the girl worked her way over to them.

"I'll have three hambugger de-luxes to begin with," said A. C. and Knox cracked up. Mr. Bob cleared his throat loudly and looked at the ceiling.

"But Mr. Bob, I'm a growing boy."

"You can grow tomorrow."

"Make that two. And some home fries."

"N'you sir?" she asked Mr. Bob.

"How's your fried chicken?"

"No fried chicken!" thundered a voice from behind the wall.

"A nuther country heard from," said A. C. "What kind of a restaurant don't have fried chicken?"

A square panel in the wall slid open and a rough approximation of an old woman's face squinted out from the kitchen. "This restaurant don't, not at lebben clock the gobdam night. Got no time to fry no chickens. You hab a hamebugger like the others an be gratefoo for it!" The panel slammed shut.

"What was that?" asked A. C.

"That's Annie. She does the cooking."

"She cooks like she looks we in a world of trouble here. That is one *home*ly child."

"Now pardner, you can't tell a book by its cover."

"Cowflop. If that woman fell down a well you could pump ugly for a week."

"Three hamburger deluxes," said Mr. Bob, "double order of French fries and a hunk of that pecan roll."

"And what'll he have?" mumbled the girl.

"Huh?"

"Him," she said, not taking her eyes from her pad but jerking her head toward Pogo.

"Who?"

"Him. The — you know —"

"Pogo? Ask him."

"He don't bite, Honey," said A. C. "He may nibble a little, but he don't bite."

"That his little boy?"

"No Miss," said Lewis, "that's mine."

"Hunh. Don't look it, do he?" She walked away.

"Real angel-puss int she?" said A. C.

"Can it, plowboy." Pogo sat with his head in his hands and his elbows on either side of the menu. The girl approached cautiously and stood in front of him, never looking down from her pad. "You got ribs this time of night?"

"Yessir."

"Okay, a plate of ribs, home fries, and a side order of yellow beans."

"I'll have the same," said Denzel.

"Since when you like yellow beans, kid?"

Denzel shrugged.

"Hold the beans," said the girl, and turned to leave.

"And a chocolate milk for the kid," Pogo called after her.

When the girl was out of sight A. C. smacked his lips and sighed. "Oh to be sixteen and full of vinegar again."

"Instead of thirty-one and full of shit," said Mr. Bob.

"Teenage stuff'll wear you down, pardner. I'd say that

37

little girl is about right for our young mound ace here. They both such friendly children. Whatsay Pitcher?"

Pitcher drank his ice water.

The Okies began to help themselves to whatever was loose on the counter, sugar cubes, packets of salt and pepper, napkins and placemats, stuffing their pockets while Mr. Bob shook his head asking the Lord why he had to be chosen den mother and told them that at silverware he drew the line. Then Lewis noticed Mrs. Mumps eating alone in a corner booth.

"Lo there, m'am," he said. "You so quiet we didn't know you were here."

Mrs. Mumps smiled sweetly, a gray-headed little woman. "I didn't want to bother you gentlemen while you were choosing your dinners. It's nice to see you all again."

"Been some time since we crossed paths," said Mr. Bob. "Where are you working?"

"Right now Mr. Mumps and I are vacationing, but in a few days we take the act and join with Furman Donicker's people."

"Then we'll catch you in Samson. Where's the Mister?"

The woman blushed a little. "Oh, he couldn't eat in here. You know how it is."

"No I don't." A. C. swiveled around on his stool. "Why can't he eat in here?"

"Well," said Mrs. Mumps, nodding toward the kitchen, "she said he couldn't."

"She? Which one, Beauty or the Beast?"

"*I* said so!" Annie's voice rasped from behind the wall.

"Woman has got ears like a hawk. Why can't he?"

"Cause this is my place and I said so!"

"You serve niggers, don't you?" called Mr. Bob.

"Got to."

"You servin us, aren't you?" said A. C.

"I'd prefer niggers."

"So what's the problem?"

"Hell flaws."

"Whatsat?"

"Hell flaws! Inspectors ebber found out they close me down. Don't care if he *is* wearing a forty-dollar suit. Law says I *got* to serb niggers, says I *got* to serb you, but it don't say a thing bout I got to serb any gobdam go-riller!"

"Chimpanzee," said Mrs. Mumps.

"Whatebber. It's a clear bilation of the hell flaws an besides I don't want to. Case dismissed."

Mrs. Mumps again smiled sweetly to the men. "I preciate your concern, gentlemen, but it's really no problem. Mr. Mumps and I have gotten used to it. I'll bring something out for him when I'm through. You learn to be patient." She turned to her meal.

"I'd feel a whole lot better if I knew what she's doing to that food in there," said A. C., swiveling back to the counter. "I hope to God she wears a mask when she's handling it."

"Lay off," said Pogo.

"I aint said a thing bout you."

"It gets on my nerves."

"Well don't blame me when your milk comes out all curdled with fright."

"Fuckin yokels."

"Woman must be three years oldern dirt. Aint that right pardner?"

"Face could peel bark off a tree."

"Sure as shit."

"Trying to build a ball team," said Mr. Bob, "and I get struck with Heckle and Jeckle."

The girl and Annie came out with plates of food. Annie was missing all of her teeth and a large crown-patch of her white hair. A. C. snaked Lewis's sunglasses from his shirt pocket and put them on. "If I'm to be blinded," he said, "I'd prefer it to be from food poisoning."

Pogo said thank you and Denzel echoed him. Lewis told Annie it looked very good. The men put their faces down into the warmth still coming off the food and argued over who was hungriest.

They grew silent. An inch-long roach appeared on the counter, walking leisurely before them. It tapped its feelers ahead, pausing to examine cracks and stains, strolling in front of Mr. Bob and Knox and A. C. and Lewis.

"Now who might this be?"

"Relative of yours, Burnsy?"

"Wonder if he knows the health laws."

"Wonder if he'd like to see a menu."

"I recommend the hambuggers."

Just as it was about to reach Pitcher, Annie mashed it flat with the heel of her hand, whisked it off the counter, and returned to the kitchen.

"What d'you know," said A. C., "the customer *aint* always right."

The girl brought their beers.

> *Well you aint exactly gorgeous*
> *But you're close enough for me*
> *Close enough for me*
> *Plain as you can see,*
> *On a scale up to a hundred you might get a*
> *Forty-three,*
> *It's important for a boy to have a mother.*

"They really ought to have some place to put a puss like that away," said Knox through a mouthful. "Seein as there's not a sideshow in the country would have her."

"Oh, there's a place, pardner. The Georgia State Home for the Hard-on-the-Eyeballs. Only this one excaped."

"Some people got no class," said Pogo, "no class at all."

"Aw Burnsy, we just kiddin."

"No harm intended."

"Couple of juvenile delinquents."

"Hit's not like we're denying the lady's other talents. She don't cook bad a-tall. Matter a fact I could do with another of these hambuggers, even if I got to spring for it myself."

"Kitchen's closed!" A pot clanged behind the wall.

"Voice like the whisper of an angel's wing."

"Damn straight."

Now you aint no A-dolph Hitler
But you're mean enough to be
Mean enough to be
Girl you torture me,
I would bet there is a hangman's noose upon your
Famly tree,
It's important for a boy to have a mother.

Pogo had barely touched his ribs and when Denzel mentioned it he said he wasn't very hungry. When the girl brought him another beer she laid it on the counter a few feet away and then slid it toward him with her fingertips, then snatched her hand away when he reached for it.

"Know who that is?" A. C. whispered to the girl loud enough for everyone to hear over the music. "That's Babyface Burns. The terror of the West Coast. I won't go into details with an innocent child like yourself, but someday you'll be able to tell your grandchildren you seenum with your own eyes and lived to report on it." The girl frowned a little and stacked menus. "Not many have, Sugar."

Pogo pushed his food away and told Denzel to finish for him. When he was out the door the girl came and cleared his place.

Gee I hate to be untactful
But your best friend is a witch
Best friend is a witch
A headache and an itch,
She should wake up in Antarctica without a
Single stitch,
It's important for a boy to have a mother.

"Sa matter with Burnsy?"

"Going to count his poker winnings. Lucky little fucker."

"Maybe he found some of Annie's teeth on his plate an it put him off his dinner."

"Hell no, pardner, she lost them in the Civil War. Pogo just had his eyes on Sugar here and didn't think he could hold

41

back his passion another moment. Honey-hunch, you been spared a fate worse than death."

The girl piled a tray with empty bottles and left for the kitchen, yawning. Denzel took a few quick bites, hopped off his stool and went outside.

In the parking lot shadows he saw a figure sitting alone on the hood of a car, legs dangling down.

"Pogo?"

Denzel came closer. It was Mr. Mumps, glumly waiting for his trainer.

"Oh. Lo there."

The monkey nodded.

"Ha you?"

It shrugged its shoulders. So-so.

"Well," said Denzel, stuck for words, "I got to see somebody. Mrs. Mumps is almost done in there, I spect she'll be right out. See you round."

The monkey nodded and Denzel passed on.

He entered the van quietly in case Pogo was sick and trying to sleep. Pogo was sitting on his bunk looking down the barrel of the gun. He caught his breath and tightened when he saw Denzel, then relaxed. He lay the gun across his lap.

"Oh. It's you."

"Yuh. I wasn't too hungry either."

"You took me by surprise again. Going to have to tie a can to your tail."

"Yuh." Denzel stared at the gun.

"Just cleaning a little. Got to keep her in good shape."

"Uh-huh."

"Listen kid, would you do me a favor? I forgot to tip that girl," he dug out a handful of change and gave it to Denzel. "She ought to get something for taking all that gas. Would you run this in for me? Thanks."

"You all right?" said the boy.

"No sweat. Just a headache is all."

When he heard the boy crunching back across the gravel he pulled the clip from the gun and put them away.

Wednesday

1

Denzel wandered toward them with his glove under his arm. A few were in the outfield, crowding under liners and pop-ups that a tall boy threw them. "I got it!" they called in unison, "Mine, mine!" Off to one side a dark, barrel-chested kid was playing pepper with a boy who had a bandage over his eye. The rest milled around, joking, tossing gloves and hats in the air, fighting over the remaining bat to take practice swings. They all seemed to know each other.

Denzel squatted next to a thin boy who sat on his glove at the fringe of the action, watching expectantly. He was the only one there smaller than Denzel.

"Gonna be a game?"

"Uh-huh." The thin boy looked up at him, surprised.

"They got regular teams?"

"Nope. They pick sides."

Denzel nodded.

"Hope I get to play," said the thin boy. "When the teams don't come out even I got to sit," he said, "every single time."

He waited for a word of support but Denzel just grunted and moved several feet away. Might think we come together.

The ones on what seemed to be the field hacked around a

little longer until a movement to start a game began. "Let's go," someone said. "Get this show on the road."

"Somebody be captains."

"Somebody choose up."

Gradually they wandered in and formed a loose group around a piece of packing crate broken roughly in the shape of a home plate. They urged each other to get organized and shrugged their indifference over who would be the captains.

"C'mon, we don't have all day."

"Somebody just choose."

"Big kids against the little kids!" said a fat boy in glasses and they all laughed.

"Good guys against the bad guys!"

"Winners against the losers!"

"The men against the mice!"

"Okay," said the dark, barrel-chested kid, "Whynt we just have the same captains as yesterday?"

"Yeah, but not the same teams."

"Too lopsided."

"That was a slaughter."

"We got scobbed."

"Do it then," said the fat boy, "Bake and the Badger."

"Yeah, shoot for first pick."

"Let's go, choose up."

There was a sudden movement, everybody spreading in a semicircle around two of the boys, jostling not to be behind anyone, the thin boy hopping up and running to join them. Denzel got up slowly and walked to the rear of them. No sense getting all hot and bothered. No big thing. He drifted through hips and shoulders, quietly, till he stood in view of the captains.

They were shooting fingers, best four out of seven, like the World Series. The barrel-chested boy was one of the captains, the one they called the Badger, and the tall boy who had been throwing flies was the other.

Denzel slipped his glove on. It was an oversized Ted Kluszewski model his daddy had handed down to him. Each of the fingers seemed thick as his wrist and there was no web to speak of and no padding in the pocket. Orange and gunky.

The tall boy won on the last shoot and the Badger scowled.
"Alley Oop!" Bake called without even looking.

"Haw-*raaat!*" A wiry kid with arms that hung to his knees
trotted out from their midst and stood by Bake. "We got it
now, can't lose. Can not *lose!*"

"Purdy!" The Badger barked it like an order and a solid-
looking red-haired kid marched out and took his place.

The two first picks began to whisper and nudge at their
captains.

"Vernon," whispered the wiry boy, "get Vernon."

"Vernon."

Vernon came to join them and he and Alley Oop slapped
each other's backs at being together.

"Royce," whispered the big redhead. "They get Royce
we've had it."

"Royce," said the Badger and Royce was welcomed into
the fold.

"Psssst!" called the fat boy with the glasses to Alley Oop
and Vernon. "Have him pick me. You guys need a third
sacker."

"Ernie," they said, on their toes leaning over each of
Bake's shoulders, "Ernierniernie!"

"Okay, Ernie," he said and Ernie waddled out with his
glove perched on top of his head.

"Gahs looked like you needed some help," he told them.
"Never fear, Ernie is here!"

The captains began to take more time in their picking.
They considered and consulted and looked down the line
before calling out a name. The Badger pounded quick,
steady socks into the pocket of his glove while beside him
Purdy slowly flapped the jaws of his first baseman's mitt.
Soon there were more that had been chosen than that hadn't.
The ones who were picked frisked and giggled behind their
captains while the ones who hadn't were statues on display.
"You," the captains said now, still weighing abilities but
unenthusiastic. Finally they just pointed. The Badger
walked along the straggling line of leftovers like a general
reviewing troops, stood in front of his next man and jerked
his thumb back over his shoulder. When there was only one

47

spot left for even teams Denzel and the thin boy were left standing. It was the Badger's pick.

Denzel stood at ease, eyes blank. It grew quiet. He felt the others checking him over and he smelled something. Topps bubble gum, the kind that came with baseball cards. He snuck a glance at the thin boy. His eyes were wide, fixed on the Badger, pleading. He had a round little puff of a catcher's mitt that looked like a red pincushion. There was no sign of a baseball ever having landed in it, no dent of a pocket.

Denzel felt the Badger considering him for a moment, eyes dipping to the thick-fingered old-timer's glove, but then he turned and gave a slight, exasperated nod to the thin boy. "We got him."

Before Denzel could get out of the way Bake's team streamed past him onto the field.

"First base!" they cried, "Dibs on shortstop!" Trotting around him as if he were a tree, looking through the space where he stood. "Bake?" they whined, "Lemme take left huh? I always get stuck at catcher or somethin." Denzel kept his face blank and tried to work the thing back down into his throat. They all knew each other, didn't know whether he was any good or not. No big thing.

He drifted off to the side, considered going back to the van, then sat beyond the third base line to watch. As if that was what he had come to do in the first place. Nice day to watch a ball game. He decided he would root for Bake's side.

"Me first," said the Badger, pointing with the bat handle, "you second, you third. Purdy you clean up. Fifth, sixth, semeightnon." They had full teams so Denzel couldn't offer to be all-time catcher and dive for foul tips. You didn't get to bat but it kept you busy and you could show them you could catch. Denzel kept his glove on.

He could tell he was better than a lot of them before they even started and some of the others when the end of the orders got up. The pitching was overhand but not fast. There was a rock that stuck out of the ground for first base and some cardboard that kept blowing so they had to put sod clumps on it for second and somebody's T-shirt for third. Bake played shortstop and was good and seemed a little older than the

48

others. The one called Purdy, the big red-headed one, fell to his knees after he struck out. Everybody had backed way up for him. Alley-Oop made a nice one-handed catch in center. Whenever there was a close play at a base, Badger would run over and there would be a long argument and he would win. The thin boy had to be backed up at catcher by the batting team so it wouldn't take forever to chase the pitches that went through. The innings went a long time even when there weren't a lot of runs because the pitchers were trying tricky stuff and couldn't get it close. Denzel followed the action carefully, keeping track of the strikes and outs and runs scored, seeing who they backed up for and who they moved in for, who couldn't catch, who couldn't throw, keeping a book on them the way his daddy and Pogo had taught him he should. When fat Ernie did something funny he laughed a little along with the rest of them. Once somebody hit a grounder too far off to the left for the third baseman or left fielder to bother chasing. "Little help!" they called and Denzel scrambled after it. He backhanded it moving away, turned and whipped it hard into the pitcher. No one seemed to notice. He sat back down and the game started up again.

The Badger's side got ahead by three and stayed there, the two teams trading one or two runs each inning. They joked and argued with each other while waiting to bat. They practiced slides and catches in stop-action slow-motion and pretended to be TV commentators, holding imaginary microphones and interviewing themselves. They kept up a baseball chatter.

"*Hum*babe!" said the team in the field, "Chuckeratinthere-*iss*gahcantit*iss*gahcantit! *Hum*babe! *No*stick*no*stickchuckeratinthere —"

"*Lets*go!" said the team at bat, "*Big*innin*big*innin*we*gottateam*we*gottateam*bang*itonoutthere! *Lets*go*lets*go!"

Late in the fifth inning a mother's voice wailed over the babble from a distance.

"Jonathaaaan!"

There was a brief pause, the players looking at each other accusingly, seeing who would confess to being Jonathan.

"Jonathan Phelps you get in here!"

49

The thin boy with the catcher's mitt mumbled something, looking for a moment as if he were going to cry, then ran off toward the camp.

Denzel squatted and slipped his glove on again. He wore it with his two middle fingers out, not for style but so he could make it flex a little. He waited.

The tall boy, Bake, walked in a circle at shortstop with his glove on his hip, looking around. "Hey kid!"

Who me? Denzel raised his eyebrows and looked to Bake.

"You play catcher for them."

Denzel began to rise but the Badger ran out onto the field. "Whoa na! No deal. I'm not takin him. Got enough easy outs awriddy. Will play thout a catcher, you gahs just back up the plate and will have to send somuddy in to cover if there's a play there."

Denzel squatted again and looked to Bake.

"Got to have even teams," he said. "I got easy outs too. If you only got eight that means your big hitters get up more."

"I'm not takin him, that's all there is to it." The Badger never looked to Denzel. "We don't need a catcher that bad. Not gonna get stuck with some little fairy."

Bake sighed. "Okay. He'll catch for us and you can have what's his name. Hewitt."

The Badger thought a minute, scowling, then agreed. Hewitt tossed his glove off and was congratulated on being traded to the winning side.

"Okay," said Bake, "you go catch. You're up ninth."

Denzel hustled behind the plate and the game started up. There was no catcher's gear, so though it was hardball he stood and one-hopped the pitches. He didn't let anything get by him to the kid who was backing him up. He threw the ball carefully to the pitcher. There were no foul tips. Badger got on and got to third with two out. Bake called time. He sent the right fielder in to cover the play at the plate and Denzel out to right.

The one called Royce was up. Denzel had booked him as strictly a pull-hitter. He played medium depth and shaded toward center. The first baseman turned and yelled at him.

"What you doing there? Move over. Get back. This gah can cream it!"

He did what the first baseman said but began to cheat in and over with the delivery.

The second pitch was in on the fists but Royce swung and blooped a high one toward short right. Denzel froze still.

"Drop it!" they screamed.

"Choke!"

"Yiyiyiyiyi!"

"I got it!" yelled somebody close just as Denzel reached up and took it stinging smack in the pocket using both hands the way his daddy had told him and then he was crashed over from the side.

He held on to the ball. Alley Oop helped him to his feet and mumbled that he was sorry, he didn't know that he really had it. The Badger stomped down on home plate so hard it split in half.

"Look what I found!" somebody called.

"Whudja step in, kid?"

"Beginner's luck."

Denzel's team trotted in for its at-bats. While they waited for the others to get in their positions Bake came up beside him.

"That mitt looks like you stole it out of a display window in the Hall of Fame," he said, and Denzel decided to smile. "Nice catch."

The first man up flied out to left and then Ernie stepped in. Ernie had made the last out of the inning before.

"Hold it! Hold it rat there!" Badger stormed in toward the plate. "Don't pull any of that stuff, who's up? Ninth man aint it? The new kid?"

"We changed the batting order," said Ernie. "You can do that when you make a substitution. The new kid bats in my spot and I bat where Hewitt was."

"Uhn-uh. No dice."

"That's the rules."

"Ernie," said Bake, stepping in and taking the bat from him, "let the kid have his ups. See what he can do."

51

Bake handed the bat to Denzel and the Badger stalked back into the field. It was a big, thick-handled bat, a Harmon Killebrew 34. Denzel liked the looks of the other one that was lying to the side but decided he'd stay with what he was given.

The Badger's team all moved in close to him. The center fielder was only a few yards behind second base.

"Tryn get a piece of it," said Ernie behind him, "just don't whiff, kid."

"Easyouteasyouteasyout!" came the chatter.

Denzel didn't choke up on the big bat. See what he can do.

The first four pitches were wide or too high. He let them pass.

"C'mon, let's go!"

"Wastin time."

"Swing at it."

"Let him hit," said the Badger. "Not goin anywheres."

The next one was way outside and he watched it.

"Come *awn!*" moaned the Badger, "s'rat over!"

"Whattaya want kid?"

"New batter, new batter!"

"Start calling strikes!"

"Egg in your beer?"

See what he can do.

The pitcher shook his head impatiently and threw the next one high and inside. Denzel stepped back and tomahawked a shot down the line well over the left fielder's head.

"Attaboy! Go! Go!"

"Dig, baby, all the way!"

"Keep comin, bring it on!"

By the time the left fielder flagged it down and got it in Denzel was standing up with a triple.

"Way to hit! Way to hit, buddy."

"Sure you don't want him, Badger?"

"Foul ball," said the Badger. He was standing very still with his glove on his hip. "Take it over."

This time Bake and half his team ran out to argue. The Badger turned away and wouldn't listen to them.

"Get outa here," they said. "That was fair by a mile. You gotta be blind."

He wouldn't listen. "Foul ball."

"Get *off* it," they said, "you must be crazy."

Denzel sat on the base to wait it out. The third baseman sat on his glove beside him and said nice hit. The Badger began to argue, stomping around, his face turning red, finally throwing his glove down and saying he quit.

"Okay," said Bake, "have it your way."

"Nope." The Badger sulked off but not too far. "If you gonna cheat I don't want nothin to do with it."

"Don't *be* that way, Badger, dammit."

"Hell with you."

"Okay," said Bake, looking over to Denzel and shrugging for understanding, "we'll take it over."

Denzel lined the first pitch off the pitcher's knee and into right for a single. Three straight hits followed him and he crossed the plate with the tying run. The first baseman made an error and then the Badger let one through his legs and the game broke open.

Denzel sat back with the rest of the guys. They wrestled with each other and did knuckle-punches to the shoulder.

They compared talent with a professional eye.

"Royce is pretty fast."

"Not as fast as Alley Oop."

"Nobody's that fast."

"Alley Oop can *peel*."

"But Royce is a better hitter."

"Maybe for distance but not for average."

"Nobody can hit it far as Purdy."

"If he connects."

"Yeah, he always tries to kill the ball. You got to just meet it."

"But if he ever connects that thing is gonna sail."

"Kiss it goodbye."

"Going, going, *gone!*"

Denzel sat back among them without talking, but following their talk closely, putting it all in his book. Alley Oop

53

scored and asked Bake to figure his average for him and Bake drew the numbers in the dust with a stick till he came up with .625. That was some kind of average, everybody agreed. They batted through the order and Denzel got another single up the middle and died at second. It was getting late so they decided it would be last ups for Badger's team. The Badger was eight runs down and had given up.

Bake left Denzel in right for the last inning but nothing came his way. Purdy went down swinging for the last out and they split up. Bake and the Badger left together, laughing, but not before Bake asked Denzel his name and said see you tomorrow.

Denzel didn't tell him that he'd be gone tomorrow. That they'd have to go back to Jonathan Phelps.

2

When Lewis saw Vaudie Bovis's trailer in camp he decided he'd go into town for Mr. Bob. He was checking up on the advance man when he bumped into Rags Rucker at the sporting goods store. He didn't recognize him till the old-timer opened his mouth.

"If it aint Lean Lewis Crawford looking fit as a spring colt. Buy me a drink?"

Rags had been with the old Marlins the year Lewis broke in. Rags had come down from his two-year stay with the big club. Come down for good.

"Coupla cool ones for the old pros," Rags called to the bartender, though Lewis wasn't thirsty. They were alone in the place but for a guy playing pinball. "I'm caught a little short, though, Lewis. Money's back at the mo-tel."

Lewis paid the man. Rags had been good to him when he was a rook.

"What you up to, Rags? You live here now?"

"Ohno. Just makin my way back north. Live with my daughter Eileen up in Maine. I was down for the training camps, the Grapefruit circuit. Make the trip every year, do a little scouting."

"Who you with?"

"Well, I'm sort of an independent. I like to be around the game, help bring young talent along."

"You're not on the payroll?"

"See, what it is Lewis, is I go round and dig up, you know, prospects, get em a showing, and then if they sign on anywheres I collect a little pocket money."

"Oh." They had called such people chickenhawkers in Lewis's day, and probably still did. The fellow at the pinball swore and slapped the top of the machine. "Int it a little late? Regular season's been going for a while now."

"Oh, this year I hung on with an old buddy. You member Onus Heimdall? Was up with the Browns while there was still Browns?"

"Third sacker? Stepped in the bucket?"

"Right, that's him."

"How's he doing?"

"Oh, he's dead."

"Oh."

"I run into him down in Winter Haven where he was retired, he'd taken sick and I sort of stuck by him till the finish. Had a nice place, he did. Onus was always a close one with a buck, made the right investments. Not like some of us. Funeral was Saturday."

"Sorry to hear it."

"He was a good one."

Rags stared at his hand. It shook almost imperceptibly. Veins stood up blue on the back of it. He raised it in front of his eyes and got it steady. Then he used it to signal the bartender for another.

"Every spring," he said, "every spring there's the rites. Every spring there's a new crop gone. You remember Petey DeVivo? Hotfoot Zimmler?"

"Heard of them," said Lewis. "They're before my time though."

"Gone. Crossed off the roster."

"You're lookin pretty good, Rags."

"Me? Like new, Lewis, like new. Lot of service left in the old pro yet. You take my word." He waited as the beer was placed before him.

56

"And what are you up to? You're not still with the game are you?"

"No, I'm with this show. We work the carnivals."

"Show? What do you do?"

"Play ball. Clown around."

"No kidding. How's the old stick these days?"

Lewis looked away as if distracted. "It's just softball."

"Softball?"

"It's not bad really. Actually, come to think of it, it's probably good for me. I'm working on my timin. Building up to the hard stuff." Lewis sounded like he was getting ready for another crack at organized ball.

"Yeah," said Rags. "Yeah, timing's the key. Timing's the key all right."

"It's not that bad, really."

Lewis nodded for another beer. "Um, there a lot of old, you know, ex-ballplayers down there? When you make the Grapefruit circuit?"

"Oh yeah, oh yeah," Rags perked up. "It's a regular fraternity it is. This trip I seen, lemme think, there was Bugsy LeFevre and his wife and Lou Pudroe and his wife and old Four-Eyes McNearny. Four-Eyes is a widower like me. Oh, and there was Hack Watson and his wife. He's on his third."

Lewis knew the names. "That's some good men."

"Damn right it is. Yes, there is some of the great ones left. Time don't have em all yet."

"Guess not."

"Last I was in New York I seen DiMaggio."

"Really?" Lewis was impressed.

"Yessir. Joltin Joe was there and I seen Lefty Grove and Feller and I even seen the Babe's widow. Mrs. Ruth."

"All at once?"

"Yeah, one them Old-Timers games on the television. Before the Yankees played."

"Oh."

"Some of the great ones left."

"Yup."

"I wish I could of been in on more of it."

"Mmn."

"Mismanaged." Rags shook his head. "That's the story of it right there. When I was coming up they took their time with you, kept you down for lots of seasoning. Not like today where they got high school boys puttin on the big league uniform."

"Nope."

"They waited too long on me. Timing, like you said. I was ready but they was too damn thick to see it. I was ripe and they left me on the vine, waited till my prime years were over before they give me a shot."

"It's tough." Among clubhouse lawyers Rags had been known as a judge.

"If I was with a different organization I probably would have been up there years sooner. You know Turk Devins, used to manage in the De-troit chain? He told me his organization was always high on me as a prospect, if I'd been with them they would of give me a showing right off."

"Probly."

"Same as with you."

"Well —"

"No bullshit now, Lewis, you were always right on the verge, right on the very edge of being big league material."

"I was up once, for a little —"

"First time I seen you, back with Miami when you was still leakin straw from wherever it was you come from, I said to myself this is a boy could be a major league property. Just give him a little guidance, a little push, and then watch him take off."

Yes, Rags had always been a fair judge of ballplayers.

"Mishandled, you was. They never showed any confidence in you."

"1963 I was up. Didn't see much playing time, though."

"You always had a nice-looking swing. If they'd of kept you in one place long enough to learn the pitchers you'd of been a pretty respectable hitter."

There wasn't many knew the game like old Rags.

"And you could always use that glove. A slick fielder."

Surprised they never put him on to coaching. Lewis signaled for two more beers.

"These days they bring them up from kindygarten. Just bad timing. I was born too soon."

"Guess so."

"But I wouldn't of wanted it the way it is today. Things I see make me worry about the game."

"Yuh?"

"I think it's going downhill." Rags's face darkened, he frowned into his beer.

"Things've changed."

"I think it's going to hell in a handbasket."

"I don't know about that, but —"

"I think," he said, "certain tendencies had better be reversed or the game is going to be in a sorry spot. I think Mr. Rickey's experiment has gotten out of hand."

"You mean the color line?"

"I mean the shines are ruining the sport. Taking it over and making it into what it oughtn't to be."

"Well, I —"

"Now I'm not a prejudiced man. Mr. Jack Robinson, from all reports, was a fine gentleman and a hustler to boot, and I have always admired a hustler. Some of his people in the game today are not such fine gentlemen, but that is to be expected when there is such a preponderance of them. I seen the Pirates down in Clearwater and they looked a shade darker than the old Homestead Greys. One game I saw they only fielded two white men."

"Things've changed, Rags."

"Now I'm not saying they're not talented, that they're not fine atheletes. Your shines can hit, they can throw, and Lord knows they can run. But they can not, as a rule, spare the price of a general admission ticket. That is why your attendance is down. Their own people can't afford to support them once the rent has been paid and the gin mills visited, and how many white people do you think will remain loyal fans when their team has been turned into a minstrel show? That's why your attendance is down and your big leagues are in dire straits and the minors have dried up. It's the shines and I'm not blaming them for getting what they can but it's still a goddam shame."

They were quiet for a while, a moment of respectful silence as if in mourning.

"You don't handle colored players then? For your scouting?"

"Not as a rule. Mostly what I see these days is Cubans."

"Cubans?"

"Yessir, some sharp little ballplayers come off that island."

"Aren't they pretty dark? I mean some of them?"

"There is a world of difference between a shine and a Cuban. Not a matter of color, Lewis, it's a matter of spirit. The Cubans are still hungry. And there been some good ones. You member Sandy Amoros?"

"Sure, with the Dodgers."

"Camilo Pascual?"

"Pitcher that came up through our organization."

"Cubans. And if there was something they had, it was spirit."

"Is there many left, I mean young ones? I'd figure that with the trouble and all —"

"Refugees. Fresh off the boat and hungry as can be. And weaned on baseball, every one of them."

"How do you, uh, I mean, I didn't know you spoke it. Cuban."

"No, I don't habla. I use the universal lingo. Baseball. I hear there's a boatload of them coming into the Keys I go down to the dock with a Louisville slugger over my shoulder as an introduction and things just proceed from there. Hell, the immigration people know me by now but the first time they seen me they like to shat in their pants. Thought I was some kind of demonstrator out to bust skulls, Cuba go home or something like that. Funniest thing since old Germany Schaefer stole first base. They sort of sidle up next to me, these two cops do, and say, 'Lookin for somebody?' 'Sure am,' I say, 'looking for the next Pedro Quinterra.' They don't go back that far so they don't savvy and close in a little on me.

'That so?' they say. 'Yessir,' I tell em, 'I'm lookin for the next Diego Segui.' 'Pops,' they say to me, 'if you're smart you'll be lookin for the next bus into town. Afore you get your ass busted into jail.' "

They both laughed a while at that one.

"Everybody down there knows me now, though. Call me Coach. They even help with the lingo a bit."

"You found anybody yet?"

"Oh, I've had a few, had a few. My last project turned out just fine. Young fella name of Jackie Oliveri. Shortstop. Got some quick hands on him. Gonna hear a lot of noise from this kid in a few years. Got some good pins on him."

"He can run?"

"Lewis, he can *peel*. Yup, I got him a berth with West Palm Beach in the Florida State League. He won't stay there long, let me tell you, he'll be up and out of there before the ink is dry. Boy has a natural talent."

"Can he hit?"

"Well, to be frank with you, if he's got a weakness it's his hitting. Just needs to see a little American-style pitching though, and he'll catch on. Has a little trouble with the curveball but he's a dandy with the straight stuff. You always had a hard time with the breaking pitch, didn't you, Lewis?"

"Rags, I can't say whether I did or I didn't. They all looked straight to me."

"That could of been the root to your problem right there."

"Could of been."

"Yup. So anyhow Oliveri signed on and I got me a little pocket money. It's nice to help the boys on their way."

"I'll bet."

"Though you might think an organization that has benefited from the best years of a man's life would make an effort to find a spot for a man when his playing days are through."

"It's tough."

"You might think there'd be room for a man who was always a team ballplayer, who never squabbled over contracts or none a that nonsense."

"Don't seem fair."

"You might think," said Rags, his face clouded over again, "that a man who give his all to the game would get more than a fifty-dollar finder's fee and a swift kick out the door when he tries to make his contribution."

Lewis sat back and was quiet, waiting for it to pass.

"Softball," said Rags.

"What?"

"When we was kids we wouldn't go near it. Would of used the sorriest, most lopsided thing in the world as long as it was a regulation size, afore we'd ever play any softball. That's what they had for girls' exercise class. We'd play with hard-balls had their covers flapping. And when the cover finally got tore off with a good clout, we'd wrap it with electrical tape, that black kind, and throw it back in play. Play all day and play all night under the street lights. We'd play a ball to death. But we didn't touch no softball. None a your under-handed slow pitching for us. And sooner or later that electrical tape would get knocked loose and start to peel and flap so's the ball coming at you was like a mad crow feather-flutterin into your glove. And when we got tired of repairs or run out of tape we just played her bare, and the string started to unwind and wherever it flew the ball would be trailing long streamers of twine that tangled and broke off. That pill would get smaller and smaller, harder and harder to hit, like you was getting on and the eyesight was failing or some-thing, and it kept playing out, unraveling. Unraveling."

Rags looked like he was going to fall asleep on his stool.

"So, you think you'll be heading up to Maine to your daughter's?"

"Huh? Oh, yeah. She got to send me the money though. To get up there. I been writing her."

"She just going to send you bus fare?"

"Well, it's more than that. She hasn't agreed on me living with her yet. Sometimes we haven't got on too well."

"I thought you lived with her up there."

"Oh, she'll agree all right, I'm sure she will. She only said no last time because she was afraid it would be too crowded.

But I told her how I'd only want a room and would just keep to my own and not bother them. Oh, she'll come around all right."

"Sure she will."

"You'd think," said Rags, looking very tired, "there would be consideration for who is responsible for bringing you into this world. You'd think there'd be respect for a man has done his best all his life. You'd think there'd be a place for a man."

When Lewis excused himself he left the old pro with a ten-spot. Rags had been good to him when he was a rook.

3

Knox excused himself as he slid past one of the browsers and headed for the rear of the shop. He passed the power tools and rolls of wallpaper and stopped in the middle of the caged parakeets. His fingers slipped over cuttlebone and kitty litter, ceramic deep-sea divers and tank tubing, catnip mice and flea collars until they finally settled on a little packet of fish food.

He laid it down before the old man at the cash register. The old man rang up 39 cents. Knox brought out a key from his pocket. "Say buddy, think you could make me a duplicate of this?"

"Sure thing." The old man took the key and turned it over in his fingers. "Be ninety-eight cents."

"Uh-huh."

"I'll be right out."

The old man disappeared into a little room behind the cash counter. When Knox heard the grinding wheel start up he looked to the Coca-Cola clock over the door, his lips counting silently. The grinding stopped and there were a few zips of a file. The old man returned with two keys.

"That be all?"

"Yessir, that's it." Knox paid the old man.

"If it don't fit you just bring it back and I'll do another for free."

"I'll do that." Knox turned to leave.

"What kind you got?"

Knox turned back. "Huh?"

"What kind of fish?"

"Fish? Oh, yeah, uhm — groupies."

"Groupies?" The old man frowned. "Never heard of em."

"Well, they, uh, they kind of rare. They sort of like groupers and sort of like guppies. Not many around."

"Groupies, huh? Have to look em up in my catalogue."

"Right. Well bye now."

"Come again."

Knox closed the door silently behind him.

A. C. was across and down the street a ways, leaning on a parking meter. Knox strolled behind him, then stooped to tie his shoe. They didn't look at each other.

"An old man at the box," he said, lacing intently, "two customers still inside. Clock over the door, easier to check than your watch. He grinds in a back room, like you guessed, two minutes and ten seconds. It's a piece of cake."

"Good work. Whud you get?" A. C. squinted up at the sun.

"Packet of fish food."

"Fish food?"

"Yeah, you know, you sprinkle it on top the water an they come up —"

"Jesus-God, what we want with fish food?"

Knox shrugged and untied his other lace. "You could pinch some fish."

"Backwards sumbitch. What we gonna keep em in? You need an outlet to plug in the tank. No outlets in the van."

"Just an idea. I don't even like fish."

A. C. sighed. "Okay, business. There's an old green job behind us — don't look, just tie your shoe. Nigger-lookin fins, no hubcaps, box of Kleenex on the dashboard. Anybody starts to come in on me you reach in and honk the horn three times."

"Got it."

"One of the customers just left."

"Good. You got the keys?"

"Right here. Don't fit a thing anymore, but they sure's hell gonna open up the Pidcock Pet and Hardware. Here comes the other one."

"Go to it, pardner." Knox turned and went back down the sidewalk a ways, crossing both his fingers.

A. C. took a long, deep breath and crossed the street. He winked at the Bimbos poster on the window of the shop, slipped on his sunglasses, and gimped inside favoring his left leg.

"Hey there." He made his voice low and husky.

"What can I do for you?"

"Got some keys here I need copies for."

"Sure thing. Ninety-eight cents apiece."

"Uh-huh." He handed three keys to the old man.

"Them summer colds are a bitch, aren't they?"

"Huh? Oh yeah. Just awful." He tried to sniffle.

"Be right back."

When the grinding wheel buzzed on A. C. pulled a canvas sack from down his pants and scurried down the aisle on his tiptoes, plucking items left and right off the counters and peeking over his shoulder to the Coca-Cola clock. He was careful to ease them quietly into the sack, going down one aisle to the pet section, then returning up another. One minute. One and a half. One forty-five. He snuck past the cash register as the grinding began for the third time, closed the door carefully, and cut down a side street.

Knox was waiting for him a few blocks away.

"Hoo-boy!"

"Hot diggity damn!"

"Like fuckin *clock*work."

"Never know what hitum." The Okies clapped their hands and punched each other's shoulders.

"Let's see, what we got here." Knox fished down into the bag as they walked together. "A — four — whatsit? Four-speed blender."

"Hit's a Jap one but it looks nice."

"Lectric hair dryer, just what I always wanted — uhm — a — waffle iron?"

"Makes just regular toast too."

"A staple gun — you get any staples?"

"Naw."

"A tube of caulking — a paint brush — box of Phillips-head screws — a — uh-oh, what's this big one down here at the bottom?"

"Don't know, I just grabbed it."

"A — let's see — Ever-Green Lawn Sprinkler. Quite a haul, A. C."

"Pardner, it's a wide-open world if you got some balls and a little know-how."

"With our talent and a good fence we be sittin pretty."

"No fences. That's how you get in trouble, pardner, letting other people in on it. In some businesses it don't pay to advertise."

"Damn straight."

"Hey, int that Pitcher over there gawkin in windows?"

"Sure's shit. Hey Pitcher! Pitcher!" They began to trot across the street, grins smeared over their faces, loot rattling in the sack, "Lookut we got!"

They burst through the door together, the Okies with an arm each around Pitcher, sandwiching him, Knox dragging the loaded sack behind.

"Ho-lee shit!" said Knox. "This room is got the D.T.'s!"

Every inch of wall space surrounding them was covered with colorful designs, shouting, snarling, writhing, twisting together.

"This is the place all right," said A. C. "What you think, Pitcher?"

Pitcher shrugged, almost beaming beneath their touch, almost turning tail to run.

"Hidy-doo, fellas. Rainbow Reynolds is the name." They strained to make out a breathing patch of wall topped by a pink globe. "Specialist in epidermic art. What can I do on you?"

67

The patch separated itself from the wall and came forward. It was a round, shaven-headed man whose arms and torso and legs were inked solid with tattoos. The man wore only shower clogs and madras Bermuda shorts. He extended his hand and the three shook it gingerly.

"We aim to get this boy here ignitiated," said A. C.

Rainbow narrowed his eyes and sniffed the air. "He eighteen years of age?"

"Yessir, he is that."

"He sober and in his right mind?"

"Sober? At one in the afternoon? This is a fine young athelete we got here, not one of your degenerate sailor boys."

"No problem then. Sorry, but I got to ask ahead or I'm in trouble with the law."

"I can understand. You mind if we look around?"

"Please do. Got over five hundred designs to choose from and if you don't see one you like just tell me what you got in mind and I'll knock it off freehand."

"Pitcher, we got us a *profes*sional here."

They pored over the walls, Pitcher looking strenuously disinterested, leading the way through tigers and sharks and spiders and dragons. Rainbow followed them proudly, his hands clasped behind his back.

"I can give you one the size of a dime," he said, "the size of a grapefruit or the size of a frying pan. Thirteen glorious colors to choose from."

"It's the boy's first," said A. C. "I figure he ought to start small and work up."

"Very sound advice."

"Though them big ones are awful impressive. What's all that on your chest, if you don't mind my asking?"

"Not at all. It's called 'The Garden of Earthly Delights.' Saw it in a picture book and spent two thousand dollars up to Chicaga to get it done."

"Handsome piece of work."

"The best. If you're out to decorate yourself you might's well go first class. You got no idea the number of butchers there are in the business."

"I can imagine."

"You're lucky you come upon a topflight parlor like this one."

"We are indeed."

"If you're so good," asked Pitcher, "what are you doing in Pidcock?"

"A very good question. This is a sharp young fella you got here." Rainbow winked at the Okies. "This is only my home base. Most of the year I'm on the road. The carnivals? I'd rather stay home but you got to go where the business is. It's no bed of roses, believe you me. You got no idea the number of shady characters work those carnivals."

"I can imagine." Knox giggled and nudged the sack under a chair with his foot. "I spect you get some strange birds wander in here?"

"Oh, a few. A few."

Pitcher led them through guns and daggers and skulls, bleeding crosses and dripping swords. He would stop before one and look at it, then at his arm or leg or chest and then back at the design.

"Had a little girl in here a week ago, cute thing, some kind of Spanish. Worked the orchards. Had me stencil 'Sunkist' on one of her tits."

"That so?" A. C. perked his ears. "You get many women?"

"Now and then. Mostly small stuff though, beauty marks and butterflies and such. Not too interesting. The drawing I mean. Some of it comes under what you might call cosmetic surgery. Had a fella wanted me to put little squiggly lines in between the hairs of his chest, give him a fuller crop. I done a good job on that one, two feet away you couldn't tell the difference."

"What happened to yours? Hair, I mean. I don't see none growin in the Garden there."

"Oh, I had it lectrolized off before I went to Chicaga."

"No shit."

"It detracts from the artistic effect."

Pitcher led them through hula girls and mermaids, nymphs and hookers, blonds, brunettes and redheads.

69

"If you don't mind my asking," said Knox, "how come you covered all over but for your top? Or are you gonna have some hair tattooed onto it?"

Rainbow passed his hand over his naked skull. "To tell you the truth, fellas, I'm waiting on an inspiration. I figure anything I put up there has got to be appropriate and tasteful. Can't have folks staring at my head. So till that inspiration comes I want to keep it a blank canvas."

Born to Raise Hell said the wall. Don't Tread on Me. Death Before Dishonor. Christ Is Risen. U.S.M.C. Go Navy. Mother.

"I've tattooed my share of heads though. Tattooed just about every anatomic place on the body."

Pitcher paused before a snake wrapped around a panther.

"Had a fella wanted me to do that one on his weenie."

"No!" The Okies were shocked.

"God's truth. Now that design has got to be a goodly size for it to read as anything more than a blob. I says mister, your eyes are bigger than your equipment. He settled for an eyeball."

"On his *thing*?"

"Whoah now," said Rainbow earnestly, "don't get me wrong. I wore gloves the whole time. Isn't a thing unnatural goes on in *my* establishment."

"How much is that one?" Pitcher pointed to an eagle with a sword in its claws.

"Thirty dollars."

A. C. whistled and rolled his eyes to the ceiling.

"All these middle-sized ones on the wall are from twenty-five up. You come to the best, and the best costs money."

"That's a major investment you're talking about there."

"You can have a name for ten. Thirteen colors to choose from and four different kinds of script."

Pitcher made a face and considered a moment. "Does it cost extra if it's somebody else's name?"

"Not a cent."

Pitcher shrugged. "Guess I'll have a name then."

"Sold. Take a seat, my friend, and we'll do you a name."

70

"Attaboy Pitcher," said A. C. "You joinin the society of men."

Pitcher was led to a vinyl-covered chair and sat down. Rainbow rolled a table over bearing racks of ink. "What color you want it?"

Pitcher looked to the Okies for advice.

"It's your skin, buddy."

"Well first, where do you want it?"

"You figure Mr. Bob would mind if I put it on the back of my pitchin hand?"

"Fuck Mr. Bob. He don't own you, son."

"Does it leave a scab or anything?"

"For a week or so," said Rainbow, "but it just itches a little."

"Okay, the back of my hand."

"In that case I'd advise against blue. Looks too much like veins. And yellow or orange don't read that well alone. How bout a nice crimson red?"

"You're the doctor."

Rainbow went to a corner bench and came back with a shining electric needle. "Okay, what's the name?"

Pitcher said something but none of them could make it out.

"Whatsat?"

"Charleen."

"Oh-*ho*! Charleen, is it? All this time you been holdin out on us. I tell you pardner, hit's the shy ones you got to watch for."

"Damn straight."

"Is that e-n-e or e-e-n?" asked Rainbow.

"E-e-n."

"Pitcher, buddy, whoever she is, I can garntee you she'll be impressed. If there's one thing a woman admires in a man, it's commitment. Diamonds may drop down the drainpipe, but a tattoo is for*ev*er."

"It don't hurt but a little," said Knox.

"It'll sting some," said Rainbow.

"Let it," Pitcher told them, setting his face to stone. "let it hurt all it wants to." The needle came on with a high whine.

"Lookit him, pardner, not a flinch."

"That's gonna be pretty."

Pitcher casually studied the designs on the walls around him, now and then blinking against the sweat drops that rolled down to his eyes. Rainbow worked quickly, flicking what blood there was off with the back of his little finger, forcing the name under Pitcher's skin in a flowing script till all the letters burned together on the hand. He dabbed them cool with an alcohol pad.

"Easiest job I had in weeks," said Rainbow. "You got your-selfs a young spartan here."

A. C. peeled off a ten and laid it on the table. "I thank you for your services, friend. It's been very instructional."

"Anytime. Tell your buddies where you got it."

"And watch out for them carnival people," said Knox from the door.

"I will, don't you worry. Don't scratch it too much," he called after them, "it could get infected."

He came across the sack when he was cleaning up. If they didn't come back for it he could maybe get a deal from Lester at the Pet and Hardware. And the packet of food he could take home for his parrotfish.

4

According to the posters a carnival had been there about a week ago. They didn't say whether there was a ball team or not. He'd have to check with the local bloods and then see if they could scare up some real food. If nothing came up he could push on to Savannah for the night, because this next town was hardly on the map. Stone *no*where.

As he drove Dred went over the reasons why he had to kill the freak. It wasn't just for the others' sake, to show them what happened if you fucked with Dred. He could have stayed back on the street and done that, gotten everything he had lost back without this hunt. And it wasn't just the code of getback. The white man had disappeared and it didn't make business sense to waste any more time on him. So why was the feeling so strong? Why did he grind his teeth to the gums dreaming about some whiteboy sideshow who got in a cheap shot?

It wasn't that he had called Dred's bluff. It couldn't be that. Because it wasn't a bluff. No *way*. But how to let people know for sure that it wasn't, that Dred was real, Dred was undeniable? All that counts is action, straight and clear. So he was beating the bushes to find the man who challenged his hand. And the killing would be no bluff.

He took the gun from under the seat and hefted it in his hand, not taking his eyes off the road. He liked the weight of it. More than that he liked the way it felt the one time he had shot it. It had smacked against his palm, tearing to be free. The most kick, the biggest bang of any handgun made. More than you needed just to kill a man. But Dred wasn't just killing anybody, he would have more than that. He felt the dammed power of the gun in his hand, felt all his hate trapped under pressure inside it. Oh, it would be real, all right, Dred would be real in killing. He would let it come screaming out from the barrel and all kinds of dues would be paid.

Buildings appeared up ahead and he put the gun away.

Dred coasted across the main street of the town behind tinted windows and wraparound shades, checking out the expressions on the sore red faces as he passed. Cracker country. Land of the peckerwoods. The word tickled him and he bunched his mouth as if to smile. Peckerwood. Something small and red and nervous, something that fly off quick when you say boo. Like the boy at the filling station who tried to give him the runaround. Who would want to live down South? went the old street riddle. Only a pecker would. Something small and red and nervous.

The faces did not seem as impressed as Dred had come to expect. Maybe it was the finish, it had lost some of its luster. He would have to get it washed and waxed when he had a chance.

There was a diner with a Coca-Cola sign and a gas-pump grocery store and a barber shop and an ancient Woolworth's with empty display windows. There was an insurance office over a funeral parlor and that was just about it. Main Street. Some sad-assed people, these crackers.

Dred poked about the edges of the Main Street nucleus as he had learned to do, searching for the tracks or bridge or end of pavement used for the color boundary. He found a likely looking patch of dirt road that took a rapid dip to reveal a shacktown at its bottom. A hollow, thought Dred, crackers must call it Black Hollow. He stopped for a moment to check the road ahead, not wanting to disembowel the car on a root or rock. He wondered why he heard no children playing.

Dred descended into Black Hollow. He slid silently over the roots that had taken over the road. There was nobody outside.

The Hollow was a shadow image of the white town above, a single sad main street with little roadlets branching off from it. There was a barbecue joint with a Cola-Cola sign and a grain and grocery store and a barber shop and a church over a funeral parlor. There were no cars anywhere and when Dred turned off his stereo, when he took off his shades and rolled down his window, it was silent. There was no music. Dred frowned and thought of the gun under the seat. He stopped the car and got out slowly. Didn't know they still made them this way. Must all be out choppin cotton.

Dred explored the buildings of the main street, creaking up the drooping porches and peering through boarded-up windows. The doors were nailed shut but gave with a dry-rotted crunch when he pushed them. He went from wasted building to wasted building, leaving size-fifteen tracks in their dust, taking everything in with his eyes, touching nothing. There was nothing, no one, to touch. There was nothing left but the smells, the aged funk of spicy cheap pork and mustard greens, of fried hair and Congolene, of black sweat and black sickness. There was one long, empty coffin left in the funeral parlor.

There had been no black faces visible above on the hill so it wasn't that they had moved up. And they didn't lynch an entire town. Not enough peckerwoods in the state to pull something like that off. Sides, they didn't lynch people these days. Crackers gotten subtle.

In the light again, outside the funeral parlor, Dred heard the shout of a small, distant voice. There was somebody alive somewhere back in the Hollow.

He followed the sound away from the main street, down roads that were paths, snaking around shacks in various states of ruin. He wanted to go straight at it but that wasn't how Black Hollow worked. The paths twisted and doubled back on themselves, the shacks gave no landmark in their abandonment. Some had been painted once and some had never borne that pretension, some looked livable but for the vines that spilled from the windows. Dred could hear stomping and chasing and high-pitched laughter now, he walked a little faster through the maze. If there were kids playing it couldn't all be gone.

Dred stopped in front of a large house, in reasonably good shape, that stood above the others in the Hollow. It was two stories and the yellow paint had faded but not peeled. The other houses off of the main street had smelled of musty furniture but this one held odors more familiar to Dred. Thick perfume lingered, and the smell of sour wine vomit. There were low, green weeds carpeting the path that had led in a beeline from the back door up the hill to cracker town. He heard them inside, singing —

> *What do you bring to your lovin spouse?*
> *Black Missy, Black Missy*
> *Back fum you work in the white man's house*
> *Black Missy, so fine.*

> *What did you catch out a runnin wild?*
> *Black Missy, Black Missy*
> *Pocket fulla change and a blue-eyed child*
> *Black Missy, of mine.*

There was a tittering and then they broke into whispers. The front door was open. Dred entered a dust-coated parlor, the walls papered a tired red patched with squares and rectangles of bright scarlet where pictures had been hung. There was one picture left, tilting over a spot where the floor sagged in memory of a couch. It was of a woman lying on a rug. But water had gotten to it, and time. The woman had wrinkled and her oils had bled and cracked, so you could tell neither age nor color, only that her mascara had run to her chest. The picture was titled "The Wedding Night." Dred breathed through his mouth to avoid the perfume of musk and vomit.

76

They were somewhere upstairs. What were they doing here and why that song, of all the things kids could sing? This is a strange little town, thought Dred, stand to reason it breeds some strange little niggers. The stairs gave a weary moan with his first step and the whispering stopped above.

He found them in one of the little bedrooms upstairs, hiding behind a bedframe that still supported the skeleton of a canopy. Found four of them, banjo-eyed with fright, grown pale beneath the soot smudged on their faces. Little peckerwood kids play-acting. A minstrel show.

"Come on out from there." Dred's voice boomed deeply in the empty house.

They edged out and stood in a group against the far wall.

"What are you doing in here?"

They shrugged, white lips and eyeballs frozen.

"Where is everybody?"

They shrugged again.

"What are you doing," Dred asked them, "in other people's houses?"

"All the color fokes gone," said one.

"Nobody ever live here," said another.

"People just passed the night," said another. "My daddy said so."

"Where did they go? The people who lived here?"

They shrugged again.

"There must be some black people left. Where are they? Where can I find them?"

"Bugbear."

"Who?"

"Bugbear left. Bugbear th'ony one."

"Where is he? Where does he live?"

"Daytime he be at the Woowuth. Up on Main Street?"

Dred took a step toward them and they pressed together. "How long has it been this way? How long have the people been gone?"

"Don't member," said one.

"There was some old people," said another, "but I never seem em. My brothers did, but I never."

77

"Asn't never been anybody in Spook Holler," said another. "Ony Bugbear, he tells stories bout when there was."

"Okay," he said, "okay. You get out of here now. Don't you ever come back here." He took a step aside to let them pass before him. "This doesn't belong to you."

The children scurried by and down the stairs, blond hair sprouting obscenely from their blackened heads, minds already racing with the story they would tell the other guys about what they'd seen in the Perfume House.

Dred walked back to his car through the Hollow. One of his tires was flat. He fixed it, the first time he had ever changed one of his own tires. He had to read the directions for the jack through twice and got a spot where he knelt on his canary-yellow slacks. There was no visible puncture, no sign as to why the tire had gone flat. It had just emptied. Dred flowed out of the Hollow.

He parked across from the Woolworth's and got out. There were five of them, crackers, lounging out in front in chairs and rockers. He put his shades on, it was high noon. Dred looked across the street at them and felt that he was sweating. From changing the tire. Peckerwoods don't bother me. He had to cross the street, straight at them. He felt vulnerable for a moment in the open, flat space, missing the shelter of tall buildings. Behind enemy lines. So what? Just white boys is all, peckerwoods. They fly off if you say boo. But his lean, the bop of his walk felt suddenly ridiculous on this street.

He stood on the sidewalk before them. They were large and calm and red, the smug red of sunbaskers. Straight at it, got to go straight at it.

"Where can I find Bugbear?"

"Bugbear?" said one. "Bugbear who?"

"They only told me Bugbear. They said I could find him here."

"Well I'm not Bugbear," said another, "thas for goddam sure."

They all crinkled their eyes and a laugh passed among them, though it was kept inside.

78

"You kin of his?" said another.

"Is a certain fambly resimblence."

"What you want with Bugbear?"

"I want to talk with him."

They pondered this for a moment. "You wouldn't kid us now, would you? You wouldn't be here to take our boy away?"

"I want to talk with him."

"What about you want to talk?"

"That's my business." Dred stared straight through them to the entrance of the store.

One, a fat one in a rocker, hooted and smiled at the sun and another silent laugh passed among them. "His *business*. You hear that, Reeves? So it's a business call, is it? Whynch you say so in the first place?"

"Business call for Bugbear, at's no problem."

"Should of told us. We're the boy's receptionists."

The fat one gestured to the door with his hand. "All the way down the center aisle and then to your left. Thas Bugbear's office."

"Don't bother to knock."

Dred went through the door and heard scrapings and creakings as they got up to follow him in.

There were only a few customers picking over the goods. A girl with a bad complexion played with a salt shaker behind the lunch counter. All turned to watch Dred stride down the center aisle. He came to the end and turned left. There was a swinging door that said MEN. Another word above it had been painted over. There were no other doors to the left.

Dred looked inside. It was no longer a restroom, there were stacked crates of merchandise, some broken open and spilling out onto the floor. He heard snatches of the crackers' voices through the door behind him.

"See them clothes —"

"See them shoes —"

"Biggest goddam —"

"Whaz e want th'our boy —"

"Got to be crazy, *got* to be —"

79

Before him, from the far corner of the room, Dred heard humming. The voice was high and thin, the song a children's rhyme. Dred took off his shades and went forward. The humming was from behind the headless body of a naked white woman who was striking a summerwear pose. An old, long black man sat with the head in his lap, stroking the hair as he hummed.

"Old man?"

The old man stopped humming and looked up from the head. "Yassuh? I hep you suh?"

The old man had cotton-white hair and a mottled brown sugar color. He lay the head gently by him on the crate then eased himself to the floor. He was well over six feet, though not so tall as Dred, and hung his head like a scolded dog. "You lookin for sumn?"

It was a trick. The kids had told them he was coming and they had set it up. It had to be a trick. "Are you Bugbear?"

The old man smiled a brilliant full-toothed smile. "Yassuh, thas just who I is. Them fokes out theyuh need sumn?"

"You can drop the darky act, old man. It's just us."

"Whatsay? What ack you speaking of?" The old man's eyes were hidden in hollows of flesh. Dred strained to see if there were anything in them.

"It's just us, old man."

"Name Bugbear. This yere Miss Maggie." He indicated the head on the crate.

"Don't fool with me, old man. I have to know some things."

Bugbear smiled. "Atcha suhvice."

"Where did they all go? All the black people?"

"What black peoples?"

"The ones who lived down the hill. In the Hollow."

"Nawf, I guess."

"When did it happen?"

Bugbear shrugged. "She just happen over time. There uz less an less an finely there's just me."

The old man was wearing an ancient pair of overalls that carried all the smells of the Hollow. "They weren't forced out? Nobody drove them away? Took their land?"

Bugbear giggled a little. "Oh *no*. They tried to make em stay. White fokes allus tryin to make em stay."

"Why didn't you go?"

Bugbear shook his head, wondering at the question. "I was *bawn* here, Mista, I got nobody up Nawf. Got nobody take care me anywheres but here. They want me here. They *needs* me here."

Dred was sweating heavily now, the old man gave him the creeps. He could feel the crackers behind him, a burning on his neck. "You're crazy. You're a crazy old man."

Bugbear laughed out loud. "You hear that, Miss Maggie? Man come in here, dress in *yal*lah fum head to foot, axin stupid questions, wearing *sun*glasses in the stawge room, an he call Bugbear crazy. That is a man got a funny notion of what is *crazy*."

Dred saw that the old man's teeth were false as he laughed, and caught himself looking to the mannequin to see if she was laughing too.

"How do they need you? How can you stay here?"

"Need me to tidy up the stawge room. Need me to wash them winduhs. Need me cause they allus had Bugbear to do f'them. Wunt know what to do th'out Bugbear. I wuhks here an Mista Reeve he gimme a cot, gimme a room my own. Let me come in here I'm not busy, talk wif Miss Maggie. Give me the run of the sto. Send they chillun to me, learn em bout the old days. Where else I belong?"

"Nowheres." Dred saw that the old man was barefoot. Long snaky toes. "There's nowhere you belong anymore. Cept maybe on somebody's lawn holding a lantern."

"An jus where you think *you* belong, child?"

"Anywhere I want to be."

The old man laughed softly. "Young man, you don't know *she*-it. You got to *earn* belongin. It don't just come to you. Got to pay the *price*."

"I've paid. I'm a black man."

"Child, one look at you tell me you aint paid squat. You aint neb been hurt. You got all the scream without none a the scrape. Jus a evil-lookin nigger pretend he be bad. You can't fool Bugbear, he *see*."

For a moment Dred wanted the gun, wanted to unleash it on the crazy old liar. Town was about to lose its last darky. He worked to keep up his stare.

"What you name, son."

"Dred."

Bugbear's face perked and he seemed to try to peer out from the eye-hollows. A crooked smile grew on his face. "*I* know *you*," he said with sudden discovery. "I *know* Drayuhd. Known him all my life." He walked toward Dred, reaching out with a trembling arm.

"Wrong, old man. You never seen me before. I never been South before."

"You uz bawn here," said Bugbear, "This where you *from*. You know me, you allus known me. We fum the same *blood*, son. Don't you deny me."

Dred began to move back but the old man had him in a bony grip.

"Say Mista Reeve! Mista Reeve, you out theyuh? Mista Handy? Got a homeboy come back to visit. Got a homeboy come back to Spook Holluh!"

Dred turned and was halfway out the aisle before the old man stopped shouting. He heard the crackers laughing behind him and remembered to put his shades back on. The Coupe squealed into an A-turn, facing him with the church. The clock above it had no hands.

He was five miles down the road before he realized he never asked about what he had come for, never asked about the carnival.

It was all a trick, a cracker trick. It had to be.

5

The lot man gave Mr. Bob the phone number that had been waiting and showed him where the office phone was. Mr. Bob brought his money book.

"Hello?"

"Phil Dodge?"

"Speaking."

No secretary, thought Mr. Bob. A small-timer.

"I'm told you're interested in doing some business with the Bimbos."

"Oh, it's you. Why yes, I am. Very interested."

"Can I ask how you happened to hear of me?"

"You know Mrs. Pinkham? Handles the wrestling and a few other things in Atlanta? Well, she put me on to you."

"Mrs. Pinkham, huh?" Mr. Bob was impressed. "How's she making out these days?"

"Like a bandit. She's a shrewd lady."

"That she is. A real businessman."

They both paused a moment to wonder at Mrs. Pinkham's success.

"I hear you have an open date."

"And I hear you have a proposition." $ $ $ $ wrote Mr. Bob.

83

"You're open tomorrow and I need an attraction tomorrow. I can get you three hundred up front, that's with no promotion or kickback at your end."

"Three hundred?" Mr. Bob made his voice sound unimpressed. His pencil did a quick dance in the book. He'd tell the boys a hundred seventy-five. Twenty-five each with an extra ten on the side for Pogo. The midget had made himself a separate peace and promised to keep his nose out of the books. Fifty was understood for Mr. Bob. That made one eighty-five. Figure fifteen for gas and a meal and that left —

"You still there?"

"Three hundred is getting close, Mr. Dodge, but it's awful short notice. The boys might not be interested —"

"That's good money for two hours' work. The midget still with you?"

— that left about a hundred-dollar cushion for Mr. Bob. The bigger the cushion the softer the landing if things should collapse. A man had to protect himself. "Star attraction. How far are you from here?"

"Hour, hour and a half from Pidcock. On the other side of Valdosta."

Mr. Bob sighed dramatically over the phone. "I'd like to help you out, I really would, but I got to think of my boys. They're pretty tired." He was probably desperate if he was scrambling at this late hour. "If you could sweeten the deal with a little slice of the gate they might be put in a better state of mind."

Phil Dodge sighed dramatically over the phone. "Five percent?"

"It sounds so insignificant is the problem. They'd have more confidence in a double figure. Put on a much better show."

There was a long silence at the other end of the line. ? ? ? ? wrote Mr. Bob.

"Okay, make it ten."

"That's white of you, Phil." He'd shoot straight with them about the percentage. They were irresponsible but you had

84

to keep their trust. And if Burns smelled anything he'd use it to shake down another raise. "We'll bring our own tickets for you to use at the box."

"Your tickets? You don't trust me?"

"Now, now, it's not a matter of trust. It's a matter of good business practice."

"Okay, we'll see."

"I mean it's going to be hard to talk my boys into this. It's not me you got to sell the idea to."

"No."

"I'm always ready to join in a profit-makin venture. But with the boys there are emotional factors to deal with." They had been pushing him for more pocket money for some time now. This might get them off his back. Plus that cushion.

"I understand. Well, three hundred in front and ten percent of the gate. Is it a deal?"

"Hold your horses now. There some details I want to know about your operation before I make any commitments."

"Details?"

I got him running, thought Mr. Bob. Phil Dodge is on the bad end of the old bulldozer treatment. "First off, what time you expect us to go on?"

"Seven-fifteen."

"A night show? Valdosta's the only place for miles has got a field with lights."

"No more. I got them at my stadium. We're halfway between Headlight and Colon, brand-new facility."

"Brand-new, huh? What kind of shape is it in? My boys won't tolerate any half-assed conditions."

"Won't find much better in the state of Georgia. This will be our inaugural attraction. It's quite an honor for you to be chosen."

"That remains to be seen. Where you gonna find a crowd?"

"I'll find it all right."

"I hope so. Ten percent of nothing is nothing. Who lives out there?"

"Oh, people."

He's caging, thought Mr. Bob, be careful.

"You're not risking a thing."

"Financially, no. But I'm putting the regard of my associates on the line. Labor relations are a delicate matter. I gotta think of my boys."

"I can understand. It's a deal then?"

"We'll be there early to put things on paper."

"Fine. Glad we come together on this."

"Same here. And say, Phil? You think we could keep the monetary aspects of this just between us two horse traders?"

There was a laugh on the other end of the line. "Only way to work it."

"Anything else I should know ahead of time? I don't like surprises."

"Can't think of a thing."

"Nice doin business with you then, Phil. See you tomorrow."

"Look forward to it."

Mr. Bob did a bit more scratching in his book on the way from the office, blending the windfall in with the big picture. Pulled a nice little transaction there, he thought. Almost too easy.

6

Pogo was alone in the little locker shack when he found it under a pile of wet towels. The usual cover — women in their underwear chained to a dungeon wall, demon-eyed Nazi torturers. Ah, thought Pogo, see what the Active Male is up to.

The stories were nothing. They all started at the end, a description of whatever predicament involving half-dressed girls was shown in the title picture and then a flashback to explain how the hero got himself into such a mess. Maybe one or two paragraphs to get him out of it and get the girl. There was the Nazi story and a story on young girl hitch-hikers luring men to their ruin and a phony detective thing about a wife-swapping blackmail ring in L.A. "The Other Side of the Keyhole" by Steve Mann, Private Investigator.

Private eye my ass. Krauts and robbers and wet dreams for the working stiffs. Private eye. Think it's glamorous do they? Think it's bargirls and divorcées. A con job is what it is. Make people want what they can't get. Wet Dream Magazine.

He skimmed over the stories and then began to get to the ads. The meat of the magazine. The con job in the con job. Oh, they could fix you up all right, no matter what your problem was, from bad breath to leprosy. Fix you up to win your-self a real knockout.

First on the agenda, get your act together. Are you fat, Buddy? Bald-headed, broke? Well, first things first, pal, dough is what makes the planet spin. You want to be an irresistible ladykiller you've got to shell out. Takes some capital to build up a harem.

EASY MONEY!
HOW TO BECOME RICH BY BEING LAZY!
"MOST PEOPLE ARE TOO BUSY SURVIVING TO GET AHEAD."

Mr. Moe Kargill told how he had forsaken the 18-hour days and 7-day weeks of the rat race and developed a sure fire system that had brought him a $100,000 house, two boats and a Cadillac while doing a lot less work. Out of the goodness of his heart he was willing to let his secret out for the meager fee of $10.00 (check or money order). Was that so much to risk when riches beyond *your wildest dreams* were at stake?

Dear Moe, said the order blank, you may be full of beans, but what have I got to lose? Send me a copy of EASY MONEY! Please rush!

Dear Moe, I think you are full of beans and I do not have ten bucks to lose. If you are so hot on "sharing your good fortune," on "spreading the wealth," why don't you just keep your book and send me some EASY MONEY itself? This will cut out the middleman and make it so I can "reap the benefits of an early retirement."

Please rush.

All right now, see what we can do with the green stuff when Moe sends it.

OVERWEIGHT?

A little.

UNSIGHTLY BULGES?

88

In spades.

Then try our — Insta-Thin TummyToner Belt
Just slip it on and WOW!
"Inches Disappear"

The man in the picture had undergone an amazing be-
fore/after transformation. The TummyToner had not only
erased his hanging midriff, it had shaken off the flab from his
thighs and the jowls from his face. It had put a smile on his
face, muscles in his arms and chest, had turned his baggy
striped boxers to tight bikini briefs. There was a beautiful
mane of hair sprouting from his head and an equally beautiful woman sprouting from his side.
Wonder if it comes with batteries.

HIGH POTENCY PROTEIN FORMULA!

Uh-oh.

LET'S BE HONEST WITH OURSELVES.

Sure, sure.

NOBODY LIKES TO LOSE THEIR VIRILITY.

A man gave a tough, no-nonsense look from the page. He
said that to lose your hair was to lose your virility. Straight
stuff. And if you think you could stop it by pouring fancy
goop on your head you're kidding yourself.
Virility, healthy hair, come from within. The man was selling a high potency, enzyme-treated protein and vitamin E
formula that you drank from a bottle.
Good old vitamin E.
The man looked like he had been swimming in the stuff.
He had huge bushy gray sideburns and jet black hair on top.
A model who stood behind him reached around to bury her

long fingers in the fur rug of his chest. He looked like he had to shave his square-jawed face three times a day.

So I'm rich, slim and hairy. Bring on the broads.

The who?

Love-hungry widows!
Pick your Chick!
1200 Ladies!

Clubs, directories, addresses and phone numbers. Hundreds of lonely, anxious girls in our files. Learn who's hard up in your neighborhood.

Swedish Girls
Oriental Girls
Beautiful, eager Mexican Girls

Pen pals and hookers selling snapshots. Women trying to get into the country. No broad who put her name in a grab bag could afford to be too picky, could she?

She could. The further away the women were the less expensive to get a line on them. And even if you did connect with somebody you still had to go through all the rest.

This offer will NOT be repeated
if we get enough men for our women.

Remember our slogan:
"No man is any good without a Woman."

You could always send away and keep the pictures. Free looks. Wet dreams. Wishful thinking. You could track them down even and follow them, put on a tail and see how it wagged. Or call them up. But there was still all the rest. Free looks is safest.

X-RAY SPECS!
AN HILARIOUS OPTICAL ILLUSION!

Optical illusion, that's more like it. That's about all you could count on. Like writing a letter, you can do it from a distance. It's the face-to-face stuff that gets hairy.

How to Pick Up Chicks
Surefire advice from successful studs!

Technique. Style. What to say and do. Moves and how to make them. Oh yes, we can all use more of that.

> Now you can get the girl of your dreams. Not ugly, fat or dumb girls —

I'll take 'em. Not choosy. Give me your dumb, your fat, your ugly. . . .

> but beautiful girls with long soft shiny hair, pretty eyes, lovely soft breasts, long sexy legs, delicious lips —

Right, okay. Real knockouts.

> Learn how they give you signals they want you to "pick them up." And they Do!

They do?

> Of course they Do! PLUS 25 great opening lines!

Hiya beautiful, ever fuck a midget? Oh no. Rich and slim and hairy as I am, lonely and eager as they are, it's still a bad bet at five bucks. Even with the testimonials.

> *"Don't use my name, but let me thank you in behalf of my husband and me. We thought Jerry was a homosexual, but after we gave him your book . . ."*
> *A Mississippi Housewife*

PRIDE OF THE BIMBOS

"It used to be I couldn't get past second base, now it's BANG BANG BANG each and every time."
Troy Satzger, PFC, U.S. Army

"What if you give them the willies?"
Pogo Burns, Shortstop

Maybe "chicks" is a little too much to hope for at my age. All that chasing, all that scoring. Could wear a guy out, even a TummyToned one. Better shoot for something a little more mature, a little more permanent. Something a little more money-in-the-bank. It could be rough on a guy's nerves having to "pick them up" all the time. A guy could strain himself.

1 OUT OF 5 WOMEN WANTS <u>YOU</u>
FOR HER NO HOLDS BARRED, NO STRINGS ATTACHED MAN!

By a Doctor no less. A distinguished American scientist. Now we're getting places.

Every step preplanned for you! From the first smile to the Most Intimate Caress!

When to attack. When to retreat. When and where to blow your nose.

We take all the risk from the first kiss, the first touch, the first night of Lingering Ecstasy!
MENTAL FOREPLAY
The Psychological technique that starts her *squirming with curiosity!*

No risk? Sorry Doc, for that you pay them or you rape them. There isn't a thing you can do with women that doesn't mean some risk. Straight dope. Only machines are surefire. Only broads in cartoons and wet dreams go down automatic, with the rest it's always a gamble. And Doc, I'm on a losing streak you wouldn't believe.

FOR LONELY MEN ONLY

He swore and threw the magazine against the wall. It fell open to a picture of a luscious, naked woman. He swore again. Then he went to look at it.

Hi! I'm Candy! I want to be your Playmate!
So round, so firm, so flexible

Wonder if she comes with the bars over her tits and the star on her crotch.

ONLY Candy has electronic-type ACTION mouth,
molded breasts and ALL female parts!

Including a price tag.

You can make me thin, you can make me well-rounded, you can make me pleasingly plump, in fact Tiger, you can make me ANY way you desire!

If you aren't careful you can make her pop.

Dress her in lingerie, bathing suit, dainty under-clothes, tight-fitting sleek dresses, mini-skirts or leather-

Paint GOODYEAR on her side and float her over a football stadium.

Not a toy. Designed for the ACTION–MINDED man.

No risks there. The perfect dame. Latex love for people who don't want to get involved.

SEND ME CANDY AND _____ OF HER FRIENDS (SPECIFY WHICH). IF I AM NOT TOTALLY THRILLED AFTER A 10-DAY TRIAL, MY MONEY WILL BE REFUNDED.

93

There were dozens of hard-to-get items and novelty products, rubber goods and stiff-necked women getting the tension release of "good vibs." Vibs were a hot number, whatever they were. There were cremes and ointments and unmentionables from France and Denmark. There were all the forbidden fruits from Yucca Street in Hollywood. There was the Pogo Burns Method.

NOT A CLUB, NOT A SPRAY, NOT A NOVELTY. A SIMPLE EXERCISE WITH THE ACTIVE MALE IN MIND. ABSOLUTELY NO RISK OF TURN-DOWNS OR MESSY ENTANGLEMENTS. WITH THE AMAZING TECHNIQUE OF TOTAL MENTAL LOVEPLAY WOMEN ARE NOT NECESSARY! THE POGO BURNS METHOD IS SUITABLE FOR USE IN THE PRIVACY OF YOUR HOME OR OFFICE. WHY BOTHER TO STOP DREAMING AND DROOLING? START JERKING OFF TODAY!

On the last page there was an ad that he didn't have to read. He knew it by heart. Learn to be a PRIVATE DETECTIVE at home! Your key to an exciting, rewarding life. Be somebody, be a private eye. The biggest con job of them all. Wet Dream Magazine.

He put it back under the towels and gave the pile a half-hearted kick. Wouldn't it be nice, though? Wouldn't it be easy, wouldn't it be nice, if it were all true? Love-hungry widows, lonely Oriental girls, picking up chicks?

Until that day there was always the Pogo Burns Method.

7

Vaudie looked into the mirror at Bouncy Bovis and began to
rub her away. There were two hours before the evening
teaser. She smeared cold cream on her face and then on the
breasts, hoisting each one up gingerly with a hand and daub-
ing it on with her fingers. The breasts were sore again. She
wanted to lie on her back and rest them but she had things to
do. She blotted the cream away with a damp wad of Kleenex
and the stretch marks on their sides were revealed, the net-
work of dark blue veins was uncovered. As soon as the
breasts were dry she cinched them up snug in her bra. They
hurt a little less. Then she turned to her face.

Gayle pushed in through the hung blanket that served as
their dressing-room door and nodded to Vaudie's reflection.
She quickly pulled her clothes on over her costume and left
with her makeup intact. Vaudie had told her and told her that
was what made for the pimples, but Gayle was young yet and
in too much of a hurry to bother taking it off in between. She
liked the makeup.

There wasn't time to make it over to Fat Fanny's tent for a
shower so Vaudie patted a little water from the sink on her
and dried. The water smelled like swamp. She threw some of

95

the Johnson's powder under her armpits and between her legs.

Vaudie put on her gray cotton pants and one of Theron's old shirts. She shook her hair out and brushed it a little, then pulled the dark hairs from the brush so they wouldn't get in her blond bubble wig when she had to work on it. Gayle had lost her other brush somewheres.

There was no back way out but none of the eyeballs loafing around the entrance of the tent picked up on her. They were always hanging there, looking at their watches to pretend they were waiting for someone, jawing with the other eyeballs about Lord knows what and all of them sneaking glances at the poster Theron had had a hippie in Ormond Beach paint up. Bouncy Bovis and the Sexsational Sabrina. You couldn't recognize either Vaudie or Gayle from the picture. Bouncy looked like sort of a blond Racquel Welch and had smooth ripe boobies that stuck straight out from her chest, imitation rhinestone nipples curving up to the sky. Forty-eight inches of Wiggling Wonder, said the poster, you gotta see em to believe em.

"Must hafta put em in a wheelbarra," said one of the eyeballs, peeking sideways at the picture, "so's they don't tangle with her knees."

Vaudie had told Theron he should just put the poster up in the tent and shine lights on it. Business would double up. She said scuse me and slipped through the eyeballs.

She found Theron helping to shill for Earl Terkle's Wheel o' Fortune. Things were slow and Theron had had a few. It was only a little past two. When the wheel hit his number he shouted and carried on, overplaying it like he always did when he had some under his belt. Vaudie tapped him and he backed out of the group at the wheel.

"I need the keys, Theron. Grocery shopping."

"Already?"

"You complained last night cause we were out of everything."

"Take em." He offered out the keys to the Falcon, his attention pulled back to the wheel action.

"I need money, Theron."

"What?" he said, distracted. He followed the game as if it were on the level.

"Money."

"Get it from the afternoon take. Just write down how much."

"I don't want to be fooling with no nickels and dimes in no supermarket. I want paper money."

Theron sighed and turned his back to the suckers. He fished through his wallet, passing the twenties by. Theron liked to lay a twenty on the edge of a bar and say, "Take a chip outa that, Murphy, bourbon on the rocks." Since he had been stationed in New Jersey during the War all bartenders had been Murphy to him.

He gave Vaudie a five.

"I need more, Theron."

"For what?"

"Groceries. What the fuck you think things cost, anyhow? I need more."

He gave her another five and said he'd want to see change from it.

"You'd want change from a penny."

"Don't start, Vaudie, just don't you start." Earl Terkle bugged his eyes and raised his voice to cover Theron. He didn't want another ruckus, not in front of his game.

"Well just don't you complain about what I feed you, that's all. Spect to eat for nothin." She began to move away with the money before he changed his mind. The ten he had given her and the five she had shaved from the afternoon take would be enough.

"And you hurry back," he called after her, "we got the evenin show!" He turned to the wheel. "Say Mister," he said loud enough for three counties, "I'm feeling lucky. How's about another crack at er?"

On her way to the car Vaudie passed the Bimbos' big van. She wondered if he would come over and say hello. If he was still with them. There was nobody outside the van. If Mr. Bob was still running the show then he'd be there too. He

97

followed that man around like a puppy dog, like they were married or something.

The supermarket was where the Pepsi-Cola jobber had said it would be. It was a brand-new one and big. Vaudie took a cart and padded through the aisles in her worn tennis shoes, parked beside the other women turning jars and boxes in their hands and tried to figure out the Unit Pricing. Everything was new-looking and bright and when you paid money you really got something for it. Nobody looked at her especially. Music came from the walls and ceilings, nice quiet music. There was a snack counter where you could sit down while you ate and a place where a man would wrap up pieces of meat or fish or specialties that you pointed to. When somebody stepped on the black rubber mat the doors whooshed open for them. Vaudie wondered if she wanted to go down Bakery Goods or Canned Fruit first, whether there would be enough time to look at everything. It seemed like the nicest place she had ever been in.

She went to the delicatessen counter to see what they had there. There were hams hanging behind the man in the white jacket, red, hickory-smoked hams hanging from hooks on the ceiling. It had been the longest time. Theron couldn't take the spiciness, it hurt his stomach. Everything was too much for Theron's stomach, but let her tell him to go easy on the liquor and it would be a fight. She hadn't had good smoked ham in the longest time. Her daddy used to put them up himself, back before he left. It seemed like it had been every Saturday he had brought a ham from market but it couldn't of been. She would watch him putting it in and barely be able to keep her eyes off the smoker every time she went past it, knowing the ham was in there sweating and stewing and getting good. Her daddy had been a machinist and brought hams on Saturday.

They lived on the right bank of the Tombigbee in the little two-room house where her mama had been born. In the summers Daddy would stay with a cousin down in Mobile to fix cars on weekdays and hitch a ride back home for weekends. There weren't so many cars to fix then and there wasn't work for most of the year. Mama didn't want to give up her home. There was plenty who had and were sorry for it, didn't make sense to up and walk away from what you owned outright. Mama had been to Mobile in 1930 and seen men and boys on top of a freight train and had not ventured far from the house after that. There are people live in boxcars, she would always say if Daddy mentioned moving to a city, and each one of them had a home they wish they never left. Mama thought all trains were covered with transient men and boys, even though the worst had ended years ago.

One summer all the boys suddenly wanted to wrestle with Vaudie. Before they had preferred to wrestle with each other or with Dutchie Volk, who was tough as any one of the boys, but this summer they all came after Vaudie. She sort of liked the attention but it hurt sometimes, they did, and sometimes they hurt when she wasn't wrestling or doing anything. She pestered her mother about letting her wear a foundation garment for her top. She asked Mama when they would stop growing and Mama said soon, honey, very soon, the way mines did. That was the only big thing Mama was ever wrong on.

It was Archer Hyte who challenged Vaudie to go down by the Nigger Barge. Her older brothers had been even though they weren't allowed but Vaudie had only heard stories. There was men who went there to drink sometimes and other goings-on. Sometimes if she was mad at her mama, Vaudie would decide to go to the Nigger Barge just for spite, but she never did.

"What you scared of?" Archer was a year or more older than her but in the same class at school.

"Nothin."

"Then why won't you go?"

She shrugged. It was hot and school was out and Daddy wasn't due back till late. There was nothing to do. She and Archer were sitting on the bank throwing in sticks and garbage and watching it float away. Down to Mobile. Archer wanted her to go downriver to where the Nigger Barge was.

"You ever been there?"

"Nope."

"Then why don't you wanna come?"

"Aint nothin there."

"How do you know? You neb been there. What you scared of?"

She shrugged.

"Your mama won't find out."

"Not scared of my mama. She let me go whereb I want."

"Won't nobody bad be there do nothin."

"How do you know?"

"S'daytom. Nobody bad comes there in the daytom. What you scared of?"

"Not scared of a damn thing, Archer Hyte. I uss don't feel like going, is all."

"C'mawn. Won't hurt nothin."

"Uhn-uh."

"Won't nobody find out."

"No."

"It's not like it was nighttom."

"No," she said, but fainter.

"You're just about the only person I know neb been down there."

"Oh hell, just so's you won't *bug* me to death. But there won't be anything there worth seeing."

Archer led the way down the bank. Vaudie felt a little nervous because she was going where she wasn't allowed and because she was swearing again after she'd promised herself she would stop. It was a very bright day and the river looked pretty, but she was nervous about what would be at the Nigger Barge.

As they worked their way down along the bank it was less and less built up with logs and mortar, the sides less protected, the undergrowth wilder and more dense. They didn't say anything, some kind of tension growing, and Vaudie stumbled and sweated. Wet stains spread out from under her arms and made half-circles under her breasts. She undid another button at the top of her shirt, buttoned it back up, then unbuttoned it again. When Archer got a little too far ahead of her he would wait up till she was with him again.

The Nigger Barge was called that because it was from the time when there was slaves. Nobody remembered or seemed interested to know if they had pulled it or ridden on it or what. It had gotten snagged on a sandbar and couldn't be pried loose. Over the years most of the barge itself had broken or rotted away, but other debris had stuck there and accumulated until there was a little island a couple hundred feet long, roughly in the shape of a barge. There was boards and bits of rope still embedded in the island and at one end a rusty iron pole stuck up a few feet. There was a chain at the base of the pole with its linkholes rusted in. That was where the slaves had been attached, people said. Generations of high school boys had tried to pull it free but none was ever able to. People said that the pole went right down and was anchored to the bottom of the river, that if you could take hold of the chain and yank that pole out the whole Nigger Barge would wrench loose and float down the river to the sea. But nobody could ever do that.

Vaudie and Archer stood on a small ledge with high weeds at their backs and crumbling bank at their feet and looked out at it. It looked like a trashy, overgrown sandbar. Archer had to dare her twice before she agreed to go out with him.

They started out a little upstream to provide for the current. Archer took his shirt off and swam ahead, leaving his shoes back on shore. His arms and neck were so dark and his body so white that it looked as though he still had a shirt on. Vaudie took her shoes off and tied them together and looped them around her neck and rolled her jean cuffs down so they wouldn't catch water and drag. She didn't want to be barefooted on the Barge. When Archer pulled her out of the water she tugged her shirt away from her chest cause of the way it was sticking and turned sideways from him to look over the Nigger Barge. She sat and put her shoes on and made a face. The Barge had a strong odor of decay.

"Smell it, don'tcha?" said Archer. "All these years and it's still here. Nigger smell."

"Don't smell like niggers. Just smell like trash is all." She got up and began to explore, trying to look as unimpressed as possible. The place gave her the creeps.

Mostly there were bottles from liquor and other garbage people had left. There were names and initials and hearts drawn on the scraps of board that ribbed the island, and there were pictures of men and women being together and words that Vaudie knew were awful even though she couldn't remember ever hearing them said. There were some campfire traces that looked recent and down where the rusty pole stuck out there was a silky pink rag that looked like it was some woman's underthings. Also near the pole was a breadboard that someone must of brought out specially. It was propped up and there was things about niggers written on it, about what they were like and what should happen to them. That gave her the creeps too, she was glad it was daytime that she was there. At night with fires or torches and all the wild bushes and twisting driftwood and the sound of the dark river passing by it would be too much. It would be too scary. And then there was the stories of what people did out here at night.

"Just trash is all," she said and turned to Archer.

Archer was gone. There really wasn't that much he could hide behind and she couldn't see him anywhere.

"Archer!" she called. "Archer Hyte you stop that! Show yourself out here." Vaudie hated being left alone, always had. When she had to be alone at home she would catch the two cats and bring them inside and shut all the doors and windows so they would stay with her to talk to.

"Archer? Dammit, where are you?!" She walked toward the center of the Barge. There was a shallow pond formed there by the rain, waterskaters zipped over the surface. She thought maybe Archer was in there holding his breath, though it was a scummy-looking thing. The sun hit it so there was a reflection. Vaudie saw the top of her head and then her face and then there was something looming up suddenly behind it. She screamed and turned and Archer yelled boo! and gave her a little push backwards by her shoulders. She felt her heels go into the water.

"Damn you!" she cried and went to push him back but he grabbed her wrists and they were wrestling. She had had to wrestle most of the boys around that summer but never Archer, and it was clear he knew more how to do it even when he wasn't using all his strength than the others. He got her down on the ground but she kept her elbows out in front of her and he rolled her onto her stomach which hurt her breasts and made her madder. She tried to stand up but he had her by the waist and she only got halfway before they went down again rolling and she ended up on top with him still holding her. She was on top but didn't feel like she was winning and it was an awful peculiar kind of wrestling, it made her feel peculiar. They were both breathing hard and rested for a second and she looked at his face. She expected him to be grinning but he wasn't, not really, and then he bucked her off him and they went rolling down into the pond. She was wet again and it felt oozy and she heard herself giggling though there wasn't anything that she felt was funny happening. There was a lot of splashing and Vaudie fought to keep her hair from getting dipped into the pond scum and then she felt something clammy under her shirt. She slapped down and there were long spiny things but it wasn't Archer's hand. She screamed, screamed so loud that Archer jumped away out of the water and stared at her. She looked down her shirt and there were three of them, bright green, clinging. First she slapped and then she clawed, tearing the shirt open and giving out a terrified panting scream with each breath and hopping in a little dance in the water.

"Help me!" she called, "help me!"

Archer pulled her from the water. He made a face and tried to pick one off. It was hard because Vaudie couldn't stay still and he was being careful not to touch her where he shouldn't. He got a hold of one of the leeches finally and pulled on it but the breast was attached and it moved too. Vaudie was crying and hysterical and he stepped in and took hold of them and peeled the leeches off them. There were little red dot patterns left.

He sat her down and apologized a lot and tried to get her to stop crying and shaking her head that she wouldn't go, until he started wading into the river and she saw she would be left alone on the Nigger Barge. She-cried while she swam, gulping in wet sniffs of air. On the bank he gave her his shirt and turned away while she put it on and apologized some more. She followed him back up the river, stopping to bawl then trotting not to be left behind. When they got to her house she wouldn't let him go in with her.

Vaudie burst in the door and took her mama by surprise.

"Suckers, Mama! There was suckers!" she cried and ran for Mama to hold her. She calmed a little and got the story out. Mama took her into the bedroom and dabbed calamine lotion where they had been and said it would be nothing.

About then Vaudie saw that her mama's eyes were red-rimmed and that she'd been crying, too. Mama said that Daddy wouldn't be back this weekend. That if Vaudie felt up to it would she go down to Mose Brewster's for a chicken, as there wouldn't be ham next week. And then she said, as a special thing since it had been a tough day for her, that she would let Vaudie have one of her foundation garments to wear the way she'd been pestering for. Mama took a fancy-looking new one out and helped Vaudie put it on, sucker bites and all. Even though it was Mama's it was a little too snug.

Later that week she told Vaudie how she'd had a note from Daddy saying he was going up North to Mr. Ford's plant for a job and would send for them. That was always what men told you when they was running off, she said, I'll send for you. It was what Grandmama's husband had said to her when he went to California to work on the railroad. I'll send for you.

Mama waited a year and then traded the ham smoker to Mose Brewster for a little henhouse.

Vaudie left the delicatessen without picking anything up. She zipped through the snack section, leaving all the treats behind, all the Coke and candies and barbecue-flavor potato chips. She cruised past the breakfast cereals till finally her cart slowed to run aground in the dehydrated foods section.

Minute Rice.

Theron ate Minute Rice at almost every meal. He liked it unseasoned, with a little butter melted in it. He said it made him full without bothering his stomach.

When he had first gotten back from the War, Theron Bovis prided himself on his ability to eat hot food. He told of the pepperoni, the hot meatballs and pizzas he had experienced in New Jersey. He made a great show of asking for Tabasco sauce so he could spice things up a bit. It can't *get* too hot for me, he would say and splash on a double dose. He washed his meals down with a lot of beer.

He was twenty-one and a veteran come home. Vaudie was fifteen. Some of the boys her age or a little older would take her out to the after-hours roadhouse now and then and that was where he first noticed her. Honey, he said the first time they were introduced, you're a mighty big girl to be just fifteen. You must be drinkin your milk. And everybody around laughed and whichever boy she was with felt proud that he was with her.

It was a time when she was having screaming fights with her mama. Grandmama was gone and her brothers were scattered around in the postwar army and the cats had died or gone wild into the woods. Vaudie was all that was left. They fought over how she dressed and that she put makeup on at her friends' houses and how late she stayed out and that Mama didn't like some of the boys she was around with. They circled each other warily in the house, conscious that every move was grounds for battle. Vaudie spent as little time as possible at home.

Theron would wink at her whenever he saw her and tell her how she was growing into a fine one, like he was some old relative or something. He was always with one girl or another and the center of attention, full of stories and games and tricks he could show you that he learned when he was away for the War. He would grab the nearest girl and plop her into his lap and make like he was going to squeeze her where he oughtn't in public but then go lower and dig into her ribs the tickly way. They can't *get* too hot for me, he'd say. He was always trying to start card games with the boys and at first everybody was wary of him count of how sharp he'd gotten in the army, but after a few games they saw he lost as often as anybody else, maybe oftener, and so he had a lot of takers. When you walked into the roadhouse and he was there you heard his voice booming out first off before you even saw him and right away it was like a party in the place, whereas if he wasn't there people mostly drank and wondered if there was a party going on somewheres else and complained about the deadness of the nightlife in the area.

One afternoon Theron found Vaudie and asked her to come out with him that night. He had the loan of a buddy's car. Vaudie made some story to her mama about going over to a girlfriend's the way she had started to do. Mama was tired of fighting and knew Vaudie would only defy her and sneak out if she ever tried to keep her in again so she had stopped questioning the stories. She was that tired.

Theron was quick and funny that night and kept giving Vaudie little pinches and pats as she sat or stood by his side, though he really didn't talk much just to her. She was part of his audience as usual, but every once in a while when he'd move on to something new he'd say c'mawn, honey, and put his hand on her back to nudge her in the right direction. So it was clear to everybody that she was with him which made her part of the center of attention too. And when she danced he stood back and watched her. Vaudie loved to dance.

Theron was hard to keep up with. His attention bounced from one thing to another, from one person to another, as if there were so many possible things to do or say he had to hurry to get them all in. The only thing that held his attention was the card game he started up, it took him completely in and everything else just melted away around him. Vaudie was left standing behind him not knowing what to do so she put her hands on his shoulders and watched his cards although she didn't understand how the game worked. She rubbed his muscles a little from time to time and he would roll his neck and mumble sort of distantly that's nice, honey, you just do that.

Afterwards in the buddy's car he took off her blouse. These are beautiful, he said, holding them and weighing them in his palms and squeezing on the nipples a little so they stuck out. She told him the card game had ended pretty late and maybe she ought to be getting home but he said honey, this won't take a minute, and he was right. It happened so quick that she really didn't feel guilty at all when she tiptoed in past her mother who she knew was pretending to be asleep and didn't feel any different the next day and so had to make the whole trip a few more times to be positive of what had really occurred. What all the fuss people made about it was she just couldn't fathom, if that was all there was to it. She knew all about girls had gotten into problems but it was hard for her to think of babies coming out of that little moment.

So when Theron came up empty-handed one night she said she didn't mind and would do it with him anyway. Putting them on took twice as long as the together part, and they were cold and slimy. He came by the house only once and it was clear Mama took him like poison though she never came right out and said so. She only said she didn't think the local possibilities could hold an active young man like Theron.

He took off without telling Vaudie. He had had her in the car several times and once on the bank of the river and once in the afternoon real quick behind the feed and grain. Vaudie took it as a kind of agreement, better than words. A lot of the other boys kept asking her out but she said no, that Theron would send for her, even though he had never said he would. The letter came about six months after he was first gone. He said he was lonely and needed a woman and would marry her if she would come to the address he gave her in Atmore within a week.

Vaudie took a lunch and what little money she could find and left her mama a note. By the time you read this I will be a married woman and don't you try and stop me. She hitch-hiked because she was afraid Mama would get the bus company after her. There wasn't much of a road to Atmore, not direct, and Vaudie only knew what general direction it was in.

The landlady of Theron's furnished room in Atmore said he was with a carnival and had gone on the road with them. Gone to Andalusia first, she thought. Vaudie told the people who gave her rides she was trying to find her mother and they gave her food and places to sleep. She just missed the carny in Andalusia and caught up with it in Enterprise.

She asked for Theron and a crowd gathered around her.

There were a lot of rough-looking types and some people who were just unnatural. They circled her and looked her up and down.

"What you want with him, girlie?"

"Gone to marry him."

"That so? Does he know bout this?"

"Course he does."

"You wouldn't be carryin an extra passenger, would you?"

"Pardon?"

"He didn't make you big and run off on you, did he?"

"No!"

"How old are you, honey?"

"Fifteen, most sixteen."

"Maybe she's the one he's allus cayin on about. One he said aint hardly out her crib and she like to wore him to death."

"Where you from, honey?"

"Same place as Theron."

"At's her. She's the one. Like a brick shithouse he said."

"We didn't think you uz real," said a dark little fellow with a broken nose, "we thought e uz bullshittin us. Gone to be a bride, huh?"

Then they all oohed and aahed and smiled and a fat lady told Vaudie to stay with her till the ceremony.

Theron seemed a little surprised to see her.

Sunday that week Vaudie was a married woman. The man who ran the Wheel o' Fortune put up a little tent just for them. They were honest now and Vaudie knew it was going to be good, to be together in a bed, indoors with no hurry. All the time in the world. It was their wedding night and now they could really do it, like it was for the first time.

Theron was tired from all the celebration and drinking he had done and he just did himself on her quick like before and fell asleep with his mouth over her breast. He said he liked being in a bed more cause it wasn't so cramped and her breasts didn't get goose-pimply from the cold. It turned out that sleeping was another thing that could hold his attention.

Vaudie had never been to a carnival. The people were

gruff and a little scary at first, but then she saw they were just teasing her mostly. They called her Theron's little girl and showed her how the games really worked. They had all been to just about everywhere you could imagine and knew words in foreign languages and had pictures tattooed on themselves. Theron decided she would be a dancer for him. He said he knew how she loved to dance.

The carny men would gather round and offer advice to Theron which he would pass on to her while she practiced. Jerk them a little harder, they would say, and Theron would go up to the platform where she was working and give her the word. She would jerk her hips harder and look to the carny men for approval and they would look to Theron and nod. Shake them more, they would tell him, you got to shake them things more. No use haben um if you don't. Theron would tell her and she would shake them till they hurt. The carny men looked on with such a serious, cold eye that she wasn't embarrassed in front of them. She worked at what they told her through Theron till she could do a thing to music that had little to do with what she thought of as dancing but that they said was just fine. Just *fine*.

When she put on the costume they said she should wear it was the same, the carny men gathered round and advised Theron. A little too much there, they said, no reason to hide your talents under a barrel, they said, and Theron would have her cut her costume down.

She did shows. She got used to the things the farmers said to her, the way they eyeballed her. They're just suckers, Theron told her, they don't count. He drank more though, and never went inside for the shows. He stopped working with the roustabouts and they got their own trailer. He took tickets.

They caught on with different carnies, stuck a while then left. She learned tricks from the other dancers, from the things the customers said, from the things she heard the eyeballs say outside her tent. All their balls were in their eyes. She learned to give them what they wanted and by the time she was twenty and not yet full growed she was Bouncy

Bovis. The other carny men stayed away from her and there was no chance for someone from the outside to get near her. It was a tight, protecting world.

Sometimes, on stage with the music, the smoke and lights and men's voices would fade and she would imagine she was dancing to the music. Dancing.

And Theron got a bad stomach.

Vaudie picked up a six-pack of beer. She looked in her cart and saw all the familiar items, everything that they always ate. The other women seemed to have much more interesting stuff. But it was all too expensive or too spicy or too exotic to take a chance on. Vaudie toyed with the idea of getting something totally new, a real change of pace. But she totaled her items and saw she would only just have enough for vegetables. She went to the fresh produce counter.

Squash, lettuce, tomatoes and okra. Corn and stringbeans.

Stringbean.

She had called him that once, just once when they were together and she was looking at him. He smiled a little at it. It had only been that once though and she never felt right about calling him it since.

It started one night when he brought Theron back from a drunk. The Bimbos had crossed paths with them several times and she had seen him around and had babysat for his little boy. He was pleasant to talk to, tall and not bad looking though nothing to write home about. He was embarrassed and said he had found Theron sitting on the pavement in town, with his back propped up against a parking meter, looking kind of like he was sick. Sick wasn't the word for it and Lewis knew it, but he was trying to be polite. They poured Theron into bed, the first night he had slept there in half a week. It was a time when Theron was determined to go on binges, he was still a young buck at heart, he said. Lewis stayed and had coffee and helped her clean the sheets a bit when Theron upchucked. He was kind and tried to cover for Theron. Overdid it a little is all, he said. Nown then a fella is got to cut loose. Just for old times' sake, don't mean nothing. Don't you worry. He excused himself and she thanked him for his help.

The next night she came over to the Bimbos' trailer to ask if any of the men had seen Theron out. It was late and they were playing poker and none of them had. It was a different bunch back then, but for Lewis and Mr. Bob, but the same kind. Lewis left the game, folding on a pot he had a shot at to walk Vaudie back. He came in but didn't want coffee. She told him how she hated to be alone. He said he'd offer to stay with her a while but the guys would be giving him the business as it was and also she knew how people talked. He was going to go and she plopped herself down in a rocker and looked like she was going to cry. He was embarrassed but he came over and reached out and sort of petted her on the head, patted her hair the way you would with a hurt dog. There now, he said, he'll come back. And then she did cry, the first time she let herself in years, bawling and blubbering and grabbing handfuls of his shirt to climb up into his arms. He held her, standing, looking at the pictures on the wall over her shoulder and rubbing her back. He gave her quite a back rub, as if what was wrong was a sprain or a pulled muscle and it had to be loosened up. There now, he said, whynt you just go and lie under the covers and rest till he gets in? Maybe you can sleep some. She went into the bedroom but wouldn't let go of his hand. He had to stoop a lot cause the trailer was short for him. She climbed under the covers and he held her hand till she fell off to sleep. It wasn't but a few minutes. She thought she felt him pat her head a couple more times before he tiptoed out.

Theron came home for lunch and money and Vaudie had to just about hide because he was after a fight. He banged out after he'd eaten and said don't expect me.

Vaudie kept all the lights on that night and kept going out and looking at her watch and sighing. It wasn't exactly waiting for Theron but she didn't think on just what it was, either. She was waiting for something, to see what would happen. The way you always do.

Lewis came by about midnight. Vaudie? he whispered outside the door. You wake?

She made surprised to see him and said no he hadn't got her up, she had been worrying and she certainly appreciated his concern. She had him come in and gave him beer cause it was too late for coffee. They said things when they could think of them, but there was a lot of bad time where it was quiet and Lewis took the kind of deep breath he always took before he said he guessed he'd be pushing on. But he stayed, and Vaudie felt things coming from him, felt tight in her stomach when she brushed close to him pouring out a beer. She knew what she wanted now, it was a question of how to get from here to there. She didn't think she should try crying again, and she really didn't at all feel like crying the way she had the first time. Lewis started to get restless and his second beer was almost down to the bottom of the glass. She didn't want to offer him another, she knew what Theron was good for after three. It made her almost want to cry, knowing that she wanted to and that he probably wanted to but that there didn't seem to be a way to get it started. He drained his glass in one gulp and was going to get away and leave her alone so she did the only thing she could think of, did it automatically. Well, he said, taking a deep breath and pushing away from the table, but then he looked across at her just as her breasts were swinging free down out of the blouse.

He looked at them for a moment as if he were puzzled as to what they were. Oh, he said then, and looked to her face.

"Lewis?"

It was kind of exciting imagining that Theron might actually show up and catch them, even though she knew it wasn't very likely. Lewis expected him to crash through the door any moment and was a little breathless from trying to hurry, which was exciting too, and he stiffened and held up over her whenever there was a noise outside. Even with his rush because of the danger it seemed to take ages, longer than Vaudie had ever imagined you could do it. Lewis was very apologetic when he finished about being so quick and about it happening in the first place and taking advantage and having to run off now so there wouldn't be trouble, but she shook her head and said there now, don't you worry. She started to feel lonely the minute he started for the door but he turned and said he'd talk to her tomorrow if he could and then it wasn't so bad. He hit his head on the doorsill and cut himself going out.

Theron found the fight he was after. It was with three drillriggers who broke his nose and several of his ribs and laid him in the hospital for at least the rest of the week. The carny was only staying till Sunday.

Lewis came in the afternoons, bringing Denzel Ray over to be babysat for, and then never left. The site had a field with lights so he worked at night. He and Vaudie were together in between her shows but he didn't stay over. The boys would wonder. Denzel was little then and walked but couldn't talk too well.

Denzel played in the living-room-kitchen while his daddy and Vaudie went into the bedroom. Lewis stayed with her so long that he made her do like she did when she used her fingers. That had never happened with Theron. She had heard things from other women but always figured Theron knew what he was doing. And Lewis held her afterwards and petted her and thanked her. He let her keep her bra on while they were doing it so's they wouldn't hurt or keep getting in the way. Later, when she lay on her back resting she let them out and he touched them and was nice with them but didn't make a big deal. She thought maybe it was because he didn't like to be reminded by the teeth marks from Theron. They lay together till it was time for her evening show and then they would dress and come out. Denzel was a very quiet little boy, they hardly knew he was out there. Vaudie gave him costume things to play with, a feather boa and a big rubber snake Theron had gotten for the act but had never worked in. Once they caught him wrestling with the snake by their door, talking to it, telling it he wouldn't let it go inside to get them. Vaudie thanked him for the protection.

Sunday came and the carny moved on. Theron still had two more days. The Bimbos were open on Monday so Lewis told them he had a relative near he had to visit and would catch up. They gave him the business and asked him where he'd met her and was she a blond and how old was she cause they went hard on you for statutory in this state. He even went so far as to have Mr. Bob take him and Denzel down to the Greyhound in town Monday morning. When they hitched back there was only Vaudie's trailer left at the site, abandoned amid a few acres of garbage.

That was the only night they spent together. Vaudie made Denzel a bed on the couch. All night she kept waking up so she could feel herself still being held. In the morning Lewis said it was done.

"It's just not fair play is all," he said, upset with himself, sitting at the edge of the bed. "The man has taken a beating, he's in the hospital, and here I am with his wife. It's kicking a man when he's down. How do you think he'd feel, what he'd think of me if he knew? I'm not a man to take advantage, Vaudie, and I been wrong to have done it. I can't hold my head up coming through another man's back door. We've got to make an end to it."

He was apologetic then, and kind in his way, but he left. He was familiar enough to duck automatically going out the door.

Four months later the fortune teller woman found Vaudie a doctor to stop the baby from coming. When Theron had not used safeties and nothing had happened they just figured it was something wrong with her, that she was one of those women who couldn't, just like she couldn't do the other. She never told Theron about using her fingers. She knew she couldn't pass a baby off as his.

The Bimbos would cross their paths from time to time. Lewis came over only when she was with Theron and was polite and distant. Sometimes she babysat for Denzel till he got too big. Sometimes she looked for Lewis at the shows, but never saw him.

"Stringbean," she had called him that night, watching him undress, "you just a big Stringbean."

Vaudie looked at the other women in the checkout line and envied them. She tried to imagine their lives. She saw that they had bought garden seeds and bath freshener, so they had houses. Homes. Often they shopped in twos or threes, talking about other people who lived near them, and some of them had little children mounted on their carts. You could tell from what they bought that they were shopping for families.

The line took a long time and Vaudie saw she was going to be late. She speeded on the way back and only put the perishables away. Somehow a jar of Gerber's pureed spinach had gotten in her bag. She ran to the tent.

"Goddammit where you been, Vaudie?" Theron was stalking outside the entrance. Music came from within, "The Age of Aquarius," and there were men's voices. C'mawn honey, they were saying, atsa girl.

"The checkout line was really long."

"You got my change?"

"There's only semmy-five cents, Theron. Prices gone up."

She thought he was going to hit her and ducked toward the rear of the tent. Theron had to stoop and pick the change from where it dropped.

"Gayle had to do the goddam teaser herself and she's been stalling for you. I told em you'd be there, not to worry. You get your ass out there quick or those men'll be in one ugly mood. And we'll talk about the money later. I got business in Savannah overnight. You hear?"

When Vaudie got before the mirror there were a few minutes left to Gayle's music. She stripped and made her breasts smooth and creamy with the makeup. Rouge around the nipples. She put Vaseline inside her thigh so if she grabbed some farmer's glasses off toward the end and put them up there they could come out filmed and sticky. Something to show the boys. She gave the wig a quick fluff, pulled it on, then did her lips and eyes. It took no time, she had developed a steady hand. She slipped her costume on.

The music ended and Gayle came in with her leopard skin bundled in her arms and gave Vaudie a dirty look.

"Honey," she said, "you best be good or those men will just chew you up."

Vaudie heard the introduction and then she was out in the light and the whistles and the smoke. Drops of sweat broke from her armpits and tickled down her sides. Saxophones

115

sleazed into "Night Train," Vaudie slunk around and jerked her hips at them and made eyes and rolled her tongue slowly around her mouth. She slid her hands over her body and closed her eyes and bit her lip and then broke out of it, thrusting her thing into their faces as they thundered for her to start peeling it, baby, and whipping off some eyeball's tie and working it between her legs and shaking, shaking her forty-eight-inch gotta-see-em-to-believe-em tits till they hurt, wondering all the time if she should have gotten more milk.

8

Denzel was alone in the little locker shack when he found it under a pile of wet towels. The cover felt greasy, the colors in the pictures were smudged. Denzel was not quite sure why, but he kept an ear open for anyone coming. It had been hidden under towels.

There were some stories that didn't look too good and some ladies in their underwear. The story about Nazis didn't have any fighting in it at the start and didn't get much better. Denzel flipped past it and then stopped at a picture of a man. The man was in a jockstrap kind of thing and bulged all over with muscles.

Denzel got up and looked to see if anyone was coming, then sat near the towels so he could put it back quick. He felt nervous at the back of his neck and shoulders, like a hand was going to pounce and grab him.

INTRODUCING THE BULLMASTER POWERWORKER

There was a girl standing behind, being protected by the jockstrap man, who stood with his chest pushed out and his fists on his hips. In a cartoon picture below it showed the man stretching some kind of spring thing, pulling it out like an accordion.

REVOLUTIONARY NEW EXERCISE PROGRAM

Denzel felt his arms. They were thin and round, the same thickness for their whole length, like a fungo bat. Denzel flopped down on the floor to do push-ups. The picture had reminded him how he was going to do them every day, increasing by one each day to build up. He got to five and his arms began to shake and his face turned red and he collapsed with a whoosh. When he had started the program he could do five, and he always forgot or couldn't the next day and he never got over five. It would take forever to look like Scooter Ryan. Scooter was a halfy boy, cut short at the hips, who did the carnivals. He was all muscles, and he could hop off his chair and run around on his hands. He could crush a coconut with his grip, they said.

Denzel felt bad like he always did after the push-ups, because he could only do so few and because his arms felt sapped and powerless, too sapped to mess with anyone. He would never be able to win a fight with someone like that Badger kid. He'd get pinned down, knees tromping down his shoulders, hands on his forehead, and get his face washed with dirt. Or worse, he'd start to cry before he could stop himself. It wouldn't be so bad if your face just got all bloody like the cowboy shows, but getting it spat on or dirt-washed or starting to cry was the worst.

There was a picture on the next page of a woman who looked a lot like Mrs. Bovis. Denzel thumbed on.

NEVER BE _AFRAID_ AGAIN!

One time Mrs. Bovis was taking care of him and she had to bring him with her to her show and have him stay backstage while she went on. She was in a hurry or something and put her makeup and her wig on in the trailer. Sometimes the guys had to put theirs on in the van cause there wasn't a

118

dressing place by the field. It was afternoon and they were going across the site and some men started following and saying things.

"She's the one, all rat," they said.

"No mistakin them things."

"Yoo-hoooo! Miss Bounceeeee!"

"Bounce over this way honey."

"Bounce-bounce-bounce-bounce — hey, it's like basketballs!"

Denzel glared at them but they kept following. Mrs. Bovis made like she didn't hear but walked faster. Denzel had to hurry to keep up. She took his hand.

"Hey sonny, yall wanna take a walk? We wanna talk to your mama."

He remembered that. They had thought she was his mama and he sort of felt like she was, just then. "Denzel Ray," his daddy always said, "you be good now and take care of Mrs. Bovis."

If he was big enough he would of chased them all away.

"Wonder if he's weaned yet?"

"Shit no. Would you be?" They all laughed. Mrs. Bovis hurried more and they were chased by laughter.

No Size or Muscle Needed!

Even small, slight persons, using the Secret Techniques of the Ancient Oriental Masters, can become a total self-defense Fighting Machine!

There was a picture of a man, built about like Pitcher, who had already knocked out two big men and had the third in a death grip.

The DEADLY arts of KARATE! JUDO! SAVATE!
JU-JITSO! combined to immobilize any attacker
— destroying him!
Hands with the power of an ax, elbows, knees and feet become death-dealing sledgehammers. Reduce any assailant to cringing helplessness!

119

He wouldn't want to kill them or hurt them bad. Just knock them out if they wouldn't go away.

Regardless of Age or Build
YOU CAN BECOME MORE POWERFUL
THAN ANY OTHER MAN!

Powerful.

Finally they had come closer and he already had water in his eyes so he couldn't see too good, and he tried to swing at one, seeing only a leg, but was caught by the wrists and held. They laughed and then he really started crying, and they laughed and Vaudie called them punks and they laughed a little less and she pulled him away and picked him up all the way to the show tent. Even his daddy didn't pick him up anymore. She said thank you for sticking up for me but he saw how he looked crying in the mirror and put a towel over his head.

WALK THE STREET WITH A NEW CONFIDENCE!

Please send me the Free Fantastic information on
how to become a Self-Defense Fighting Expert!

The information was free but the course cost five dollars. He could probably get that much money, sometimes Mr. Bob or A. C. and Knox would give him a quarter to run an errand. Daddy didn't of course, and Pitcher never talked. Denzel did errands for Pogo as a favor and Pogo sometimes gave him money to get things as a favor.

But even with the money it still wouldn't work. Sending away was a mystery to him. You had to stay in one spot and have an address. They wouldn't come and find you. And he couldn't tell anybody about it or ask for help, they'd give him the business and punch him on the arm where the muscle should be. They had laughed that time when he was little and had asked Daddy if the Bimbos would be playing at Battle Creek Michigan so he could cash his boxtops in.

Something caught his eye.

CLOSE BODY CONTACT!

What?
He heard something outside and stuffed the magazine back under the towels and untied his shoelace. He waited. Nobody came. He tied his sneaker back up and checked out the door. No one. He dug the magazine out and found the place, right near the last page.

CHINESE KUNG-FU!

The art of instantaneous death — requires no strength or CLOSE BODY CONTACT!

A man was throwing bodies through the air. There were at least five tough-looking guys with x's for eyes sailing away unconscious.

Instant self-defense for the weak, the defenseless, the fearful and the Untrained.

There were times when he wanted to beat them all up. The Bimbos would come out, Pogo, his daddy, and they would hoot and whistle and stomp, point and say things and laugh in that bad way they did. He wanted to wipe all those smiles off.

Flick-of-the-wrist technique that needs no strength, size, or undue exertion. You could be in danger of being hurt — or worse, humiliated — and KUNG-FU could make the difference. A centuries'-old fighting secret that will keep you safe in most* situations.

*We do not claim that physically handicapped or other disadvantaged persons can perform these feats. Nor do our techniques claim to be effective against anyone armed with a loaded gun.

They were coming. He got the magazine hidden again and

was just sitting on the bench across the way when they burst in.

"Ho, Denzel buddy! Whatcha say?"

"How's tricks, kid?"

"Ready to getem Tiger?"

They were all there but his daddy, who was off getting the wig box. They were in a horsey mood.

"Where's the wimmin?!" A. C. went down the line, checking in every empty locker. "Where you got em stashed, Mr. Bob? You know what it says in our contract."

"No lay, no play!" Knox had a bat between his legs. "Boinnng!" he said and stuck it straight out from him. Denzel laughed at the noise and the cross-eyes Knox made. "Take a gander at my thirty-eight-incher!"

"No stick, no stick!" called Pogo. "The man is batting zero."

"Choke up a little pardner, I think it's your grip."

"Clowns," grumbled Mr. Bob. "Like a bunch of school kids."

"Mr. Bob, can we tape Burnsy's mouth shut during the game? He's been sayin some awful things."

"Fuck yourself, hayseed."

"See? Can we Mr. Bob? Aint right for good clean atheletes like us to be influenced by a dirty ol sucker like he is. It's bad for baseball, is what it is."

"Tell the plowboys there that being the senior member of this ball club entitles me to certain privileges. Saying what's on my mind is one of them."

"Well, you're no example to the Youth of America, Pogo, an that's a fact. I hate to think of the oaths you put in their little mouths."

"If there's a cuss word you didn't know by the time you could crawl, A. C., it wasn't invented yet."

"An it was disrepittable old men like yourself what taught em to me. What's poor Denzel Ray gonna come up like, being round you all the time?"

"Hey Denzel! Denzel Ray! Do Pogo for us!"

He put his head down and shyly started to do the walk. They chuckled. He took a bat and held it over his shoulder the way Pogo did and did the walk and then turned and gave an imaginary audience the Finger. They laughed.

"See? See what I mean? E's pickin up all your bad habits."

"You got it kid," said Pogo, smiling. "You learn to move with that kind of style and you won't be able to beat the dames off you with a stick."

"Hey do Mr. Bob. Do Mr. Bob with the advance man."

Denzel twisted his face into a scowl and paced up and down, holding his breath till he turned beet red and then gave a locker door a vicious kick.

"Beautiful!"

"You gotim."

"All you need is some pennies to pinch and you got the whole act."

"Denzel for Manager!"

Their laughter was all right, they were laughing at the people he was doing, not at him.

"Can you do A. C.? See you try him."

Denzel squinted and made a huge tobacco chaw in one cheek with his tongue. He took the first sacker's stance, hands on knees, then turned to wink at somebody cute in the stands.

"Atzim, atzim all right. Allus on the quail hunt."

"Now do Knox. Aint fair to just get me."

Denzel thought a minute. They were chuckling while they waited. He squatted in the catcher's position, squinted his eyes, and pushed the plug into the other cheek. He mimed a big juicy spurt from the side of his mouth, then made a face and carefully took off the imaginary catcher's mask, dripping with tobacco goo. They broke up.

"Great, great!"

"Use that in the show."

"Kid is sharp."

He leaned back on his haunches, waiting for what they wanted next. He hoped it wouldn't be Pitcher. He knew what he could do for it but wasn't sure how Pitcher would take it.

"Lessee, who else?"

123

"How bout Bouncy? Do Bouncy."

"Bouncy Bovis."

He hesitated a second, then went to the costume trunk, high on the laughs and backslaps and hair musses. He took Knox's fake tits out and hung them over his neck, the cups reaching down to his thighs. Then he stooped over as if the weight were too much to stand erect, and did an elephant walk around in a circle, tits dragging the floor.

The men fell out, even Pitcher laughed. They all agreed that Denzel ought to do his own show. He felt good. Then his daddy got there with the wigs.

"Okay you clowns," said Mr. Bob. "Let's go. Showtime in fifteen minutes."

The men took turns at the mirrors and put their makeup on. Eye shadow, liner, rouge, lipstick. Beauty marks. They put on their bloomers and panty hose and dresses. A. C. helped Knox strap his tits on. Denzel sat in the corner by the pile of wet towels and felt funny. He felt funny a lot of times before shows but this was different, it was like it was something he had already done. Hair fell over his daddy's shoulders as he fitted on a long black wig.

There was a little time before the show started when they were dressed. They sat quiet for the most part, punching glove pockets, chewing gum or tobacco. Pitcher spun the ball in his hand constantly, fingering the laces. They listened to the crowd noise grow outside. Every now and then one would go over to the drinking fountain, then come back to his seat. The drinking fountain didn't work.

Then Mr. Bob slammed in and said it was time. He and Denzel lugged the equipment out, the Bimbos waiting inside for their introductions.

It was a clear night. Denzel could see the constellations up beyond the field lights. He couldn't really see any faces in the stands, just restless shadows. And voices.

Mr. Bob began the introductions and the Bimbos took the field one by one. The voices roared, shoe clerks and pump jockeys, they whistled, bartenders and barflies, they stomped and hooted and catcalled. Shopkeepers, churchgoers, housewives and undertakers. They laughed, one loud grating raucous laugh that seemed to stretch out into the rest of the carnival, as if all were watching, as if the screaming lights of the Ferris wheel and Rocketride were in on the joke. Denzel wanted to punch the lights out, to face each and every grin, to cram each voice down each throat. He would never let anyone, anyone, laugh at him that way.

Yes, Honorable Master KUNG-FU, I wish to know the age-old Secrets of your Ancient art. In return I promise to use deadly knowledge of KUNG-FU for defense only and never to employ its Secrets toward evil ends.

PLEASE RUSH.

9

Rubella shifted her body on the bench. Her fingers slid over the organ till they settled in a familiar position. From the corner of her eye she saw the dark one, sitting motionless as he had all night, nagging at her mind, a hole in the wall of righteous faces. She took a large breath of pine-smelling air and waited, tense in her pure white robe.

The congregation had been whipped and preachified up to the edge. Some laid back in their seats gulping and sweating while others rocked slowly, ready for the night's climax. The local Rev, a dark little frog of a man with a thin moustache, made the introduction. Orison rose and Rubella met him with the theme, soft little panting notes that whispered a song.

> *Jesus walked*
> *Upon the water,*
> *Jesus searched*
> *Through desert sand.*

Orison stood erect before them and gave a smile, kind-eyed and seductive. "Brothers and sisters," he said and the congregation squirmed pleasantly in their seats, for his voice was deep and soothing, smooth like pouring molasses. "My dear friends in Christ," he said stepping into the light, and the sisters loosened inside, for he was pretty to look on, a honey-headed man peppered with gray at the temples who gazed into you with large sad eyes.

"Do you know, my brothers, of the tempation of Adam? Have you heard, good sisters, about the wickedness of Eve? Do you know," he asked them, teasing, probing, "the story of Man's Fall?"

Yes, thought the congregation. I do, thought Rubella.

"Of course you do. And are you familiar with the tragedy of their offspring? With the sibling murder that branded Mankind forevermore? Do you *know*," he barked, face darkly clouding with memory of the crime, "of Abel and of *Cain?*"

The congregation shifted in their seats, unsure now of the story.

"How did it begin?" he asked them, soft now, circling, gathering himself, "How does it ever begin?"

Now, thought Rubella, start it now.

"THE MAN KNEW EVE HIS WIFE AND SHE CONCEIVED AND BORE CAIN SAYING 'I HAVE GIVEN LIFE TO A MANCHILD WITH THE HELP OF THE LORD!' "

Rubella gasped with the congregation as she gasped every time he did it. His voice when it thundered frightened and thrilled them at once.

"With the *help* of the Lord. And later she bore his brother. Abel." He cocked his head back and looked down at them, the teacher and his initiates.

"Who made Cain?"

They didn't answer, afraid to be wrong.

"Did Eve make Cain?"

They hesitated.

"No!" he answered for them, "she did not."

"Did Adam make Cain?"

They met him tentatively. "No."

"Did he?"

"No!"

"No he did not!" He leaned into them, they had the feel of it now. "Did Adam and Eve make Cain together?"

They pulled back, worried, what did he want? Wait, thought Rubella, you have to wait for it.

"No!" he thundered, "they did not. Adam and Eve made a son with the *help* of the *Lord!* Whatever we cre*ate*, whatever we do that is *good*, we do with the assistance of our Heavenly Maker. We are the Lord's vessels, he creates new life *through* us. When we build a house of worship, who drives the hammer?"

"The Lord," they answered.

"When we plant a field, who drives the root?"

"The Lord!"

"When we make a new child, who sparks the seed?"

"The Lord sparks the seed!"

Rubella clenched and loosened her hands, rested them on the organ for a moment, then flitted them up to her face.

"But what of evil? With whose help do we sin? It was Satan who seduced Eve into sin, but *why* did she open herself to him? Was it with the Lord's help that she took of the Forbidden Fruit? No, it was not. Eve fell because she was *hu*man and she was *proud*, because she was flesh grown from Adam's rib. Good can only be done with the help of the Lord but evil is natural to the flesh, issues straight from the pride of man.

"Now Abel was a keeper of flocks and Cain a tiller of the soil. In the course of time Cain brought to the Lord an offering of the fruit of the ground, while Abel brought some of the firstlings of his flock with their fat portions. The Lord was pleased with Abel and his offerings, but for Cain and his offering he had no regard. Cain was angry and downcast. The Lord said to Cain, 'Why are you angry and why are you downcast? If you do well, will you not be accepted? But if you do not do well, will not sin crouch at the door like a hungering beast that you must master?'"

When he spoke the Lord's word they knew that was just the way it had sounded, that it had made Cain ashamed as it made them ashamed, not knowing quite why.

"The Lord accepted Abel's offering, but turned Cain's aside. There, my good brothers and sisters, there is the in-equality, the unfairness of the world. The Lord works in strange ways and Life is his mystery. Have you ever been turned down when you knew you were good enough? Fallen short when you gave your best? Victimized when you were unguarded? Accused when you were innocent? Struck from above and behind with no reason at all?"

They had. They sighed and rocked and nodded.

"And how did you feel?"

Lost, thought Rubella, empty.

"Lost?"

They nodded.

"Empty?"

"Yes."

"Angry?"

"Angry."

"Downcast?"

"Oh yes!"

"Did you feel like the Lord himself was against you?"

"Yes!"

"Oh, but you were wrong! Wrong to doubt the Lord!"

They pulled back again, he wanted something deeper.

"Life is hard and life is unfair because we have made it that way. When Adam fell Paradise was lost, equality was lost, innocence was gone — lost forever! And it is our fault, it is because we are human that troubles befall us. Do you think the Lord would stoop to purposely torment one puny soul? Do you have the conceit, do you have the audacity to say 'Why me?'? If you turn your bitterness toward the Maker you are sadly deluded, for He is too great to bother with your little worries.

"Of course life is hard," he said, building again, coming at them, "of course life is unfair! But if you are among the righteous, what of it? If you are set for the Kingdom of Heaven what consequence are the trials of this world? If you do well, will you not be accepted? Do you question the De-sign of the Creator?"

Rubella was sweating now, arching toward him, hanging, knowing the answer but wanting it from him.

"Cain said to his brother, 'Let us go into the field.' And when they were in the field CAIN TURNED AGAINST HIS BROTHER ABEL AND *SLEW* HIM!"

The last resistance broke in the congregation, Orison's voice entered them and they let themselves go to ride upon his words.

"Pride!" he called, closing his eyes with the pain of the killing. "*Pride* goeth before the Fall! Cain was *jeal*ous of his brother, *en*vious of his brother's good fortune. He was a proud man and would not see another above him in the eyes of the Lord. So he took the *life* of his brother, *mur*dered one of the Lord's most precious creations out of his sinful false pride, and then was so *full* of himself that he thought he could put one over on his Maker."

"The Lord said to Cain, 'Where is your brother Abel?' and he answered, 'I do not know. Am I my brother's keeper?' Pride, sinful pride! *In*solence to the Lord! The Lord said 'What have you done? THE VOICE OF YOUR BROTHER'S BLOOD CRIES TO ME FROM THE GROUND!'"

A moan escaped from the congregation and they heard the blood of Abel. Orison glowered down upon them and they felt the fear of Cain.

"There is *no shel*ter from the *judg*ment of the Lord. A sin of pride is a raw and festering thing, it speaks out more clearly than virtue. *Pride.* Not talking about self-respect. You can always fight the good fight and respect yourself as one of the Lord's children. But sisters, tell me, what is it that makes you puff up and strut yourselves before another woman's man? Pride. What makes you backstab and gossip against your neighbor?"

"Pride," said the sisters.

"What makes you rag your own man for the job he's got, for the money he makes, for the things of this world?"

"Pride," they said, "it's the truth."

"Brothers! Tell me brothers, what makes you slip around with your best friend's woman and then tell the whole world about it?"

"Pride!" said the men, eager to prove their sinfulness.

"What makes you hard with your woman when you should be soft, angry when you should be kind, out when you should be home?"

"Pride! It's pride does that."

"What makes for all the showdowns, all the cuttings and shootings, all the ugliness between one man and another?

"Pride!" he shouted joining the men, "*sin*ful pride!

"And do you think it goes unnoticed?"

"Uhn-uh."

"Do you think you can get away with it?"

"Oh no!"

"Do you think you won't pay for it, right here on *earth*, as well as in the Afterlife?"

"No way."

"Got to pay!"

"*Judg*ment day!"

Rubella was rocking now, ready for it to come, her fingers poised rigid over the keys. And yet something snagged, a tiny hook of uneasiness held her.

" 'And now,' said the Lord, 'cursed are you in the soil!' "

"Cursed!"

" 'Soil which has opened its mouth to drink your brother's blood by your hand!' "

"Goodgawd, blood in the *ground!*"

" 'When you till the soil, no more shall it give its fruit to you!' "

"No more!"

Rubella paused on the edge and suddenly felt a chill, something unholy, someone in the congregation who was cold, moving against the flow. She swept her gaze over the intent faces, heads haloed in blue from the light of the neon cross entering through the window, sweat beading their brows and then there he was. The dark one. Eyes hidden by a blank mask, body still to the breaking tide, his stone presence bottled the feeling in Rubella for a long moment of dread until Orison sent her crashing over.

" 'A FUGITIVE AND A WANDERER SHALL YOU BE ON EARTH. FROM MY FACE SHALL YOU BE HIDDEN!' THEN THE LORD PUT

A MARK ON CAIN AND HE WENT OUT FROM THE PRESENCE OF
THE LORD AND DWELT IN THE LAND OF NOD, TO THE EAST
OF EDEN."
Rubella's fingers stiffened and dug into the organ, her toes
curled down on the pedals and her wail lifted her from the
bench, matching the wail of the chord and the anguish of the
sinners in their seats.

> *Jesus walked*
> *Upon the water,*
> *Jesus searched*
> *Through desert sand.*

Wrenching each word from her body, bending them so
they weren't words but rocks and briars on a painful
journey —

> *Jesus trod*
> *The lonesome pathway*
> *Leading to*
> *The Promised Land.*

A shudder passed through the congregation, and they
joined her in release, all the preaching and squirming of the
long night overflowing in song —

> *Through this world*
> *We're bound to struggle,*
> *Fighting sin*
> *To win His love.*

> *Always strong*
> *Yet always humble,*
> *Meek before*
> *Our Lord Above.*

When the meeting broke up Rubella had to work her way
through the brothers and sisters to get back to Orison. The
regular organist, a middle-aged sister who had stepped down

that night, bared her teeth in a smile and complimented Rubella on her musicianship. The brothers admired the shape of her pure white gown. The froggy Reverend laid his hands on her in thanks.

By the time she reached the dressing room Orison was not alone. She heard a flat, probing voice and peeked in. It was the dark one, the one she had seen, sitting now across from Orison with shades in his hand. Rubella ducked back into the shadows behind the door to listen. She saw a mirror in the corner of the room, could see in it her honey-colored Orison and the impassive face of the dark one.

"What do you want with him?"

"Business."

"What kind of business?"

"Personal kind."

Should she make a noise and go in? She was his business manager now.

"I don't know."

"You've seen him. I can tell."

"We crossed paths. This show he's with played the same carnival as we did about a month back."

They talked like they knew each other. Rubella was jealous of his mysteries, of his life before he knew her.

"Who is 'we'?"

"Me and the woman I'm with now. Rubella."

Yes. Let him know how it is.

"She's my partner."

"Married? You?"

"Yuh."

The dark one frowned. "Orison, you gone soft. What kind of game you running here? I saw the take, it wouldn't feed a flea for a week."

"It's not a game anymore. It got serious."

A long silence and Rubella held her breath.

"So. The Revrund Orison Obeah got religion. The baddest Jesus-hustler ever was has gone and taken it serious. You must be stone crazy! Have you been around this country down here? These people are ignorant, a bunch of burr-heads. You should be copping with every word you say. These people just crying to be cleaned."

"They're poor."

"They're poor but they breed like rabbits. You could nickel and dime your way to Fat City. Who you think supports the number but poor people? You could work these farmers for some heavy dust, Orison."

"Man doesn't live by bread alone." He mumbled it.

"Don't hand that to me. Why aren't you pulling in the money?"

"It isn't enough."

"So take more."

"More isn't enough. Money isn't enough."

"Shit it isn't. Now that doesn't sound like Orison at all. This bitch has got you cunt-struck."

"I'm getting *old*er, man."

"But not *see*-nile. What's with you?"

"I don't know, the words I guess. I started listening to what they said."

"They're just words."

"That's what I used to think. But since Rubella come, hell, they've been making sense."

Tell him.

"You think these people listen to your *words?* All they after is your big black voice and a little crying gospel music. They come for the *show*, not for the snake oil. Think these people clean up their act after they been down here? You're not *that* old!"

"It must help somebody."

"Lord helps them what helps themselves. So help yourself."

"No."

"Why not?"

He thought a little while and then said hesitatingly, as if confessing a secret sin, that he didn't want to take advantage of them. Just didn't want to.

The dark one turned his gaze away until the embarrassing moment was over. "Never thought I'd see the day. You be-*lieve* it?"

"I want to."

"You think it do you any good? Here and now, I mean?"

He shrugged.

"The Lord supposed to take care of his own, right? Be with you in the lions' den?"

"Yes."

"You think he'll protect you from anything down in this white man's country? You think if the shit hits the fan he's gonna be there to get splatted? You think all your religion gonna stop some cracker who's got his sights on you? You think you not just another nigger?"

"You don't go testing it or it's no good. You just believe."

"Why?"

"For a man who used to have all the answers you sure asking a lot of questions."

The muscles of the dark one's face bunched as if to make a smile. "Two points for the Rev. Now why?"

"It's a feeling I got. I want to believe something."

"Hah. Wanting to believe aint believing. You so full of shit, Orison, you such a blue-ribbon bullshitter, you even hooked on your own game. How can you believe the thing is true when you get the same wailing and testifying when you're straight as when you were in it for the hustle? Buddy, I think it's a little fuckin late for be*lief*."

"Okay, then I want someone to believe in me."

"They always do."

"But to have it be *real*. You have to keep up a game twenty-four hours a day you're not real. You're not all preacher and you're not all hustler, you're just an actor can't ever get off. It's not like you, man, you were always just one thing, just pure badness. But when you got to be both in one you lose track of yourself. I don't have the heart for it anymore. I'm tired."

"You're dead."

"No."

"Wasted. Crawled back in some woman's belly."

"She looks up to me."

"She still lets you on top?"

"Don't *be* that way, man."

135

"Cunt-happy after all you've had. I can't see it, Orison, can't *see* it. You could always take your pick, anyone, anytime you wanted to. Kept on the move so's the morning after never happened, so's the older sisters never put the word out on you."

Resist him. Resist him. Rubella's stomach rose and fell with the talk.

"No telling how many little Orisons you left running around on the gospel trail. And now you got that gray up top you should be copping twice as much. Older sisters think you distinguished-looking now and trust you with their daughters. All those fine, Jesus-struck little bitches, Orison, laid out and waiting, hot and excited and spread open for salvation."

Fight him. Beat him back.

"And the money? Shit, man, you know what this country is doing? Fucking *Je*sus *revival*. Dragging the old jew back for an encore. The time is *ripe*, Rev, all you got to do is reach out and grab it. All you have to do is admit that everything else is bullshit and that you were meant to take all you can get. You want it, don't you? You still want it?"

"No."

"You want the money."

"No."

"The women. You want the women. You haven't gone queer, have you?"

"I don't want them."

"You sure, Rev?"

"I don't. I know I don't."

The dark one put on his shades and shook his head. "You turned into one sorry sumbitch, Rev."

Praise be to God. Rubella deflated with a huff but they didn't hear.

"That carnival the midget was in — did they stay with it?"

"Maybe. They were skipping around. They might leave it and come back."

"Where does it go? Where does it stop?"

"The carnival? Somewheres in Florida, some dead end.

136

What business you got with Burns? Back in the City he was just a game, just for jun. What's up?"

"It's not a game anymore, Orison. It got serious."

There was another long silence. "Him?"

"Yuh."

"Why?"

"I got my reasons."

"You that desperate to take yourself serious?"

"Got to believe in something, man, you said it. I believe in me."

"You better go now. You're some bad news."

"That's right. And you taught me every little thing I know."

Then the dark one left and Rubella appeared in her pure white robe to attend to her man.

10

Pogo's legs nearly failed him crawling out of the bunk. He crossed slowly to where he hid the pain pills, stopping every few steps to listen for the breathing of the others. His fingers wouldn't work right and he had to suck the cotton out from the bottleneck. He swallowed the pills dry. His eyes began to find solid edges in the van and he made his way past the sleeping men to the door.

It was no cooler outside. Cicadas and peeper frogs pulsed the night with their shrill whistling. Pogo sat on a front wheel guard and strained to see across the grounds. He massaged his legs, squeezing heavily at the thighs but lightening to barely a touch around his knees.

The cicadas and peepers cut dead.

Pogo snapped alert, gulping in a breath and holding it. The outlines closest to him were fuzzy and melted into black a few yards away. There was no movement.

"Come on," whispered Pogo. "Please. Come. Now."

An owl skreeked and there was a second of frantic rustling. It was silent again for a moment and then a frog ventured a single tentative note. It was answered by another and soon the night was pulsing again.

"Damn."

Thursday

1

"You take the pieces and dredge em up in your egg batter," said the dark-haired fat woman, "and then you sprinkle on your condiments."

"To taste," said the blond-haired fat woman.

"To taste. Then you can pan-fry them in anything, oil, shortnin, butter, though personally I prefer Lord have mercy look-it this."

Pogo had two full canvas equipment sacks, one over each shoulder, and Denzel had a bulging plastic trash bag that hung nearly to the ground. They walked by the fat women to the last machine in the row.

"Butter," said the dark-haired fat woman without taking her eyes off the new arrivals. "Makes for a sweeter taste all round." And then, softer, "I wonder if they just moved into the neighborhood."

"Takes all kinds," said the blond.

Denzel read the instructions out loud as Pogo rooted in each of the bags to see what was what. "Looks like two full loads here," he said.

"We got enough change?"

"Plenty of change, kid."

"So whynt we put the other guys' stuff in one and ours in the other."

"No good. We'll put my stuff in one machine with half of their jocks and socks and your stuff in the other machine here with the rest."

"Their stuff is mostly all white and our stuff is got colors. Why don't we do it my way?"

"Because," said Pogo, "I don't like to get my things mixed up with yours. When they're the same size they're hard to sort."

"Oh. We'll do it your way."

They stuffed double handfuls of clothes into one machine or the other till the bags were empty. Pogo closed the lids and laid change in the slots and Denzel shoved them in to start the machines.

"Shit," said Pogo.

"What?"

"No soap." He put more change into a vending machine and came back with two packets of soap. The machines stopped what they were doing while the lid was open and began again when it was closed.

"All set, kid."

"Pogo? I think those ladies are whisperin bout us."

Pogo looked across the laundromat to where the two fat women sucked innocently on their cans of Fresca. The dark-haired one was draped in a loud print dress and had glasses hanging from her neck by a black ribbon. The blond-haired one wore a lavender smock and a pair of pedal-pushers that had been worked on. Her front threatened to spill out over the stretch panel that had been sewn into the waist. Both wore tennis shoes and white ankle socks. "Nah," said Pogo. "Just woman talk is all. Food and clothes and babies. Probably didn't even notice us come in. They only see what they want to."

"They keep looking over here."

"Looking isn't seeing. They got a kind of female tunnel vision. They only see things that concern them. Food and clothes and babies."

"Uh-huh."

"They're practical people, women."

"Yuh."

The fat women giggled about something.

"They look but they don't see. And they hear but they don't listen." Pogo started to use his hands the way he did when he gave Denzel the inside dope on life. "That's why you have to take everything a broad says with a grain of salt. They never say what they want and they never want what they say. You take some hard-as-nails old hooker, some tough old bird, and what she really wants is to settle down and get married to some straight-arrow, have kids and do knitting. And then you take a couple settled housewifes like the pair over there and what they're really itching to do is cut loose and chase around with men."

The blond cracked up over something, nearly snorting soda through her nose.

"But don't ever tell them that," Pogo lowered his voice a little, "don't let them know you're wise to their act, cause they'll go for your throat. They're not a rational breed."

"I thought you said they were practical."

Pogo thought a moment. "Kid, I think you got to the bottom of it right there. Inconsistency. That's the worst of it all. They're inconsistent."

"Oh."

The first wash cycle ended and the spin lights went on. The blond fat woman went to the soda machine for two more Frescas. When she walked she held her arms out from her body and bent slightly, the flesh under them jiggling.

"Were you ever married?"

"Huh? Why do you ask that?"

Denzel shrugged. "Don't know."

"Hell of a question. Was I ever married." Pogo tried the cigarette machine but it kept returning his money.

"Were you?"

"No, kid, I wasn't ever married."

"Why not?"

He sighed. "Well, first of all, I'm a guy who doesn't like to be tied down. I like to be able to roll with the action."

"Oh."

"Marriage is strictly for the birds as far as I'm concerned. It's an overrated occupation."

"Uh-huh."

"It's a sucker bet."

Denzel was silent.

"Never found one was worth the plunge," said Pogo, almost to himself.

Denzel boosted himself to sit on top of one of the machines. It buzzed under him and made him feel tingly.

"See, kid, you've got to put an awful lot of work into a woman if you go marrying her. Even if you don't get that far it's still a job." Pogo gestured with a dead cigarette butt. "You got to call all the shots but not let them wise to it. They want you to run their lives for them but they don't want to admit it. So you can't be nice to them the way you can with a guy, they'll just take advantage of it and make themselves miserable. You got to get them where they don't know where they stand, where they don't know whether you're going to belt them or what, so when you don't they feel like they've tricked you and are happy with what they get."

Denzel nodded in the spaces Pogo left to show that he understood.

"If you just give them stuff they won't enjoy it, they won't respect you for it. With women you can't treat them fair, just firm. And all the while you got to make it seem like you're doing a big favor even to be tough on them. All that is a lot of work, it's a lot of time you got to invest in broads. Personally I could never see it."

"Oh."

Pogo put his ear down to one of the machines as if he could hear how clean the clothes were. "These got a while before we need to switch them over. You want to keep an eye on things while I go get some cigarettes?"

"Sure."

As soon as he was gone the fat women came to Denzel.

"Mornin Sonny."

"Mornin."

"Got quite a load you're doin there."

144

"Uh-huh."

The women smiled and pulled at their sodas on either side of him, squatting slightly to lean against the sorting table.

"You must come from a good-sized family. You have a lot of brothers and sisters?"

"No M'am. Just me."

"Oh. You and your daddy couldn't hardly carry all the clothes."

"Snot my daddy."

"Oh."

"Sa friend."

"I see."

"Are you-all doing the laundry as a treat for your mama? Or does she work?"

The machine stopped spinning under him and rumbled into the second wash cycle. It was uncomfortable but Denzel didn't want to hop off with the women there. "She works."

"How nice. What does she do?"

"Waitress."

"How nice. And what about your daddy?"

"What about him?"

"What does he do?"

"Works."

"Oh."

"How nice."

"And how old are you?"

"Nine. Most ten."

"Well you're a big one aren't you."

"No M'am. I'm small for my age."

"Oh."

"Did you-all just move in?"

"No M'am."

"Oh really? How long have you lived here?"

"We don't."

"You're from out of town. How nice."

The women emptied their soda cans at the same time, crumpled them in their fists and laid them back on the sorting table.

"Where at is your mama a waitress?"

"In a restaurant."

"Oh."

"What she meant is where do you-all live?"

Denzel gave them the first name he could think of. "Samson."

"Oh."

"That's in Florida."

"How nice."

"And your daddy works down in Samson."

"Yuh."

"And what does he do?"

"Say," whispered the blond-haired one, nudging her friend's elbow, "he's comin back."

The top of Pogo's head crossed in front of the window. The fat women mumbled that it had been nice talking to him and hurried back to their seats.

What my daddy does, thought Denzel, is mind his own business. The edge of the sorting table had left a deep crease in the bottoms of the fat women. The machine went into the last spin cycle.

"What did those two want?" asked Pogo.

"Nothin. Ask some questions."

Pogo scowled. "Nosy bitches. That's another thing about women. They can't leave well enough alone."

"Yuh."

"They're never satisfied with what they got. Always think there's greener pastures next door. Think the world owes them more than they've been getting. But they're not brave enough to go out on their own and look for it, they expect some man to lay it at their feet. Women got no balls."

Denzel slid off the machine. "That why my mama went?" He took the twisted soda cans and tossed them in a trash barrel.

"Huh?"

"She thought things were greener somewheres else?"

"What makes you ask that?"

Denzel shrugged.

146

"Those two didn't say anything, did they?"

"Naw."

"They got some nerve, digging at other people's affairs." Pogo glared at the women through cigarette smoke. "I never met your mother, kid."

"I know."

"I really couldn't tell you why she left."

"Yuh."

"Maybe she got tired of hanging around while your father played baseball games."

"Maybe."

"Maybe she couldn't take being on the road all the time."

"Yuh."

"It's hard to guess, kid, when I never knew the lady. Just one of those things, I guess. Ask your father sometime."

"Yuh."

Pogo went to the candy machine and bought a Snickers that he split with Denzel.

"Maybe," said Denzel, "she just didn't want to be a mother yet. Maybe she didn't want to be settled down."

"That could be, kid. Nothing personal of course. She never got to know you. But maybe she just didn't want the job."

They ate their candy and the machines shut off. Pogo relayed lumps of damp clothes óver the sorting table to Denzel, who put them in dryers keeping the two loads separate. Pogo handed dimes across and Denzel set the clothes tumbling. They sat down together in plastic scoop chairs.

"That's another reason I never got married. You can never tell what they're going to pull on you. So my policy has been don't get involved. You can't win."

"You said that man is after you cause of a girl."

"Oh. Yeah, well that's different."

"Did you do something to his girl?"

"Do something? You mean like hurt her? No, nothing."

"Did you steal her away from him?"

Pogo considered for moment. "You could say that. In a way. Yeah. I stole his girl from him."

"Why?"

147

"You're full of em today, aren't you?"

Denzel shrugged. "Just wondrin. You don't have to say if you don't want."

"He didn't treat her right."

"How? Whud he do?"

"Oh, he was mean to her and made her do things she didn't want to. She didn't have any say in her life cause she was scared of him."

"I thought you said that's how you got to be with women."

Pogo frowned and jammed his cigarette out. "Oh, well that's for dames in general. There's exceptions. Some of them are, uhm, special, and you treat them different. She didn't deserve that crap."

"Oh."

They watched the clothes somersaulting behind the dryer portholes.

"That's the kind I'd want to have if I was ever to have one. The exception kind."

"Good luck, kid. There's not many of them around. Few and far between."

"What happened to her?"

"Huh?"

"To the girl you stole."

Pogo shrugged. "Went to live with some relatives."

"Oh."

Pogo smoked and Denzel wiggled his toes inside his sneakers until the clothes were dried. They piled everything on the table and began to separate the other men's socks and underthings from their own clothes. They were only halfway through when Lewis popped in to tell them Mr. Bob was ready to roll. They stuffed the clothes away quickly, both refusing to surrender a bag to Lewis. They nodded to the fat women as they were leaving. The women told them to come again and resumed their conversation.

"Food and clothes and babies," said Denzel.

"And men, kid. That's one I forgot."

148

2

The radio sang fuzzily through the open window of the car, competing with a muted snoring sound.

Fill up my casket
With sweet bonded bourbon,
Fill it up – all cozy and nice.
Won't you fill up my casket
With sweet bonded bourbon,
Gonna fly – up to Payridise.

Pickle my body
In Tennessee moonshine,
It will cover the deathly smell.
Won't you pickle my body
In Tennessee moonshine,
Gonna float – down easy to Hell.

The shoeshine boy put Dred onto it. Drunken cracker weaving around town in his car. Beat-up old Falcon, buff-colored. Stops to ask the shoeshine where he could find a little poony-tang. Dark or light, so long as it was lively. And then, when the boy had steered him, tried to tip with carnival tickets. The Ferris wheel and the bumper cars. A day-old pass to a baseball show. And then threw up on the sidewalk.

Dred found the Falcon parked in the shade of an alleyway at the side of the address the boy had given him. He parked a block away and walked back, holding a paper bag by the bottom.

The cracker was sprawled in the front seat, face turned into the seat crack, one arm hooked through the steering wheel. He smelled like stale beer and whorehouse disinfectant. Dred slipped carefully into the back seat, reached forward and tilted the rearview mirror to the floor. He turned the radio off. There was a clink of metal against glass as he pulled the gun out of the bag. He hung it over the seat and lay the side of the barrel to the cracker's skull. He lifted it a few inches, then let the weight thump down on the man's head.

"Whubfug?" The man's voice was muffled in the seat. He settled back to sleep. Dred lifted the gun higher. Thunk! "Aaaaow!" he whined, turning to see what was falling on him. "Cuddadow!" He opened one red eye and Dred poked the nose of the gun into it.

"Morning, boy. Rise and shine."

"Wh —?"

"Don't look. All you got to see is this gun. Move your head and you lose it."

"Ohmagod." The hand hanging down from the steering wheel began to shake. "If I done anything last night that I don't remember, I'm sorry bout it." The man stared up cross-eyed at the gun looming over him, afraid to look to the back seat. "Whatchew want with me?"

"I want answers. I want a man."

"Well I'll try to be of help. I surely will."

Dred pulled a poster from the bag and unrolled it. He lowered it in front of the man.

"Uh-uh-uh-*uh*! Don't look at me, muthuh! I'll spray this car with your brains."

"I aint seen a thing."

"Just look at this poster. You know him?"

"Well, uh, not exact —"

"Do you *know* him?" Dred squashed the man's nose back with the gun.

"Oh yes. Yes indeed." The gun let up. "But what you want with him? Feller who never done nothin? Like my wife Vaudie says, she says 'Old Lewis a good-hearted feller, he just none too swift.' Man who —"

"Not him. The other one in the picture. The freak."

"Burns? Don't *know* him — I mean not personal, but I seen him —"

"Where is he? Is he with this team? Are they at your carnival?"

"Oh no. He's with em all right, but they're gone. Long gone."

"Where?"

"Don't know where they're at today but I believe tomorrow they booked into Samson."

"Where's that?"

"Florida. It's between —"

"I'll find it."

"What you want with Burns?"

"Said I wanted answers, not questions."

"Sorry. What now?"

"Say 'ah.' "

"Ah?"

"Like in the dentist chair. Ah."

"Wh —?"

"Say it!"

"Ahhhhhh —"

Dred stuck the barrel of the gun down the man's throat. His eyes bugged out and he gagged.

"Ohwhygog. Weez oank. Weez."

"What you say, boy?"

"Oank gill gnee. Ah woang ock."

"You say you won't never breath a word of this cause if you do I'll find you and kill you? That it's none of your business and if you stick your nose in it I'll blow it off? That what you're saying?"

The man nodded enthusiastically, teeth clicking on gunmetal.

"Smart boy." Dred pulled the gun out. He smelled piss. "Since you been so helpful I'm giving you some breakfast. A little mornin sunshine."

Dred lifted a full bottle of tequila from the bag and twisted off the cap. He propped it on the man's chest. "Drink."

"Well thank you kindly, but I'm strictly a beer —"

"Drink!"

"My stomach don't —"

Dred rested the hole of the gun between the man's eyes. He untangled his arm from the steering wheel, took the bottle and tilted it to his lips.

"Drink it." Bubbles rose in the liquid but the level stayed the same. Dred reached over with his free hand and pinched the man's nostrils shut. He spluttered, eyes growing even wider, and the tequila began to jerk down in deep, glugging swallows. The eye nearest Dred filmed, then rolled, and liquor streamed over the man's chin. He passed.

Dred put the bottle, the poster and the gun back in the bag. He left the cracker sprawled in the Falcon and walked out into the bright morning of the street.

The street.

See what it is and then walk straight at it. If it don't disappear altogether it at least turn tail and run. Straight at it, that was Dred's style, was Dred's power. He came straight at you pushing fear up front of him like an odor. Standing erect and relaxed at once, conserving his words, saving his eyes for the important. Big and bad and black. Half the dudes from the street hustled to catch those eyes and the other half hustled to avoid them. Dred's eyes could stick you, bore into your stomach and push up into your throat, or they could look clear through you to the wall. And if he gave you a word, for one word was usually enough from him, he either wanted something from you or had something to sell you. And there would be no bargaining, take it or fuck it. He was a hustler who never hustled, never broke a sweat or cracked a smile, a stone businessman. The street dudes didn't bother to think of a nickname for him because Dred was good enough, Dred was who he was.

Nobody remembered when he came, where he came from. It seemed he had always been there. Rumors followed him, things he had done in other days, in other towns, things you wouldn't want the man to do to you. But nothing anybody could report for sure. It just didn't make any sense to try the man, so he went unchallenged. The street was full of bad young bloods, full of grudge and getback, full of budding Dreds. And it seemed the younger the bloods were, the less real niggerhood they had gone through, the angrier and badder they came on. If anyone from the street ever noticed something ass-backwards in it they never said so.

And they all knew Dred, knew who he was, the ones who had dealt with him and the ones who didn't dare. He could sit at his booth and not move a muscle, not so much as grunt and everybody would know he was there. Because his hard eyes and straight talk was a style, announcing him as much as Honeythroat's walking stick or Zeno Turner's bored yawns or Little Snatch's dashiki and mojo bag or the smile and quick jiving of Odell Pittman Jr. The bright vines he wore only worked to point out his skin, his deep, solemn black. All you had to do was catch a glimpse of that black, feel the shadow of his big straight self looming over you, catch the slight forward lean and the insinuating slow-motion bop and you knew that the man meant business. Not a wasted motion. Because Dred was a serious man and if you dealt with him you damnwell took him serious. Nobody messed with Dred's working bitches, nobody poached in his territory. When he walked into a place everything about him warned you, Don't Tread on Me. Nobody wondered about it or tested it. There was death and there was taxes and there was Dred.

If one of his bitches got silly and started acting up, the way that bitches will sometimes, he would buffalo her. He would find her and she would start to sweat, he would walk at her and she'd start to shake, he would stand almost brushing against her and look down through his shades, his size fifteens blocking escape to the sides, her back to a wall or bed, and she would begin to tremble and plead and swear she'd get right fast. That was all. The slap never came because the threat of it was more powerful, Dred left a tension behind him that was binding, where a bruise would have been release.

He never blew grass or snorted coke like the others, only chipped a little high-grade heroin now and then, a serious drug, and nodded solemnly through a day. He never carried a gun because everyone knew he would. He saw everything but looked at only what concerned him. He had no enemies and he had no friends. There were only other black men who he dealt with as men, and people not worth seeing.

One time Fresno Willie owed him some money. The day when Fresno Willie was supposed to pay up passed and everybody knew it. They licked their lips and asked each other where Willie had been seen last and where Dred had been seen last, hoping to plot the point where they would meet and be there when it happened. But nobody had seen Willie, and Dred, from the look of him, didn't seem to have noticed. Dred went into Lebo's one afternoon and everybody knew something was up because Lebo and Fresno Willie had once been brothers-in-law.

Dred sat at a booth, waiting alone in his shades and his Dresden blue vines. Lebo finished with his bar customers in a hurry and went to the booth.

"Hey, Dred."

"Hey."

"You drinkin?"

"No."

"Waitin for somebody?"

"No."

Lebo tried to be cool but it was hard, wearing his apron in front of the bar.

"So how is every little thing?"

Dred didn't answer.

"How's everybody on Folsom Street?"

"Ask them."

"Is Porkchop loose yet?"

"He still got twenty days to do."

"What about that fire down to Django Green's? You think he had it torched on purpose? *In*-surance?"

"That's his business."

"You seen old Fresno Willie round lately?"

Dred took off his shades and stretched his legs under the booth table. The conversations at the bar lowered a bit to take in the answer.

"Willie," he said, "is on a trip. Got some business to take care of. Won't be back till he makes it right."

"Oh," said Lebo. "A bidness trip."

And the word went back to Fresno Willie.

In about a week people had forgotten about it. They just wrote Willie off their lists. The turnover was that fast on the street. Him? they would say to someone who had been away, oh he aint been round for *ages*, man. Must gone back to *Fres*no. Less old Dred got to him first.

Then Ahmed the Younger, the one who worked the game in the rear of The Soul Shack, brought the word and started people talking again.

Ahmed came by Dred's daytime office, the shoeshine stand in front of the Continental Club. There were two chairs, one for customers and one for Dred to sit and prop up his mammoth feet. The kid who worked the stand got him Cokes and newspapers and ran information. It was a business arrangement.

Ahmed sat in the chair by Dred and immediately his shoes were being shined. Dred did not look up at him.

"Say hey, Dred."

Dred didn't speak. Ahmed the Younger was only a little jiveass who was coming up too fast for his own good.

"Where you been keepin yourself, man?"

It was hard to tell whether Dred's eyes were open under the shades. He could have been napping, but Ahmed didn't want to touch him to find out.

"Aint see you down our way in a long time."

The kid popped a rag at his feet and began to hum.

"Old Lebo was sayin just the other day how it been too long since you been by his place. Lebo say you got some mail."

Ahmed waited for something, an answer, a grunt, anything to bring back. He waited until the shoeshine kid cleared his throat and held out his hand and said that's all Mister, I got customers coming.

Ahmed left the kid with a five to show Dred how high he was living. The shoeshine kid ran to check on the number so Dred would know if one of his bitches had hit. It was a business arrangement.

The next day Dred walked into Lebo's and Lebo gave him an envelope.

"Somebody left this for you," he said.

Dred counted the bills and put them in his wallet.

"Been a while since we seen you," he said.

"That's right."

"Haven't seen old Porkchop in a while neither."

"No."

"I wonder if Fresno Willie done with that bidness trip he was on."

"He's on his vacation now." Dred told him, turning to leave the bar. "Willie doesn't like the heat. Plans to stay out of town till things cool off. About a month I'd say. One month."

And the word went out to Fresno Willie. In a month he was back in town and people smiled and whispered whenever he was in the same room with Dred. Man squirmed his way out of that one, they said, an damn lucky he did, too. Hadn't been lucky the man wouldn't *be* here now. Be somewheres else entirely. An I don't mean fuckin *Fres*no.

It had been a bitch, an itch, a something not worth a rat's ass that had brought it all down. There had been a Chinese bitch who needed bus fare to Boston and a white man that the street dudes kept around for kicks, a freak.

The Chinese bitch had floated in from Hong Kong with a six-ounce bag of pure heroin taped between her breasts. She spoke English passably and had people in Boston. She tried to sell a pinch on Little Snatch's block and he heard of it. A meeting was set up and Little Snatch lifted the whole bag from her. Took it from between her breasts and said that stuff's against the law in this country, sister, I better get rid of it for you. She had no one behind her to face Little Snatch, no one to report him to without fixing herself and no way to get to Boston. She wasn't even sure which direction it was, not even sure the people she had were still there. Dred heard about her. He checked her over. He started putting his hooks in her.

She was small but big-breasted, pretty in an Oriental way and young-looking. She wore her hair long and straight the way the young bitches did. Dred wanted to dress her in college-girl clothes and use her downtown for the conventions. They liked to think they were doing a college girl. She would bring more money that way, telling them she was working her way through San Francisco State or Berkeley. The high cost of education.

Dred lay her money for a room and said he'd see about getting her a job. She was afraid of him which was fine and didn't trust him which didn't matter. She had no way to get to Boston.

He sat back and took his time with her. He didn't think about it much. She might work out and she might not, it was hard to tell in the beginning with bitches, even ones who were citizens. Even with the ones who had nowhere they thought they wanted to go. Dred could take his time with her because she didn't know anybody and had no way to leave and nobody on the block would dare step in with her. The other street dudes would check her out from a distance and smile but leave her be. The word had gone out that she was Dred's and that was all anybody needed to know.

He had a party one night with some of his bitches and a few of the men he did business with. He hand-fed her coke and took her off and did her when there was no way she could refuse. After that he did her now and then but didn't push it. She still told anybody who asked that she had people in Boston.

The freak was named Pogo Burns and he called himself a private eye. The street dudes, all of them, from the lamest dice-chuckers to the biggest hustlers, called him The Man.

"Better get right," they would call out as he entered a bar, glaring up through their legs, "here come The *Man*."

"Uh-oh," they would say if he hopped up on a stool in some soul-food kitchen, "someone goin to be burned. Someone under a*rrest*. Someone bout to get *wast*ed. The Man is here."

He peeped through keyholes for divorce lawyers, fingered debtors for the insurance companies and the bail bondsmen.

"Ohshit," they would say. "Rent must be overdue. The Man just walked in."

"Honest Mista Burns," they would call, "that was my twin brother you seen with that woman. Turkey has got no morals a-*tall*."

He would ask straight questions that got crooked answers, always fishing out the private detective's badge he'd had engraved for himself.

"Goodgawd!" they would cry, "The Man flashing his shield. I confess, I con*fess*!"

"Look like something you find in a box of Cracker Jacks. Kind of fuckin badge is that?"

"The Man, he look like *he* come out from a box of Cracker Jack too. Ha!"

They would sputter their beers and double up and slap five. He was a pest and sometimes he brought the credit people down on you but he always was good for a laugh. Took hisself so *ser*ious. You could mock The Man all day and he just keep coming, just stare up with his little hardeyes and wait you out. So they laughed The Man away, and with him could laugh away a little of the real Man out there, the Man that Burns was only a cartoon of.

For the most part Dred ignored him. The only white men that were visible to Dred were real cops. Once he almost had to deal with the freak, but it never came to anything.

Burns had hired out to a finance company to steal cars back when the payments had stopped short and the home addresses turned up phony. He waddled around the neighborhood toting a thick cushion and pedal extensions he had made. He did good business the first week, checking off his list of names and plate numbers, sneaking away with the Caddies and Imperials and Deuce-and-a-Quarters that were always parked just a few blocks from where the delinquent was living. He was careful about who he hit, stinging only the lame types and leaving the hustlers and bad bloods alone. One day he read the wrong name for the wrong plate number and copped a burgundy Coupe de Ville.

The word went out to Dred that his car was not in its parking place.

The word came back from Dred that this could not be true, that nobody would steal a man's car right off the street. That when he walked to his parking spot the next morning he was sure the car would be there, untouched.

There was a boost that night at the finance company's storage garage. The next morning Dred walked to his parking space and there was his car, untouched but for a full tank of gas it hadn't had before.

But for the most part Dred ignored him. He was no one worth the attention of a busy man. So it all happened right under Dred's nose without him really being aware of it. It was like a color too dark to see or a sound too high to hear. Like something you only dreamt was happening so you didn't bother to wake up and stop it.

The Oriental bitch liked Burns because he would talk to her and he wasn't frightening and he was funny. Not funny like he was to the others, just because of what and who he was, but funny because he tried to be, because he had a joking, paternal way with her. He called her Dragon Lady and bought her drinks. She was learning to drink. At first he hung around her because he had heard about the heroin and thought that maybe she could finger bigger people behind her. Even if he didn't do anything about it, Burns made it his job to know all the deals that were going down. After a while he hung around her because she was pretty and only laughed at him when she was meant to.

"Dragon Lady," he would say, "I get the idea that you are independently wealthy. You must be to lead the life you do. Sit in this bar all day and play the jukebox. What's your secret honey? Daddy own a jade mine? Brother-in-law own a chain of laundries? Or maybe you got a pile of that top-drawer horse banked away somewheres?"

"Midda Burn," she would say, "If I got moneys I don be here. No more." She would sigh. "Midda Burn, you play song for me?"

"If you'll have a drink with me. A guy doesn't like to drink alone."

"Hokay."

And he would hop off the stool and plop a quarter in the box, punching out songs he knew she liked, then scoot back up on the stool. There would be two sloe gin fizzes waiting.

"Dragon Lady," he would say, "you're a good kid, but there's things you've got to learn. There are drinks that dames drink and there are drinks that guys drink. This Kool-aid here is of the former group. Herman, Scotch on the rocks."

He didn't check her out like merchandise the way the other men did or smirk and wink behind her back like the women did and he was funny and shorter than even she was. And she had nothing but time to kill, time to worry about how to get across a big country.

"Midda Burn," she would say, "is possible for me to get job on a railroe? Work till they stop Boston? How mutt it cost to take a bus? Can woman hit-hike?"

"Dragon Lady," he would say, turning into his drink and growing quiet, "you'd better ask your tall dark friend that one. Put the touch on him if you want to go to Boston."

She would smile and agree, just to let him off the hook, but she knew Dred wouldn't help her leave.

Convention time rolled around and Dred started to reel her in. There was another party with a lot of sloe gin and a lot of coke and somehow she ended up not with Dred but with some lame named Tyrone who had showed up from Daly City. He left money on the bureau in the morning. Dred

160

came in and asked what the idea was. She asked him not to be mad with her, it wasn't her fault, she had almost been knocked out with the high. He slapped her once, hard but not hard enough to leave a mark. The smack of it scared her. He told her he bet she even took money for it. She cried and he found the money on the bureau and called her a whore. She asked him not to blame her, if he had stayed with her it wouldn't have happened. He made to hit her again and she flinched and cried. He didn't hit her. He said if that was what she wanted, to be a whore, it was fine with him. He didn't want her anymore, but she owed him money and he wanted that. She owed him for all the room and board and drinks and clothes and jukebox he had given her. She owed him for not telling the police what she had brought to the country, for protecting her from bad men like Little Snatch who would take advantage of her. She cried and said she didn't understand, she just wanted to go to Boston and find the people she had there. He told her she was free to do whatever she wanted as soon as she paid him back for everything she owed him. He would tell her when they were square. He would even help her make the money. She didn't understand. He told her it wouldn't be hard, that you didn't have to be a citizen, that it was only using what came natural. She cried a little and then she didn't cry anymore.

She began with people Dred called friends of his, though she knew Dred had no friends. They came to her room and were gone in the morning. They told her to ask Dred about the money. A couple times it was Tyrone from Daly City.

Dred told her the money didn't come to much. Just enough to pay the rent, for a meal and some drinks. He told her that all the work was in the finding, not in just laying up in your room. If she wanted to get the money herself and start to get out from under him she would have to go out and do the finding. He told her where and he told her how. The idea of Boston stayed with her though, and she had not yet admitted to herself any of the names, the names that would mean there was no point in leaving anymore.

Burns met her in a bar downtown one night. She was

dressed like a pimp's idea of a college girl. He bought her a drink.

"Dragon Lady," he said, "I've missed you lately. Got a new boyfriend?"

She smiled a little. She was nervous.

"Looks like you've gone coed on us."

She laughed, just a little.

"Must be studying up to go to Harvard when you hit Boston."

She looked around the bar. She didn't know Harvard. Burns noticed her eyes skip over him as she looked. He talked a little about how his business was going, about what was coming down on her old block. She half-listened and looked at the new watch she was wearing. She didn't know why she had bought the watch. She was trying to save for a bus trip and Dred never left her too much. She didn't know why she bought a lot of things she bought lately.

"Dragon Lady," he said finally, "I get the feeling I'm in the way. You waiting for somebody?"

She nodded and blushed, an unhappy blush.

"Anybody I know?"

She shook her head. It was cool in the downtown bar but he saw sweat beading her makeup.

"Anybody *you* know?"

She looked at her feet.

"So it's night school," said Burns, nodding as if he'd known all along, as if the knowledge fit well with his view of things. "Tell me, Dragon Lady, what's tuition these days?"

She looked at her feet. She was still a shy bitch. Spooky.

"Twenty and ten? Or a hundred for the night plus expenses? This is a classy bar."

She looked down and was afraid he would make her an offer, that he wanted to do her like the others. But he only bought her another and left. She changed seats and tried to look available. She knew Dred was never far away, though she never saw him.

"Study hard," Burns had said, "that's the only way to make it."

That Saturday Burns boosted a '72 Caddy for the finance

company. The last three digits of the Caddy's plates were 982. The number Saturday evening was 982. The midget flamed and partied all weekend, buying drinks for all the street dudes who were interested. And on Monday the Oriental bitch was gone.

Dred waited for her in his nighttime office, a booth at the rear of the Continental Club. She didn't come. She was holding out on him. He went to her room and her clothes were gone. There was a note that said she had paid him enough and that she wasn't afraid of him anymore. There was no forwarding address.

The word went out to Dred that The Man had sprung her.

The word came back from Dred that the little cocksucker had joined a sideshow and left the country. That he wouldn't be back anymore.

But when the dust cleared Burns was still there. The street dudes buzzed and licked their lips. The Man was crazy. The Man was doomed. Wherever it was he had come from he didn't know enough to go back there. The Man was as good as wasted away. They invented reasons, business, to hang by Dred so they could drop the word.

"You seen The Man lately?" they would ask. "You seen old Burns?"

"Joined a circus," Dred would tell them. "He's gone forever."

"Yeah?" they would say. "I thought I heard bout him fingering some turkey down on Mission yesterday."

"That so?" they would say. "Somebody told me they seen him again taggin some married bitch up by Lincoln Park."

"No shit?" they would say. "Thought I saw the dude at Lebo's last night."

Dred found him in Lebo's. It was afternoon and there were just neighborhood men loafing, nursing beers. Little Snatch was in, shooting pool with Upstairs Jimmy. As each of them turned and saw Dred's big self blocking the door they grew quiet, the way men in bars grow quiet in cowboy movies. A space cleared around the little white man. He turned and there was Dred.

Dred began to walk toward the freak on the stool. He was

more aware of the faces of the street dudes to his sides than of Burns. But he knew what was there and he walked straight at it.

"He got a gun," said Little Snatch and a question touched Dred's mind. Gun? Who? But it wasn't time for questions. He walked straight at it, the way he always did, but this time someone thwacked him in the leg with a baseball bat, someone he never saw, and he fell to the floor bleeding and trying to find where his knee had gone. His shades fell off and everybody saw his eyes blink and waited for him to pull his gun. But he didn't carry a gun. He lay on the floor crying and holding his leg and watching them see him, see right into him. See into his eyes and see that he had no gun, that he drank milk for his stomach and ground his teeth down to the nubs at night and that he had never shot or cut or killed anybody, that he was years behind on his dues. He looked around at them and saw a white man pointing a gun at his head and passed out.

The Man, the midget, disappeared to wherever it was that midgets disappear to. Dred was taken by the hospital. The street dudes got used to living without either of them. The turnover was that fast.

An artery had been popped and a bone shattered. Dred was in the hospital three months. He was a slow healer they said. It was another month in a room in San Jose working the limp from his walk before he came back to the City. When he hit the street again it was like he had never existed.

His bitches were scattered. Irene was with Honeythroat and Doris was with some wop down by the pier and Maria had split for L.A. Little Snatch had fucked his parole and was back in Q and Porkchop had gone lame, marrying some church lady and opening a beauty parlor. Almost all the fast movers were new to Dred, kids who had come up without him ever having noticed them. They knew his name but had never done business with him. They knew him from some street story about a midget.

Little jiveasses he had never seen before sat in his booth and ignored him. New bartenders asked him to repeat him-

164

self. He heard laughter everywhere and was sure it was leveled at him.

He went to the shoeshine stand, the one on the corner in front of the Continental Club. Ahmed the Younger was sitting in the chair, propping up his sandaled feet and reading a paper.

Dred walked straight up and stood by him. Stared at him through his shades. Ahmed let the paper drop but didn't leave his seat, reaching his hand under his shirt to a sagging lump. The kid came up and asked Dred if he wanted his shoes shined. Dred felt a twinge in his leg. He sniffed and walked away.

The word went out that Dred had lost his heart. That he had come back looking mighty pale. That he was washed up. That maybe The Man had shot something sides his leg. Cause *some*thing sure's hell was missing from old Dred.

The biggest change was with the bitches. All of a sudden it was work. He had always been on top of it with them, no sweat. If he and some bitch didn't hit it together that was her problem, not his. Let her sit on her lonesome tushie and weep. Some worked out and some didn't, nothing to get all hot and bothered about. But now he feared the loss, feared the failure ahead of time. Dred caught himself caring.

And the fucking. Fucking had been to where he took it without breaking stride, he'd had it down like eating, scratching an itch. A couple bad months and it was like he had to do it new every time, to prove it again. I'm Dred, he told them with his cock. Shouted it on them. I'm Dred, I'm Dred and you got to see who that is.

"Make it, don't break it," they told him.

"Ease up poppa," they said, "you tryin too hard."

"Never knew fun was so much work."

Once one of them started laughing and he thought it was at him and threatened to waste her with an iron pot. It was a bitch he had just met, way too early to be playin Big Daddy with. The bitches talked with each other and the word went out that he was wrong. Was *strange*. That the ride wasn't worth the ticket.

Dred's knee hurt when it rained and late at night. He made the rounds, no longer able to be still and have action come to him. In each bar he would have one or two drinks, nudged and spilled, just one of the customers, his voice drowned in laughter and no takers for his hustles. He pawned some of his clothes and saw them walk by on some skinny teenager a week later. He found himself thinking about everything that had once come natural to him, that once was thoughtless. How should he walk, talk, drink? Who should he move with and who should he ignore? How could he show them who Dred was? The only place he wanted to live was in the street people's minds.

One night Dred was sitting on a barstool in Lebo's. Somebody was in his old booth. Fresno Willie came in shitfaced.

"Say hey, Dred," he shouted, "Where you been, my man? Take a little business trip?"

The old hands smiled and winked at each other.

"Yall go on vacation?"

There was a little buzz as the old hands told the newer kids how it had been.

Used to be, Dred heard them buzz.

Once pon a time.

Was a day.

Lost it.

No more.

Gone lame, Dred heard them buzz.

Fresno Willie came over and held Dred's arm. "How's bidness, ol buddy?" he said. There were snickers. The street dudes could smell Willie's breath from where they sat, all of them had been hit up close with it one time or another. Smell like some scumbag of a bus-station wino crawl up in the man's throat and *died*, Jim. And old Dred was getting the gas full in his face right now.

"You been to the circus lately?"

Another snicker began but cut off to listen. There was a snarling sound, a deep rumbling like somebody had swallowed a bad dog. It came from Dred. He sat stone still and stared at Fresno Willie, still but for the vibration of his chest.

166

The sound grew till it was like water boiling inside of him then it boiled over into a roar and he picked Fresno Willie up off the floor and bounced him, bounced him like a man would bounce a basketball, off the back wall. Willie landed in a heap and lay puking on the floor. Dred turned to the bar.

"Lebo," he said, "you know that gun you always holding for Little Snatch? That cannon? I want it. Pay you fifty."

Lebo had his eyes fixed, like the rest of the room, on the dent Willie had made in the wall. "Don't know anything about no gun. What give you that idea?"

"It's in a cigar box next to the Scotch," he said. "You going to give it to me or am I going to come back there and get it?"

"That used to be my brother-law, man," Lebo pleaded. "How can I give over the gun?"

"Don't worry about him. He's got his already." Dred laid fifty dollars in ones on the bar and Lebo gave him the gun.

The street dudes looked at each other and looked at Dred.

"What you gonna do'thit, Dred? What for you want a gun?"

"I'm going hunting," he told them. "Going hunting for some white meat."

The street dudes showed their teeth and squirmed in their seats.

"Midget season is officially open. Going to get me a trophy."

"What you gonna bring back?" asked one of the jiveasses.

"Know how you see the greasers ride round with Jesus statues on their dashboards?"

"Yeah."

"Or how the guineas got those peppers and fuckyou fingers hanging from their mirrors?"

"Yeah, yeah, or how ol Porkchop got plastic dices hangin from his."

"Right."

"So what you bringin back? What your trophy?"

"Shoes," Dred told them. "Next time you see me roll by in my car I'll have a pair of shoes hanging from my mirror. Bronzed shoes. Midget shoes. And the feet will still be in them.

"That's why I've got to go hunting."

And goddam if he wouldn't bring them back. Old bad Dred. Man was born bad. Just has to take care of first things first is all. God*dam* if he wouldn't.

3

"Mr. Bob I sure hope you know what you're doing."

"Just drive the van, Okie. And Knox, you keep your eyes open over there. I forget whether he said on the left or on the right."

"It's probly on both sides. The mound will be in the middle of this cowpath and Pitcher will be dodging traffic."

"No problem there, pardner. We *are* the traffic."

A. C. and Mr. Bob and Knox were crammed in the front seat. A. C. was driving slow, they combed the shoulders for a turnoff.

"I think somebody's puttin you on, Mr. Bob. Aint no ballfield out here. Nothing out here but niggers and weeds. You been had."

"Nobody's been had. If it's a phony then all we lose is a little gas."

"And a little time."

"It's an open date. What were you guys going to do all day, play with yourselfs?"

"If you'd promise to umpire."

"You're a comedian. If this pans out it's all cream. No advance, no expenses, a flat twenty-five apiece and a slice of the gate. That's what the man said. It's all cream plus a little sugar."

"That's what the man said over the *phone*. Man calls *me* up on a telephone and tells me to come out and meet him at — where at is this place spose to be again?"

"About halfway between Headlight and Colon."

"Man tells me to meet him halfway between East and West Bunghole and says he's got a fantastic deal for me I'm onna *smell* something. And it won't be *money*, neither. Over no *tel*ephone."

"I don't like that part of it either. But I got him to agree that we get the flat rate before the game and that we use our tickets for the box so nothing funny goes on."

"Still don't like it. Whatsay his name was?"

"Fella name of Phil Dodge. Said Mrs. Pinkham put him on to me. Lady who promotes the wrestling in Atlanta? He says we'll be the first show at this new site of his."

"We'll be the first audience too, unless the birds and the bees and the little forest creatures want to take a look. Uh-oh, what have we here?"

Seven or eight black men, bare-chested in denim coveralls, were picking and shoveling to one side of the road, grading the shoulder. They stepped aside and stared sullenly at the gaudy van.

"That's the ones," said a man with a towel wrapped Arab-style on his head, "that's them." The van left them behind.

"I didn't see no chains," said Knox.

"And I didn't see no redneck with a shotgun, pardner. I believe those boys were out there on their own."

"That's a strange one. I mean they were *work*ing when we come on em. Not a white man in sight and they were workin away. That's one for the books."

"Maybe they aint heard how Lincoln freed the slaves."

"Shhhh!" said Mr. Bob, "not so loud. What they don't know won't hurt them."

They laughed.

"That's your philosophy in a nutshell, int it, Mr. Bob?"

"Yeah, probly right this minute we're headin for some slave trader, you gonna sell us down the river. All the time thinking it's no use to tell the guys and get them all worried. What they don't know won't hurt em."

"Comedians," said Mr. Bob, "I'm surrounded by comedians."

"We'll be surrounded by cannibals if we go any further into these here boondocks. They'll be cooking us up in a big black pot."

"No worry, pardner, they haven't got the hang of fire yet out in these parts."

"And who'd eat raw Okie?" said Mr. Bob.

On the left of the road, about halfway between Headlight and Colon, they discovered the field. They parked behind the backstop.

The stands looked fairly sturdy, but the mound and plate were lined up almost directly east-west, making it murder to play in the daytime. There were five portable lighting units crowded along the first base line. There were no sanitary facilities visible. There was a clubhouse, an unpainted cement bunker dug into deep center field.

"Phil Dodge, huh? I never heard of him."

"I'm glad to hear that, A. C. Everybody you've ever heard of has their portrait hanging on the wall at the Post Office. Along with their fingerprints."

There was an old black man fiddling with something in the stands behind third base. Mr. Bob and A. C. and Knox made their way across to him. The others got out and stretched and took a brief look and then brought the equipment from the van out to the bunker. It would be cool inside.

"Whatsay, Pops?" A. C. said to the old man when they had climbed to where he sat. He had a towel draped over his knees and little metal parts, wires and screws and bullet-shaped things spread out on it.

He glanced up at them and returned to his fiddling. "Mr. Dodge will be here about six. He wants to start at seven. Make yourselfs at home." His fingers were long and knobby and were doing something small and intricate, some needle-threading thing, with two of the parts.

Mr. Bob took over. "Where's the toilets?"

171

"Bringing in portable ones." The old man did not look up. The crown of his head was worn, bald patches and little tufts of gray wool. "Got a shithouse on wheels."

"What about the box office? Where's that? And the concession? He said there'd be one, said we got a slice."

"Bringing in portable ones."

"How about the sound system? I got to have a microphone, it's a part of the show."

"Got that right here in my lap. If you gentlemen would excuse me, I'll put it together."

Mr. Bob made an unhappy noise and turned to see what else there was to bitch about. "How come they set this place up so the sun is always in the players' eyes?"

"Don't play in the day. People got to work."

"What about weekends?"

"Can't afford to book shows on the weekends, the prices too high. That's what Mr. Dodge says."

"Well you tell your Mr. Dodge I want to see him the minute he gets in."

"I'll come for you."

"How come everything's left for the last second?"

"We had another show but they canceled. Mr. Dodge didn't know if he's gonna get you people or not."

"Hell of an operation," grumbled Mr. Bob, starting down to the field, "one hell of a goddam business operation."

The old man stripped the end of a tiny wire with his fingernail.

There were about three hours to wait. The guys were skeptical, they told Mr. Bob they would believe it when they saw it. There was no place to go. They started a poker game, rationing the beers that were left, enough for three apiece leaving out Pitcher and Denzel Ray. Pitcher read his sports magazines and worked a grip exerciser. Mr. Bob did figuring over a brochure about cheap land around Las Vegas. The guys pressured him to play but he said why should he? He might lose. Denzel played a baseball game Lewis had showed him where you use dice to see what happens. Denzel had forgotten exactly how it worked and everybody kept getting walked. He started to change the rules with every toss which livened things up.

Pogo got a royal flush in spades, the first time ever for him, he said. Drew it straight from the deck. Everybody but Lewis had passed on that hand and Lewis had folded after a weak nickel bluff.

"A-bombs for a squirrel hunt," said Pogo. "First decent hand in twenty-five years and everybody runs away, plays dead. If it rained soup I'd have a fork."

They got tired of poker and convinced Pogo that pinochle was a man's game too. Lewis and Pogo stood the Okies.

"You guys are always talking across the table anyhow," said Pogo, "might as well make it legal."

Denzel fell asleep at his dice and Mr. Bob over his brochures. Sounds of equipment being moved, of hammering and shouting filtered in. The cardplayers debated whether they should drink up Mr. Bob's remaining beers, playing to a thousand for them, and decided against. In the far distance there was something like the sound of musical instruments warming up.

About six-thirty the old black man knocked and said Phil Dodge was waiting. Mr. Bob was pissed at the guys for not waking him up sooner so he could take care of things. He told them to get dressed.

"Let's just wait till we see that twenty-five apiece before we get all suited up."

"Yeah, no pay no play."

"All right, I'll settle with him and come right back. And keep your hands off my beer." The old man led him away.

They began to hear the crowd then. It wasn't bad.

"Near a thousand head," said Pogo.

"That's a lot of crackers. Wonder where they all hide in the daytime?"

"Gonna have to keep an eye on old Bob with this piece of the gate thing. See how much of it he tries to skim."

"Aw now, Mr. Bob int that way. Not a deceitful bone in his body. He'll just come out and say he's manager and gets semdy percent."

"Leaving us twenty-three cents each."

"What the hell," said Lewis, "it's all found money tonight."

When Mr. Bob returned his face was drained pale. He breathed as if he had been running. Mr. Bob never ran.

"They're all *black* out there," he said, as if reporting from a strange new world, "ever goddam one of them."

"What?"

"Who?"

"Black?"

"Niggers. It isn't anything but niggers in the stands."

"Go *awn*."

"Niggers at the box office, behind the concession, in the toilets, nothing but wall-to-wall niggers. All of them."

"I knew it. Doing business over a goddam telephone. What's this Dodge guy trying to pull?"

"He's one too."

"Oh shit. Couldn't you tell over the phone?"

"Now A. C.," said Mr. Bob, "who ever heard of a nigger named Phil?"

They went to the door, one by one, to see if it was true.

"Ho-leee shit!"

"Look at em all."

"Every last one."

"So?" said Lewis after he had seen. "Why not just give them a show? We've had them in the audience before, had them at every show."

"But not *just* them. Four or five maybe, scattered around, but never a crowd that's nothing but colored."

"What's the difference?"

"Just *look!* If you can't *see* the goddam *dif*ference, Lewis, you're stone blind."

"You want us to dress up like women and march out there?"

"That's what we do every night. That's the show."

"Not in front of just niggers. I don't know what it is but there's something *wrong* about it."

"Hit's *dif*ferent."

"All right," said Mr. Bob, "let's put it to a vote. Against?"

When Lewis saw all their hands he shrugged. "Hell, whatever you guys want."

"Okay now, we got to plan a getaway. Mr. Bob, is there any way to get the van out here?"

"Not enough room."

"Hey, he didn't already pay you, did he? There's nothing signed on it?"

"No, I stalled him, told him we were having a little emergency and I'd get right back to him."

"He's gonna be over here to see what's up."

"He knows we're here."

"I say we just walk out," said Pogo. "No apologies, no goodbyes."

"They'll kill us."

"You know how they gang up."

"Cmon, we got to think of something. Some reason we can't go on."

"We forgot our stuff? The costumes?"

"Never work."

"What if our star attraction is hurt?"

"We can't go on without Pogo."

"Right," said Mr. Bob. "He asked over the phone to be sure that Pogo was still with us."

"It's my old war wounds," croaked Pogo, "where the Krauts got me. I'm having a relapse." He clutched various spots of his body and lay flat on the bench.

"Shit Pogo, this is serious! War wounds my ass. Now what can he have that would come up sudden?"

"Heart attack."

"I don't want a heart attack," said Pogo. "I can't do one. No dice."

"He'd have to lay low for a while, too, if Dodge followed up on us. We got bookings to fill. Think of something he can recover from in a night."

Knox clapped his hands. "I got it. An eepaliptic fit."

"My specialty!"

"He's having an eepaliptic fit and we got to get him to the hospital fast."

"What if they got a doctor?"

"They're all *nig*gers, Pogo, use your head."

"Okay, that's what we do," Mr. Bob was in control of himself again, his cheeks reddened back to normal. "You guys have all got to make it good or we're up Shit Creek without a paddle."

"And you, Mr. Bob," said A. C., "will be the first overboard."

When Phil Dodge entered the clubhouse to see what was keeping the Bimbos he found them circled around Pogo on the floor. Pogo was wheezing and choking and bugging his eyes, shivering and writhing, bucking across the floor on his back and kicking his legs up in the air.

"Stand back! Give him room to breathe!"

"Grab his legs!"

"Grab his tongue!"

"Don't let him bang his head!"

"Whatever you do *don't* let him bite you!"

"What's wrong?" said Phil Dodge.

"Phil, we got an emergency here. Our midget's been struck down."

"Eepaliptic fit," said Knox. "He's had them before but not like this. This'ns serious." Knox had grabbed Pogo by the crook of his elbow and was stooped over following his convulsions across the floor, looking at his watch like a TV medic.

"How's his pulse?" asked A. C.

"Pretty bad, pretty bad."

"What's it read?"

Knox frowned. He didn't know what kind of numbers pulses came in and that was an awful sharp-looking nigger standing there. "It's pretty bad, pretty bad."

"We got to get him to a doc."

"There are doctors here," said Phil Dodge, "I'll run and get one."

"Oh no!" Mr. Bob jumped in front of the door. "No, they wouldn't be no good. I mean they wouldn't know what to do. See this is a special kind of umm — *mid*get eepalipsy!"

176

"Hit don't work like the regular kind."

"We got to get him to a midget doc. Specialist. There's one in Valdosta but we can't lose a minute!"

"Okay, but if you're going to move him," said Phil Dodge, "you'd better restrain him first."

"Huh?"

"Tie him down so he won't hurt himself."

"Yeah, let's restrain him."

Phil Dodge took a locker door off its hinges and they forced Pogo down on it. Pogo bit Mr. Bob on the hand in the struggle. Phil Dodge put Knox's catcher's mitt under Pogo's head and they began to wrap him to the locker door, winding him in rolls of elastic bandages they had to tape ankle sprains. When they were done they were all sweating and cursing and Pogo was mummified all but his head. He jerked and squirmed under the bandages like a moth trying to bust from its cocoon.

"You better get him to the doctor now, you can carry him to your van."

"What about the crowd? They come here expecting a show."

"I'll handle the crowd," said Phil Dodge, "you just take care of your man."

"I'm awful sorry about this, Phil. I hate to be the one stiffs somebody."

"Nothing you could have done. Come on, he's turning blue."

They opened the door to the first notes of The Star-Spangled Banner. Phil Dodge ran waving to where the band was and managed to get them stopped at the twilight's last gleaming. Then he trotted toward where the P.A. system was.

Mr. Bob surveyed the situation with one foot on the top step of the clubhouse. "Okay boys," he called behind him, "it's now or never. Over the top."

The audience was still standing for the anthem when the tight procession emerged from center field and started toward home. There was scattered cheering but nobody picked it up. A. C. and Knox carried Pogo's bier on their shoulders. Mr. Bob and Lewis and Pitcher carried the equipment. They all walked quickly but solemnly. When the microphone skreeked open the Okies nearly dropped their load.

"Ladies and gentlemenenenenen —" Phil Dodge's voice bounced back and forth over their heads.

"There has been a terriblerriblerriblemeirsfiorlteune-ortuneortune —"

"He's dead!" cried a child's voice from the stands, "the midget's dead!"

The crowd rumbled and creaked from their platforms.

"A medical emergencyergencyergency —"

They had reached the shallow outfield and faces were visible in the stands. Denzel pressed close to his daddy's leg. Pogo was still and waxy-colored on the locker door.

"Tonight's show will be canceledanceledanceled."

Their procession entered the infield where the lighting was strongest and the crowd fell silent. Denzel looked up at them, all the black faces surrounding him and felt his skin tingle. White. He was white. He looked at the other guys and they were white too and he crowded in a little closer with them as they walked in the stillness. Then there was a noise, a humming.

"Dum dum dee-dum, dum dee-dum dee-dum dee-dum." Pogo was humming the Death March. Knox choked on a nervous giggle.

"You're fined, Burns," said Mr. Bob through his teeth, "fifty dollars."

"Take it out of my pay for tonight."

"Shut up or I'll have them bury you under the pitcher's mound."

"Safe!" hissed Pogo as they crossed home plate.

They let it all out with a whoosh once they were in the van and rolling back toward Headlight.

"Yeeeee-*hah*!"

"We done it! We skunked em!"

"Put on some *kind* of a show!"

178

"I was shitting peach pits. Thought sure they's gonna stop us."

"Midget eepalipsy, beautiful!"

A. C. popped open the two beers that were left and poured one over Mr. Bob's head and one on Pogo. Pogo was still getting untangled. They slapped each other's backs and patted each other's butts and pounded and whooped forward to Pitcher at the wheel.

"I thought I was gonna kill you when you asked me what his pulse read."

"Ha! If that nigger known anything about it he'd of been on to us right off."

"Some nigger."

"Watch your language boys," said Pogo. "The man did a good job. He took good care of me."

"Only you weren't dying."

"He was doing everything else but."

"You see him bite Mr. Bob on the hand? Hotdamn!"

"That wasn't funny," said Mr. Bob.

"Is there really a midget doctor in Valdosta?"

"Sure, Lewis, he's three foot six."

"Poor boogies didn't know the real show was bein held in the locker room."

"There was a *shit*load of em, wasn't there? I never seen that many in one place before."

"An old Pogo finely found a position he can handle."

"Hey Denzel! Do Pogo! Do Pogo tonight!"

Denzel took Pogo's place on the litter, crossed his hands over his stomach, bugged his eyes and let his tongue roll out to one side.

"Beautiful! Like a picture!"

"You got the part, kid."

"Did you see Mr. Bob when he first come in? You see him? Mr. Bob was white! Just *white*!"

And laughing, the team drove toward home together.

Mr. Bob decided they should push on to Samson that night. Pitcher had his maps and assured them he'd have no trouble finding the way. They stopped at a gas and grocery to fill the tank and get sandwich makings, then settled back to food and cards. Pitcher said he wasn't hungry, he'd just drive. Every now and then one of them would bug eyes and droop tongue and make epileptic noises deep in his throat and everybody would bust out laughing again. Pogo found it was impossible to read Denzel's kibitzing in a pinochle game so he talked them all into going back to poker, playing for the last slices of olive loaf. Mr. Bob scribbled and swore, erasing the night's prospected take from the books. Pogo won the poker game and punched the olives out of the meat, giving them to Denzel. It seemed like it was taking forever to get there.

It was nearly midnight when Mr. Bob checked his watch and announced that Pitcher must be dragging ass because they were due at Samson a long time back. It was another ten minutes before he decided he would have a word with the boy and by that time there was some very bumpy terrain passing under the wheels. They came to a stop. The men laid their cards aside and piled out the rear door. They found themselves not in a trailer camp but in some moonlit patch of backwoods Florida desolation, surrounded by what appeared to be an orange grove gone sour. Mr. Bob made efforts to inquire about their exact fucking whereabouts but found the driver's seat deserted. Mr. Bob's flock gathered around him, eyes pleading for explanation. He sat on the front fender and looked into the trees with the most unconcerned expression he could muster. Mr. Bob was not one who liked to lose control of a situation.

"Say Mr. Bob?" said Knox after a while. "We aren't lost are we?"

"No," said Mr. Bob, "I don't believe we're lost. A slight deviation from plans, maybe, but not lost."

They were silent but for mosquito slappings after that, until a soggy thumping sound began to their left. It was a sound not unlike a softball hitting a catcher's mitt on a rainy day.

"The kid is screwy" was Pogo's verdict as he trailed the

line that snaked through the overgrown rows toward the thumping. "The keys are in the ignition, I say we leave him. A ball team is no place for a screwy kid." The others ignored him, their curiosity stirred, while Pogo was trying to spare his wingtips any unnecessary wear. He grumbled a little more, but when he saw Denzel being whiplashed by branches in the men's wake he ran ahead and took the brunt himself.

The thumping was regular but not machinelike. The timing was familiar to all of the men, though they could not quite give it a name yet. The sound was clearer as they made their way through undergrowth and rotting fruit, it was a sloppy, sucking kiss. There would be the loud wet smack and then a silence, till all the men felt inside them that the next one was launched and about to connect and there it would be, smack on schedule. It was like listening to your own heartbeat between ear and pillow. The men tried to make as little noise as possible as they crept toward it. Only Denzel did not yet know the sound, but he was beginning to have an idea.

The men slipped past the tangled bush and came to an opening. A clearing. They stood at its fringes blinking in the moonlight, and saw Pitcher. He stood on a little knob of land, a natural mound, and pawed an imaginary rubber. He was surrounded by piles of decaying oranges, some hard green pills, others overripe and bursting at the seams. Pitcher was taking them one by one, winding up and rhythmically ramming them home. He threw overhand, hardball style, and did not bail out as he did when he pitched for the Bimbos. He stood erect after every pitch and studied it on its way in.

His target was a hole in a Hudson. Blue and tireless, the old wreck was flopped on its back in a bed of ferns and bottle glass. Its back seat, door long gone, gaped invitingly. The opening was the height and size of a strike zone. An orange socked dead center into it and burst to liquid. Blue-green fruit mold had thrived over the years, a fuzzy carpet of it lined the walls of the hole. Pitcher kept hurling into it, juice glistened in the moon, drooling from the opening and the smell hit the men all at once, both sweet and acid-sour, a smell long bottled up. The men stood fascinated and repelled, bug-eyed as children at a freak show. Denzel was embarrassed though he was not sure why. Pitcher was throwing oranges at a car — so? He looked to the men but Pogo only shook his head cynically, the Okies grinned and squinted, Mr. Bob checked his watch and his daddy stood with jaw hung open, scratching his head like a cartoon hillbilly. The faces told him nothing but seemed as embarrassed by the sight as he was.

Finally, whether it was a noise or the pressure of their eyes, Pitcher realized he was being watched. He faced them and reddened, caught sticky-handed in his private act. He picked up a last orange and idly looped it behind his back into the waiting zone. He came toward them looking as if he had only stopped to take a roadside leak. "I'll pay for the extra gas," he said.

"We got to make time, son," said Mr. Bob.

"Tomorrow's an open date."

"We still got to get there."

"I got one more stop to make."

"Well make it fast, son, make it fast."

They turned to go back to the van and Pitcher said, as if an afterthought, "Use to live over there."

The men followed the jerk of his thumb past the resting car to the opposite edge of the clearing. There were the remains of a shack, rotting boards and crumbling stone, a planter for the weeds. It looked abandoned for centuries though Pitcher had left only three years back.

"What's this next stop?" asked Mr. Bob, trying to sound casual. You had to give them some rope sometimes.

"My wife. Not far. It'll only take a minute."

When the crop began to fail steadily and the old man stopped caring Pitcher had had a lot of time on his hands. He didn't run wild and steal and raise hell with the other boys. He wasn't popular that way. He spent hours, endless hours of endless days throwing his old man's failed fruit at his old man's derelict car. There wasn't baseball at the school or leagues so he made his own. He pitched complete games, five-hitters, three-hitters, an occasional no-hitter when he was feeling strong, never giving up anything but the scrubbiest of infield singles, the freakiest of blooping Texas League doubles and of course, the errors. A pitcher had to rely sometimes on the other men behind him. But when the chips were down, the bases loaded by a booted grounder, a squib bunt and a bad throw, well then he would rely on nothing but his own arm and whiff the side with nine overpowering strikes. When he thought of home he thought of the Hudson, or rather the hole within it. The shack was indeed an afterthought, it held only the old man, mean and liquor-sick. It was the womb of the Hudson that his life revolved around, that was the hub of his lonely hours. Hours when he had won both ends of a doubleheader and still had time to burn, hours when his boredom drove him to circus tricks, eyes-closed-behind-the-back-through-the-legs-left-handed-underhanded screwing around till everything he threw was a strike, till he could knock flies from the air as they fed from the rotting citrus.

And later in his life he would lie with Charleen in the soft ferns by the Hudson, fruit decay thick in their nostrils, sex always to be sweet and acid for them. She would run her tongue over the muscles he had grown, put his strong fingers in her mouth.

Pitcher had shown his stuff to a birddog, an ex-umpire, in Tuscaloosa. The boy who caught him made his mitt a target, moving it around the zone and Pitcher nailed it dead center every time. The ex-umpire was impressed, there were a lot of kids with speed to burn, but control, control was rare.

They put him on a single-A team in Alabama and gave him a uniform and had him warm up in the bullpen for a week before the skeptical manager gave him a try in a lost game. It was the first time he had ever faced a batter.

At first he threw nothing but strikes. The first batter went down swinging. Pitcher didn't like the swinging, didn't like

183

the bat violating his zone. The bat had pointed at him at the moment of its greatest speed. The next man up was a punch hitter who crowded the plate and fouled three straight pitches. It seemed to Pitcher that the man was standing smack in the middle of the zone. He threw his pitches to keep them from hitting the man, keep them from the bat, and walked him. He walked the next batter with four pitches, none of which went where he wanted them to. He started to sweat and shake a little and the catcher came out.

The catcher was a man who liked to think he was working his way back to the majors from a heart attack. He was well over thirty and was nicknamed Pops. He had roomed with the manager of the club back when they were both rookies.

"Take it easy," said the catcher. "Just throw to the glove like in practice. You got the weak part of the order coming up."

"They're in the way," said Pitcher.

"In the way? Who?"

"The batters are in the way. I'm not used to throwing with batters."

The catcher sighed deeply and looked up at the sun. It was a very great distance to the big leagues from a place where pitchers were not used to men with bats. He considered his aluminum siding business for a moment and then looked to the kid. "What you have to do is to make them disappear. If you look at anything long enough and hard enough you can make it disappear. That batter is challenging you, he's in a struggle with you. You have to stare him down, stare him away, look right through him to the target. Look at a point between his eyes. Every batter has nightmares about catching a fastball between the eyes. Stare at him and plant that dream in his head. Make him afraid and he's half invisible already.

"The mitt, son, just concentrate on throwing into the mitt. There aren't any batters."

The umpire called and the catcher walked back to the plate feeling like an old man, wishing he could make the kid on the mound disappear.

Pitcher stared at the hitter till the ump complained, then

struck him out with three pitches. A skinny boy, the opposing pitcher, appeared at the plate next but soon faded from view. Pitcher threw two strikes to the mitt and then threw the third. But as he stood erect, studying it as it went in, something went wrong. A ball came screaming back at him, screaming toward a point right in between his eyes and he only had time to jerk his head and feel his ear ticked and then people were running around the bases and yelling in the stands and someone gave him another ball to throw to a man with a bat who wouldn't disappear. Everybody was watching him, just him, so he had to throw it there. He threw, but before he completed his motion he was falling off the mound sideways into a crouch, glove fanned out at arm's length for extra protection. People in the stands thought something was funny and laughed. He walked the man to load up the bases. The next one hit a fast grounder at him but he was ready this time and jumped out of its way so it could hop into center field. The manager yanked him.

In the morning he handed in his gear and got a job in a parking lot. He pitched pennies during the slow hours and wrote to Charleen of his successes on the mound.

Hort Truelove awoke and Charleen was not beside him. He heard voices out front and what seemed to be the rumbling of a truck engine. Hort didn't like to be wakened at night, didn't like surprises. He brought the loaded rifle from under the bed to the window with him.

A young man with a bad complexion stood on the lawn with his hands on hips. Charleen shivered on the porch in her wrapper, barefoot, pregnant. Hort frowned and released the safety. On the road, behind the young man, there was a large mobile camper van. The sides of it were flame red and said something about bimbos. There were more men, stretching their legs and leaning against the camper. One of them appeared to be a midget or a strangely built child. The motor of the van was running and the headlights were on. And wait a minute now, one of the men, the biggest one, was fooling around with a club, swinging it.

Hort stepped out on the porch and cocked his rifle.

The men on the road were all still now, watching the porch. The big one dropped his club. The midget scurried inside the van. The young man with the pimples did not seem to notice.

Hort cleared his throat. The midget appeared again, holding a bulge inside the breast of its pajama tops.

This was real, Hort never dreamed. He licked sweat from his lip and located the trigger. This was the real thing.

"Horton, will you put that damn toy away? You gon hurt yourself with that thing!" Charleen was annoyed. Hort hoped that she wouldn't be bitchy all week again.

"Who's he?"

"My ex-husband? That I told you about?"

Hort looked the boy over from behind the rifle and was not impressed. Charleen had said her first husband was some kind of athlete. Hort had expected someone bigger, more powerful.

The young man stared back over the barrel at Hort. He stared for a long time and Hort began to get a headache. Probly from being woke up like this.

"What's he want?"

"He just wanted to talk, Horton. No harm in that."

"Okay," said Hort and sat on the porch steps with the rifle over his knees. "Talk. But make it fast."

They didn't make it fast. They talked small talk and stumbled over people and events Hort had never heard of. He was bored by their conversation. They didn't seem to have met before. They talked about her family for a while and when she was due to have the baby and how she loved the neighborhood here. It looked as if their talk had finally petered out when the young man began to cry.

"Damn, Charleen," he cried, "why couldn't you wait? Why couldn't you wait one lousy season? Was that too much to ask?"

The men by the camper shifted their feet uneasily, they coughed and looked to the ground. Hort put the safety back on and began to unload his rifle in disgust. The guy was actually standing there crying, weeping, on his lawn. The

men climbed into the camper van. The horn was honked.
The young man wiped his red eyes and sat in the passenger
seat. Hort walked down to the road, gun cracked open and
loose in his arm, to see them off. A little man, a doll with a
constantly bobbing baseball for a head grinned and waved
from the rear window.

At the Ponce de Leon Trailer Camp they found a big stink.
The bag for their chemical toilet had cracked yet another
time and they didn't have a replacement.

"Goddam Pogo wore it out," said A. C. "Poor thing just
couldn't take any more a his shit." Pogo was known on the
team as a toilet hog.

They dragged the sack out carefully and tossed it in a field
behind the trailer camp. They located the little building that
held the showers and toilet facilities.

There were two pay toilets. A. C. had Denzel crawl under
the door of the first one to open it and the men stood in line
waiting their turn and making sure the door didn't lock them
out again. Pogo called them a bunch of pikers, paid his dime
and had the other one all to himself. Pitcher was still in the
van.

"One o'clock at night is a poor time to pick for a visit," said
Lewis. "No wonder they didn't hit it off."

Denzel winced a little.

"But coming out with a loaded rifle seems a bit — *extreme*
to me."

Pogo snorted in his stall. "Stupid cracker almost bought
the farm," he said. "Pogo Burns is not a guy who likes to be
threatened with a rifle. Especially when it's for no good reason. You never show heat unless you plan to use it." The last
piece of advice was for Denzel. Yet another lecture on the
perilous ways of the world. He had a special tone of voice
when he gave out his nuggets of wisdom, you could see them
sewn on a sampler and hung on the wall.

Knox laughed. "You would of used that gun of yours?"

"Damn straight I would."

"Old Pogo gonna go out in a blaze a glory."

"Listen, when I know my number is up you can bet I'm going to take somebody with me. I don't give a rat's ass who it is, but somebody's going to share expenses. Death is too long a trip to take alone."

"You're a fearsome man, Pogo Burns. Hey, how bout old Pitcher bawlin like that? You ever seen the like of it, pardner?"

"The man is pussy-whipped. That's the whole sad story right there. I suppose there are things a man could cry over, but a woman isn't one of em."

"A man don't cry in public," said Pogo. "A man is made to take punishment."

"Never seen the like of it."

"Pardner, you remember that faggot down cellblock D at McAlester? Day his boyfriend got sprung he dropped his tray right in the middle of mess and bawled like a baby."

"Boys will be girls."

"Let a woman get to you and that's all she wrote. That's how Dillinger got hisself nailed. All over a whore in a red dress."

Pitcher walked in. Their eyes searched for corners to hide in. They were men who had seen childbirths and murders, every freak of nature imaginable, women who blew cigar smoke from their pussies and men who would kill for pocket money, but they couldn't bring themselves to look at a man who had just been crying.

"Some guys," said Pogo from his stall, not knowing who was there, "some guys let the fillies get to them. You won't catch Pogo Burns making a fool of himself at one in the morning over a piece of ass."

There was a very long silence. Knox used the sink but didn't leave.

Pitcher went to Pogo's stall and talked to the space under the door. "Burns," he said, "the blindest, drunkest, ugliest whore in the world wouldn't shit on you for a million dollars. If you ever had a piece of ass in your life it was covered with wool and went bah-bah."

Pitcher walked out. The others waited for some action

from Pogo, but when none came they too left for bed. Denzel sat on the floor. He listened but could hear no breathing. He saw the two-toned wingtips under the stall door. It was a long time before the toilet flushed and Pogo came out. He saw Denzel sitting by the wall.

"Get some shut-eye, kid," he said. "Open date tomorrow."

Friday

1

"I don't spose it's any too easy doing three shows a day. But if that's what you got to do to come out even, that's what you got to do." Denzel searched the ground for the right-sized rock, dragging the bat behind him. He found one, took his stance, tossed it up and chock! sent it flying.

"Base hit to the opposite field."

Mr. Mumps intently searched the backs of his arms for fleas, occasionally lifting his head to watch Denzel bat.

"Now in our case, it means one- or two-night stands at each spot and travlin more than most have to. It's not so bad though."

Chock!

"Shit. Ground out to the pitcher. It's different when there's a bunch of guys with you on the trip. I mean Mrs. Mumps seems like a nice lady and I'm sure she treats you good, but it can't be the same. With the number we got things are pretty lively, lemme tell you. They argue a lot but nothing serious. They're a pretty nice bunch of guys. You'd like em."

Chock!

"Stand-up double off the left field wall. That time I got under it just enough."

Mr. Mumps nodded.

"We have some real good times. I mean really. You can't beat it, the road life. Pogo says it's a broadning experience for a kid."

Chock!

"Base hit up the middle. Only thing I miss is you don't get to see much TV."

He gave the bat to Mr. Mumps and collected a handful of rocks for him. The monkey choked up a little, his hands up where the split had been wrapped in tape.

"Okay, let's see what you can do."

Mr. Mumps threw the rocks up and swung at them. Each time his swing was the same hard, level cut. Each time he threw the rock up in a different direction, off to the right, over his shoulder, away at an angle. Denzel took the bat from him.

"You got a nice swing there but you want to work on your eye." Mr. Mumps nodded and went back to his flea hunt. "You got the making of a good solid hitter, though."

Chock!

"Pop-up. I'm serious. I wouldn't bullshit you just cause you're a monkey. I mean like sometimes the older guys hand you a line just cause you're a kid. I wouldn't try that on you. Usually I can tell right off when they're pullin my leg. They get extra serious. That's a tip-off you ought to remember."

Chock!

"Line drive single to left. Though sometimes it's hard to tell. Like with my friend Pogo's stories. Some of them are pretty wild but they make sense. And he never cracks up later and says he was just putting one over on you." Denzel looked around. There was no action in the trailer camp. "If I tell you a secret, you think you could keep it to yourself?"

Mr. Mumps nodded sincerely.

"There's a man that's after Pogo. Out to kill him, probly. That's what Pogo says. Sometimes he's real cautious but other times he just lets his guard down. Like he doesn't care. Like there really isn't a man."

The monkey shook its head in puzzlement.

194

"And then other times it's like he's just waiting for something to happen. Just asking for it."

Mr. Mumps shrugged his shoulders.

Denzel took a tighter grip on the bat. "If that guy does show up, this is what I'll use on him. Right in the head. Say listen, don't let any of this out. Pogo'd be pissed."

Chock!

"That's gone. Home run. That time I got my hips around and used my wrists like Daddy says. Daddy was never a power hitter, but he says I might have the built for it. He says you ought to be compact."

Swish!

"Damn. Tried to kill it. You always want to meet the ball. He says I'm a natural at a lot of things and the rest will come with work. An when I'm of age he says I'll have a good shot at the majors. Pro ball."

Chock!

"Ground out to first. I wish I'd hurry up and get older. It'd be awful if there wasn't any majors left when I come of age. I want em to be just like they are now."

Mr. Mumps sucked a toe.

Chock!

"Long sacrifice fly. Runner scores from third. Don't take it that I'm bragging or anything. He said all of them things, not me. And my daddy is one person who never hands me a line. Never."

Chock!

"Foul ball. And you know what else?"

Mr. Mumps shook his head.

"I'm gonna be ten on Sunday. Pogo calls it my first decade in the business. He says he likes to see other people's birthdays but not his own. Says he's had all the birthdays he wants for himself."

Chock!

"Liner up the middle. I spose when you get past your prime and don't have the majors to aim at you're not in such a hurry."

Chock!

"Foul. Must of been different for Pogo though. I mean he knew all along he'd never have the size for it. No hope."

A voice called from the camp. Denzel and Mr. Mumps lifted their heads.

"Sounds like Mrs. Mumps. Probly your breakfast is ready."

The monkey got to its feet and tossed a few nearby rocks to Denzel. It turned to go.

"See you round."

Chock!

2

Dred woke just before noon and didn't know where he was. There was a Bible on the stand by him. His feet stuck out naked at the bottom of the bed. Motel room. His skin stuck to the sheet and the ribbons on the air conditioner across from him hung limp. A bug zipped along a ridge in the cracking stucco wall, an inch-long armorback mother that put the tenement roaches back in the City to shame. Sun bled through the venetian blinds, striping him and spilling past onto the new flier he'd found. He was in a motel room in the South, on the afternoon of the day that he was going to kill Pogo Burns.

He rolled on his side to study the picture. It was the white man, dressed in woman's clothes. There was a list of dates and locations, including one for the next day in Samson, Florida. Dred checked the time. He should start soon, find the place in the early evening, and come for him by night. He got up to shower.

At first the water steamed down but Dred turned it all the way cold. He didn't want the water to relax him. He stepped under and gritted his teeth against it at first, then, sucking in chestfuls of air, let it wake him up and put him on edge. On edge, a trigger, that was it. And concentrate it on the freak, the white man.

He would come for him by night. The midget would be alone, ready for bed, naked. The light would flick on and he'd be caught blinking at Dred's gun, his body pale white, obscene. Cornered. No one to yell to. Dred would stand silent and still as death, give him time to recognize, to remember, to know. To know why he was going and who was sending him, to know finally that you don't fuck with Dred and survive it. The little white man would sweat and try to cover himself and Dred would bring the gun barrel down level with his eyes. The midget would start to plead then, and Dred would blow his head off.

He dressed slowly, choosing his clothes with care. It would be black today, crushed black velvet from head to foot, with gold buttons. The strips of sun were already frying the dust they crossed on the floor, but today it would be black. He left the key to the room on top of the Bible.

He taped the flier over his rearview mirror to build his concentration and left the afternoon stink of Savannah behind him. He reached under the seat and felt the gun. He had loaded it the night before. He barreled south well over the speed limit, flicking his gaze constantly to the picture over the mirror. Off the cocksucker. Blow him away. Straight at him. Forget the rest, forget Black Hollow and Bugbear and Orison and all this place. Now it's just two. He looked at the picture so steadily that when he brought his eyes back to the road he began to see a lingering image of the white man, as if there were a picture slide on his shades and whatever he saw would have Pogo Burns laid over it. He saw the freak before him on the road, taunting in curls and woman's clothing, and he drove at it, leaning into the accelerator, driving hard to meet it, to thunder over it and as the image faded he drove harder not to let it escape and all the while there was a whine growing, heightening and loudening into a high-pitch scream till he realized it was coming from his engine.

He pulled to the side of the road and stopped.

The scream fell back into a whine, but whined steadily. Dred stood in front of his machine and tried to figure how to open the hood. He pushed and pulled at different parts of the hood and grill, burning his fingertips. Mother was hot. He crouched as well as he could in the tight pants and finally found the catch. He lifted the hood and looked inside.

The whine was louder. There were all kinds of machine parts cramped together and connected with wires and pipes. Some of the ones to the rear of the engine smoked like a fire had just been put out. It was too hot back there for Dred to get his hand near. At the front of the engine, between the grill and the propeller thing, was a flat rectangular box. The more Dred listened, the more the whine seemed to be coming from the top of the box. There was a round cap on top of it that looked like it would twist off so Dred could look inside. It was too hot to touch. He got a handkerchief from the glove compartment and gave it a twist. The whine turned into a low forceful hum. He twisted again and the cap blew off singing past his ear as a spout of steam blasted him back from the engine. It geysered straight up, smoking white and furious, and showed no sign of letting up. Dred held his arm where it glowed from scalding and wondered what the fuck he had turned loose. At any moment the entire machine might deflate like a punctured tire.

But the column began to lower and the steam cloud broke up into larger pellets of water until finally there was only a frothing around the mouth of the hole in the top of the rectangular box. Dred approached it carefully and listened. He heard water bubbling hot inside. Boiling. A boilover, it needed water.

He searched along the bank of the road until he found the cap. There were only a few wisps of smoke twisting silently from the hole now; he wrapped the cap in the handkerchief and screwed it back on. He got his road map out from the front seat.

Water. The map showed that not too much further down the road it crossed the spot where the Ogeechee and Canoochee met. If the car would start it might be able to make it there.

When he started the engine up Dred noticed a dial on his dash panel labeled TEMP. There was a horizontal green strip

199

that turned red at its right tip and an arrow. The arrow quivered at the extreme end of the red.

Dred watched the arrow and listened for the whine and drove well under the speed limit, only occasionally noticing the thing on his mirror, until he came to a bridge. A river. The Fugyouchee.

He opened the hood again. The long block parts at the back of the engine were still smoking and when he gingerly unscrewed the cap of the thing in front a hot cloud lifted out and he smelled rotting rubber. Got to cool things off. He looked down the bank to the water and wondered how to get it up where he needed it.

He looked in his car. There were no bottles or cups. There was nothing he could think of in the trunk. Finally he thought of the plastic litter bag he had wrapped the gun in.

The bag did not hold much and he had to be careful not to spill coming up through the weeds on the bank. The first bagfuls he poured on the block parts at the back sent the water bursting to hot vapor the moment it touched, droplets spattering off the metal like grease from a grillplate. Little pockets of water formed in the folds and bubbled. Occasionally a bomb of sweat would plop from his forehead and sizzle where it hit the engine. He kept dousing them till the water stayed water and ran off.

The first water he poured into the hole spat back out at him, and when after what seemed hundreds of trips the box seemed to be full, it gurgled deep inside and vomited half of what Dred had brought. He filled it to the top again and gave it a solemn warning. It remained still and he put the cap back on.

Okay, collect it. Direct it. Straight at it now. He took a long deep look at the picture and headed for the Interstate.

He was not on the highway three minutes before he saw little strings of white trailing out from the edges of the hood. The arrow was swimming toward the red. He slowed down and the arrow stopped, just short. That was it, speed. He drifted to fifteen miles an hour below the limit.

He kept on that way for a while, eyes jumping from the arrow to Burns to the road. The land was flat and uninteresting. The arrow threatened the red on the slight inclines, then retreated with the downhills. The sun made mirages, little streams that seemed to trickle over the highway just ahead but disappeared when you reached them. Dred felt the gun beneath him, loose now. He hadn't wanted it to get wet from the bag.

The arrow began to wriggle over and Dred eased up on the gas a bit more and then from nowhere there was a cop beside him pointing to the side of the road. Dred considered the gun then nudged it further back with his foot. He snatched the paper away from the mirror. Bastard had snuck up from behind, couldn't see.

The bastard got out from his car and walked back to the window. The engine whistled at him as he passed it.

"Buddy," he said, "you got problems?"

He wore the same kind of shades as Dred. You couldn't tell what he was looking at.

"It's hot."

The cop was middle-age, maybe forty. There were pale half-moons dipping below his shades. "That's a fact." He yawned a little and pulled at his nose as if he were small-talking a neighbor. "Ha come you goin so slow?"

"Engine's hot."

"I seen that," he said. "This is an Innerstate. Like to keep it movin?"

"Yuh."

"Where you from, Buddy?"

"California."

"And where you goin?"

"Florida."

The cop considered this. "Come down to catch some sun did you?"

"Business."

"Business must be pretty good. S'a nice car."

Dred was silent. The cop looked up the highway, thinking. Dred was breathing slowly, relaxed, waiting cool for whatever came next the way he had trained himself to do with cops. No panic, he hadn't done the thing with Burns yet.

"Hokay, Buddy," sighed the cop, "tell you what. You got to

get that ingin yours taken care of, can't be pokin along the Innerstate. I'll take you up the next exit and you catch semteen there, take you down same direction if you want. Or you can stop up to Rassburra get that thing fixed?" He patted the top of the roof. "Okay? You just follow me na."

So Dred had a police escort to the Riceboro exit.

17 was reasonably good for Georgia and he had it all to himself. Riceboro was six or seven miles in the wrong direction and he had no time to mess with garage mechanics, but there wasn't going to be a river for a long while.

Another jerkwater town. Used to be on the main drag but now it dried up. There was a Stuckey's that had closed down and a White Tower that had burned out. Finally he came to an A&W that was open. A sad scrawny girl came out, freckled, crooked-toothed. She was carrying a window tray and dressed in the carhop uniform. Black and orange, sheeit. Some sorry vines. Some sorry people. She did a skittish little dance around the hissing engine. He thought at first just to ask for what he needed but then decided fuck it. Not down here to be polite to cracker bitches.

"Don't bother," he said when she went to clamp the tray to his window, "just bring me a gallon jug."

When she left to get it Dred took his shades off and wiped the sweat from around his eyes. The engine began to whistle again. He caught a boy and a girl in a convertible at the far end of the lot staring at him, and made them retreat into their hamburgers. The waitress returned with his gallon.

"Be a dollar."

When he got out of the car to pay her she skittered back, unprepared for his height. The outside of the plastic jug was beaded with a cold sweat, he rubbed it against his arm where it was burned, then opened it and sent the root beer glugging to the pavement. The girl was properly impressed, her mouth hanging open as she watched the puddle spread over the oil blotches, little flecks of foam at its edges. Dred frowned, seeing that his shoes were caked with dried mud. He flipped the hood up and unleashed the spume from the thing up front. The girl made herself scarce.

There was a water tap Dred had seen at the side of the building. He poured two gallons on the parts in the back and was filling a third when some ofay under a little white hat eyeballed him from around the corner. Dred looked through him and made him disappear. The box took two gallons and he kept another full in the front seat. The soda was fried to a dry stain when he left.

A few miles south on 17 he noticed the smell. It was stronger than the hot seatcovers and came from behind him. Burnt plastic. He had left his box of cassettes on the rear window ledge the night before. They made little sucking sounds when he pried them apart from one another. He took one and jammed it into the tape deck. He could barely recognize Ornette Coleman, the notes all bent the wrong way, the energy of his charges was dissipated. Aretha was wobbly and Miles was sour and Nina Simone was just *wasted*. Shit a brick. Dred shoved them in, listened a few bars then one by one tossed them out the window. He watched them skip and shatter in the rearview mirror till there were only a few left, then caught himself. Looking back. Looking be*hind*. Worried about some sounds when it's the day a man gets killed. Now get it back.

He dumped the rest of the tapes out the window and slid the picture of Burns over next to him. You. You are the man. He checked the arrow, checked his watch and glanced at the road map. He would come for him by night. The midget would be alone, ready for bed, naked. The light would flick on and he'd be caught blinking at Dred's gun, his body pale white and obscene. Cornered.

The whine pulled Dred's ear. He had been speeding. It grew to a howl before he got the car pulled over. The eruption when he uncorked it was the most furious yet, jetting the hot mist well over his head. He stood holding the jug, in the middle of nowhere, waiting for it to be still. His clothes sucked the sunheat into him and he thought for one instant, before he pushed it from his mind, that black was not the color for the day. Thirsty gurgling rose from the hole and he filled the box.

He nudged at the arrow, lightfooting it, till he reached Darien. Just beyond it the road crossed the inlet that was the mouth of the Altamaha River. He wondered if the water was fresh and if ocean water would hurt the engine thing. The path leading under the bridge looked mucky, he thought about it and then kept his shoes on. He picked his way down carefully to the water. His reflection showed that though he was sweatsoaked on the inside his look was still together. A bad-looking nigger in black crushed velvet.

He saw that there was a noticeable coat of dust on the car now, that it was crusted with salt at the bottom. Later for that, no side trips. Straight at it.

When he crossed the Satilla it was fine but as he neared the border it began to rumble and he saw he needed gas. There were no black gas stations in Kingsland. You could smell the engine now, scalded metal, burning rubber. A knot of crackers circled it to comment.

"Put some coolant inner."

"Have it flushed."

"Could be the thermostat."

"Take a look at her?"

"Gas," he said, "fill it."

They stepped back and scratched and winked to each other and told of radiators they had seen explode, while the attendant filled the tank.

"Could be your hose got a leak."

"It's fine," he said.

The crackers giggled among themselves and leaned back against the station wall with their thumbs in their belts, monkey-wrench studs smirking at a Sunday driver.

"Just fine." He laid a patch by the pumps, not waiting for his change.

There would be one less of the fuckers after tonight.

He barely made it to the St. Mary's before the radiator boiled over again. His shirt stuck to him by now and he said what the fuck and went to the trunk for another. Someone had written nigger in the dust on the trunk. With a small n. He wasted a gallon of water on it and punched a small dent in the fender and wondered how long he had been carrying it, a Kick Me sign stuck on his ass. Had the crackers at the gas station read it and laughed or had they been the ones who wrote it there? Go back and kick shit. But no, first things first. Take them one at a time. He started lugging gallons of water to the engine. The only clean shirt he could find was orange.

Back on the road he felt something behind him, something following. His eyes went from the picture to the arrow to the road to the mirror. Signs with orange suns and green alligators welcomed him to Florida. A few sad brown palm trees bent over him like half-stiff pricks. Welcome to Vacationland.

3

What do you do with a free day in Samson, Florida?

The trailer camp kids discovered Pogo early in the morning so he was driven back inside the camper to work on his memoirs. Lewis decided it was a good day to do something fatherly. He and Denzel played pitch and catch in the field behind the camp. Mr. Bob went into Gainesville on business. The Okies sat on the grass and drank beer. Pitcher did his morning exercises.

Some boys from the other trailers appeared with gloves and Lewis threw them pops and grounders. Denzel ran to get a couple bats so they could play flies-up and the Okies returned with him. About six other men from the camp, fathers, wandered over and took turns, batting out of their hands and joking. They made bases from a cardboard box and chose up sides, trying to get an equal number of men and boys on each team. They needed one more so Pitcher was dragged over. The game began, underhanded slow-pitch softball.

The men started to sweat and enjoy themselves, they took off their shirts and joked about growing bellies. The performers, the Bimbos, felt light without their women's uniforms dragging on them. Even Pitcher stopped scowling, laying fat ones up to the plate to be hit. The boys felt like men, tagging deep-voiced fathers out, and the men felt like boys again as they rounded bases and chattered from the outfield with hands on knees. Mothers and wives appeared to watch, sitting along the baselines, talking among themselves, fetching coolers of beer and lemonade. The game broke for an improvised picnic lunch then started up again, finally ending in the late afternoon. Denzel walked back to the camper with his father, who had hit three homers and made a spectacular diving catch.

"Have a good time, kid?" asked the midget when they returned. "Glad to hear it. Nothing like a father and son knocking the ball around together."

Pogo was reading a paper and didn't look up when he talked. Denzel could smell the liniment he used on his legs. The paper was a week old and A. C. had cut out half the funny page. "The National Pastime."

But if he played, thought Denzel, it would have been a show.

4

Jacksonville gagged him with sulfur and the lane-hoppers honked and zipped past him. He left the city still on 17, heading south, hugging along the St. John's and stopping twice to water the car. The second time he saw another picture, slapped on a telephone pole. The midget. Samson, Florida. He did a steady 45 down to Palatka, ignoring the arrow and the complaints of the radiator. He turned west to Samson. It was late afternoon.

He would come for him by night. The midget would be alone, ready for bed, naked.

The engine screamed three miles west of Palatka. He used the gallon. There was nothing around but dry, scraggly brush. The side of the road was white sand, like a beach. The map showed no water between there and Samson. This shit is *got* to stop.

He rolled slowly, searching the sides of the road for anything to fill his jug with. He took his shades off to see better. There were no houses. The radiator began almost immediately, he hadn't given it long to cool off. Dred was tired, he felt like he had been steamed limp.

He saw a trickle of mud at the side of the road and stopped. Mud meant water. He put his shades back on and brought

the jug along with him. The mudpath led through the vege-
tation to an overgrown tangle of barbed-wire fence. Prickers
snagged at his velvet pants, made zipping sounds as they
rode over his silk shirt. He stomped the wire down till he
could safely step over its sag. The brush was sparse now and
the path widened into a sort of unweeded field of grayish
muck. There was a walkway through it, rotting, unpainted
boards laid end to end. Chocolate water squeezed up
through their cracks when he stepped on them, he ducked
under branches. Mosquitoes sung around his ears and the
air, acid with decay, teemed with pockets of smaller, trans-
lucent bugs. He thought of turning back but needed water.
Straight ahead.

The brush fell away and the mire widened. He thought he
saw some kind of big brackish puddle ahead. He thought he
felt something nuzzle his leg.

He looked behind and saw it and was barely able to stay on
the board when he came down from his leap. The jug flopped
in the muck several feet to the side.

The thing let out a deep angry snork and stepped forward
with its head down. Its ribs and shoulder blades showed
through the gray mud that dripped from it. One side of its
face was scabbed with black and it had only one red b-b for
an eye. Fucking razorback. Fucking *hog* wallow.

It took another step at him and he tightroped backwards
till he heard a wet sucking sound from the pond and turned
to see a mean-looking chunk of mud making toward him.
Another one. The one-eye snorked again and moved up. It
had teeth, big black curling tusks that it showed to Dred. He
wrenched the board behind him up with a loud smuck and
a lengthwise half of it crumbled off, rotten. But what he kept
felt solid when he thwacked it up side the hog's shoulder. It
paid no attention and kept coming, staring at Dred's shoetops
as if they were all it was after. Dred grabbed the board at the
middle to help his balance and stood surfer style, one foot
before the other jabbing the sharper end at the animal's
snout. It feinted and retreated, its breath coming in quick
snorts. Dred saw an opening for its eye but the razorback

209

ducked its head into the ooze and the board sliced over high. Dred raised the blunt end to chop down on it but then he was lifted by the backs of his thighs and flipped sprawling into the muck. Before he could clear himself something had clamped on his arm and tried to tear it out of the socket. He screamed, his shades mashed to his face, mud-blinded, and flailed out with his free hand feeling his two gold rings dig into flesh. The clamp loosened and he jerked his arm free, pushing away with his legs, squirming in a kind of backstroke till he felt it again against his belt, rooting around his fly. He screamed again and hammered both fists down on its skull, rolled out and away from it and pulled himself into a standing position. The new one was thinner, longer legged. It faced him a few feet away and the one-eye was to his left. The one-eye closed in a little and Dred saw his weapon half buried behind it. He faked in toward the new one then did a slow-motion end run around the left, dredging his big feet up from the slough and gasping high notes through his teeth. One-eye couldn't handle the sharp turn to its blind side quick enough and Dred yanked the board out on the move, churned a few more long strides away then turned and stood. The thinner one circled warily at a good distance but One-eye plowed straight for him. Dred crouched and waited. When it was right he feinted a chop with the sharp end, dipped his pivot knee and swung an uppercut to its jaw with the blunt. There was a crack and gobs of mud flew off the board following the arc of the swing and Dred hopped close drawing the sharp end back like a bayonet then jabbed out its light. He waded back from it, the muck shlurping off one of his size fifteens and closing over it. The razorback retched screams and turned in a tail-chasing circle to the side of his bleeding eye socket, trying to catch the last speck of brightness.

The other one wrinkled its snout back in a grimace and started a stiff-haired stickwalk toward him. Dred turned to face it and crouched again. Come on, he hissed, come and get it. He slapped the flat of the blunt end down on the mud in a slow, threatening rhythm. The razorback hesitated. Dred took a step toward it and it stopped, snorking and quivering.

He made three quick munching hops at it and snarled, slapping the board down so that chocolate water sprayed in a sunburst pattern around him. It crouched into the bog for a moment, then squealed off toward the muck-puddle with Dred digging after it, snarling and slapping and swearing. The razorback splashed in till it was mired to its belly then turned and sat heavily. Dred didn't follow it in. He took a balanced grip on the board and hurled it like a spear into the bog. It struck high on the ribs leaving a deep red gouge and somersaulting clear to the far bank. The razorback made a coughing sound and floundered to the very middle of the water, only its nostril and little red eyes bubbling on top of the surface.

Dred tilted back to where he had left the jug. The blinded one was still circling, its cries growing hoarse. The jug had been torn open.

He made his way back to the road, leaving his broken shades and one of his shoes buried behind him. He peeled his clothes off and threw them into the brush. The sun had just set, flaring orange into the road ahead. He scraped what mud he could from his body and put on the first thing he came to in the trunk. He put his remaining shoe back on to drive with. The radiator had calmed and he thought he could make it to Samson even without new water. The engine started. He left the trickle of mud by the side of the road and the sound of animal crying as darkness came.

5

Denzel Ray's birthday was to be on Sunday but the guys decided they should help him celebrate Friday night when they had some free time. He was invited to come in and paint the town with them. Never too young you can't use a little experience, they said. Usually on free nights Pogo and Denzel would stay back in the camper playing double solitaire, Pogo nursing the headache he developed whenever the guys went into town. It was a retroactive concussion, he would always explain, from a beating he took in his detective days. Denzel liked Pogo better when they were alone together, the shortstop would call him Denzel Ray instead of Kid and talk softer than when the other guys were around. Sometimes he'd tell stories about when he was a boy.

But this night Denzel was going in and so was Pogo. They stood by the highway with Knox and A. C. and Denzel got to put his thumb out cause it was his birthday. Pitcher stood across the road from them, hitching the other way.

"Just to be a screwball," said Pogo. Pitcher got a ride almost immediately.

The Okies were shaved and dressed and itching to go. Denzel was wearing his new sneakers. Lewis and Mr. Bob had stayed behind to install yet another new toilet bag and would meet them at a bar later. Pogo cussed out each car that passed them all by.

An old man in a beaten pickup stopped. The Okies climbed in the back with some junk, commenting that it was hard to tell where the trash ended and the truck started. Pogo and Denzel sat in front with the old cracker. There was a sticker on the windshield, a brassy-looking woman hiking her dress around her thighs and beckoning with a thumb. NO HITCHHIKERS, it said, BLONDS ONLY. The old man smelled of garbage and had a stubbly goatee stained with barbecue sauce. Denzel tried not to brush against him when they hit bumps. They hit all the bumps possible as the old man turned to talk with them and ignored the road. One of his eyes, the one closest to Denzel, was dead.

"Goin' in to the big town, eh?"

Pogo was fooling with a cigar so Denzel answered yessir to be polite.

"First time?"

"Whatsay?"

"This your first time?"

The old man had a crazy-looking grin pasted on his face. First time for what? "I been to a town before," said Denzel.

The old man laughed though Denzel didn't see anything funny.

"Mind the road, Pops," said Pogo. They were using most of two lanes and the shoulder.

"Nosir, nothin like a trip to the big town to change a feller's luck. I wunt but leven year old when I first got mine trimmed. Just a little tadpole like Red here."

"The road, old-timer, the road."

Denzel did not like to be called Red.

"Sixty-eight year old come September and I never had an accident yet."

"You must of scared everybody else off the highway."

The old man chuckled. "Nosir, Red, nothin like it. But you an your cautious friend here got to be careful. There are some wicked women in this world, and they will hustle the clothes right off your back. Some mean, wicked women."

"The woman hasn't been born can hustle Pogo Burns."

"Maybe so, fella, maybe so. But your safest bet is to haul your asses over to the Venus de Milo Arms. Let Mama Moon take care of you."

Pogo snorted. "She still around?"

The old man laughed for a long time and they ran through a red light. The Okies could be heard swearing in the rear. "Plain to see this int *your* first trip. Yes, Mama Moon is still in business. Most old as me and still turns a trick nown then, just to keep her hand in."

"Look out for the dog."

"Dog can look out for itself. That's what God give it legs for."

"I wonder what he was thinking of when he gave you eyes?"

"He took one back, fella. He took one back."

Pogo looked at the old man for the first time. "Yeah. So he did."

"Speaking of physical handicaps," said the old man widening his grin till it filled his face, "there's a new one at the Venus de Milo. Rubber bones. A contortionist. Freak of nature she is, they tell me she can —"

"Listen, Pops, you mind keeping it clean in front of the kid here? He's only nine years old for chrissakes."

"Almost ten," said Denzel.

"Almost ten."

The old man threw his head back to laugh and forced a Volkswagon bus off the road. "I always say, hit's never too young you can't get an education. Boy's learnin."

"Learning how to be a traffic fatality. That line in the center of the road aint a tightrope you know."

"Boy is got everthing in the world to look forrid to. Everthing makes a man's life worth the livin of. Got his work to look to, and his women. Got all that room to grow into, all that man to become. Yessir, he standin on the precipiece of a great adventure."

"If he survives this ride," said Pogo, and sunk into a frowning silence.

214

The old man began to sing. He sang with great feeling, closing his eye and thumping time on the dashboard. In between verses he checked to see how things stood on the highway.

Ah know a gal who's the peach of the South
She look like butter won't milt inner mou-houth
Giver a whirl jest a playin a hunch
She took mah heart and she ate it for luh-hunch.

Two hitchhikers, teenage boys, dove for cover as the truck sprayed them with gravel. One of the Okies whooped a rebel yell.

Giver a ring an we jumped in the sack
She give me a dose and ah caint give it bah-hack
Ah got the nuggets, she got the chest
Ah got the rooster tail, she got the neh-hest.

A girl in a peasant blouse and shorts combed her hair on the bank. The Okies whistled and offered her a lift if she didn't mind squeezing in. Her boyfriend changed a tire.

Whin ahm at work she has men by the score
Ah ought to put in a re-volving doh-whore

The old man honked and waved as he careened by a sheriff's car pulled over to give someone a ticket.

It's hard to put our affair into words
But ahm for the bees, gal, an you're for the bir-hirds.

6

A great furious wash of steam roiled into the Phillips 66 in Samson and Dred emerged from the midst of it, startling the night boy.

"Water," he croaked, "bring me water."

The night boy rushed back with a Dixie cup full from the fountain. Dred only stared at it. "Gallons," he said, "gallons of water."

The night boy took a moment to comprehend, the steam cloud settling over them like a fog, then said oh and let the Dixie cup drop. White cracker noses came to squash against screen doors across the street, Dred glared back at their dim porch lights through the mist. They came out on their front lawns, crossing their arms and goggling as if they had never see a burgundy Coupe de Ville before in their lives, as if Dred were some kind of a freak. As if there were something unnatural to a six-foot-ten black man, mud-caked beneath his rumpled mustard yellow vines, standing one foot bare in front of the Phillips. They goggled and exchanged opinions till the bugs drove them inside to check the zoning laws.

The night boy trotted out with a spewing hose and shuffled around, not sure what to start with. Dred took it from him and opened the hood, vapor condensing and rolling off his face and neck, then played the cold stream over the engine. The cloud settled and the outline of a car grew sharp. He pulled the radiator cap and stepped back from its spurt. The night boy stood with his hands in his pockets looking like he wanted to call the fire department or the police or his mother. Dred shot the hose down into the radiator until cold water overflowed in a fountain at its mouth. He put the cap back on.

"Thing else?" The boy seemed afraid to ask, his voice broke.

"Is there a carnival here?"

"Air's gone to be one. Tomorra out the fairgrounds."

"Where do the carnival people stay?"

"Where? Prolly out the trailer camp. Say, you with the show?"

"Where is the trailer camp?"

"Bout four-fi miles back on the road you just come down? Yall prolly passed rat by er. Air's a sign say Ponce Delyone Trailer Camp. S'on your left. You with that baseball team they got?"

Dred tossed the hose, still running, in his direction and was gone.

He would come by night. On the left. He would come for him by night. Dred slowed, the road was not straight and he didn't want to miss the sign. He reached down and fingered the gun. Okay now, no more shit, straight at it. But there was something about the hose. Holding the hose. Dred lay back against the seat and realized he had had to take a leak for the longest time —

Fuck that. No time for leaks now. He would come for him, straight at him, by night. He leaned forward to the meeting, leaned into the gas, headlights whipping across the gnarled brush, his eyes aching for the sign. Faster, faster, straight ahead to meet it, you do things quick and straight and nobody askes questions or raises objections or makes wisecracks or sits in your goddam *place*. You don't give them time to get their guard up, to build up some courage or gather some help. Just time to go or give, to run or die. Faster, he tried to draw the picture of the midget in his mind, the picture of how he would look when he was finished, and faster until he saw it up ahead and not believing it waited till it was too late to stop. No, he thought as he braked and swerved and braced himself for the bellyflop into the ditch, not an old darky in a straw hat, not a coon on a mulecart full of watermelons.

The ditch had originally been the road it seemed, it was flat and wide enough to catch a car. Dred scuttled out and strained to see behind but was blinded till he realized he was trying to look through the glare of his own high beams.

"Hey!" he screamed. "You! With the mule!"

There was no answer.

"Watermelon man!"

There was no sound of hooves or of wheels turning.

"I saw you nigger! I *saw* you!"

There was only the idling of his engine and the sound of his rear wheels spinning in the air. There was a sinkhole within the ditch and he had nosedived into it. He turned the engine and the lights off and put the shift into reverse. He grunted and hissed and cursed the everlasting hurts down on the whole motherfucker South but there was no way he was going to push the car back out by himself. He got the gun from under the seat. It wouldn't be far now.

7

When Luwanna and Nadine entered the Lucky Lady air conditioning and drinkers' eyes hit them full in the face. Only momentum and the knowledge that most of the attention was directed at Nadine kept Luwanna from retreating through the door and looking for another place. There were only two other women in the bar, a dikey-looking girl manning the draught pump and a huge woman crammed in a booth between two middle-sized men. Luwanna thought it wasn't too late to turn and go but she saw that Nadine was drinking all the stares in, being blond and pert and perky and flashing her cheerleader smile. Nadine seemed to brighten the dim room, her skin baby smooth and white but for the blush on the arm she had hung out the window all the way down from Tupelo. Before the week's vacation was up she would have a lotion-poster tan setting off her hair and her eyes. Luwanna knew and resented it just the tiniest bit. Luwanna's skin went from swarthy to swarthier in the sun and people took her for Puerto Rican or something.

She tagged behind in Nadine's wake to the bar.

There were empty stools on either side of them. Luwanna caught men's eyes bouncing furtively toward them from the bar mirror. Eyes and the special buzz of men's talk created a pocket around them, Luwanna felt as if they were breathing special air, air that a man would have to learn to breathe if he were to violate the charmed circle and sit next to them. Luwanna thought all this in a second and was alarmed at the busyness of her mind. Luwanna wondered what, if anything, Nadine was thinking as she rattled on retelling a story from the car trip.

Nadine lit herself a cigarette, the bargirl sullenly shoving an ashtray at her, and remarked that some music would be nice. Luwanna went to the jukebox. The selection was mostly country-western, with a few Spanish titles penciled in for the harvests. She punched out three of Nadine's favorites and turned to the bar. Nadine was flanked by two blondish, grinning men in cowboy boots. Luwanna returned and sat beside the one that wasn't as good-looking. Nadine introduced the better-looking one as A. C. and the one by Luwanna as Knox and said that they were baseball players. Luwanna felt Knox give her a quick checkover but couldn't read his verdict. They both smiled and squinted and the Knox one wasn't that much worse-looking, though Luwanna noticed a lot of his fingers were crooked. The men bought drinks.

The men bought drinks and Nadine put hers away like it was soda pop because she was nervous or thirsty but Luwanna didn't want to warn her in front of the men. The men bought more drinks. They speculated whether the bargirl was George the Owner's wife or sister and whether she was the Lucky Lady the bar was named for. "If it wunt for bad luck," said A. C., "she wunt have no luck a-tall," and they laughed. Nadine threw her head back and did her high tinkling laugh and Luwanna saw that the A. C. one kept his eyes on her breasts all the while. Nadine had little pointy breasts, cheerleader breasts, and you could see them down the tank top almost to the nipple when she moved her shoulders a certain way. A. C. said that the bargirl was probly George the Owner's brother and this time Luwanna noticed that Knox too was waiting for Nadine to laugh and move her shoulders that certain way. Nadine always wore a bra in the office but tonight had said oh fooey, it's our vacation isn't it?

and gone without. Luwanna tried not to laugh too hard because bra or no bra her big breasts always wobbled when she laughed and she wasn't sure if it made them look good or just droopy. Luwanna was all tearshapes, tearshaped brown eyes in a large tearshaped face, low-slung tearshaped breasts and a torso that floated out at the hips. In the mirror she saw herself studying her features and the blond men studying Nadine. She tried to think of something clever to say. The men bought drinks.

I lost my prudence, I lost my pride, sang a husky-voiced woman from the jukebox, and then I lost my man.

The men bought drinks and Luwanna began to feel good even if she was on the outskirts of the conversation. All you really had to do was be cheery and laugh at their jokes, and their jokes seemed to be getting funnier even when she couldn't understand them. Knox and A. C. played catch telling wild stories about each other, with Nadine as the monkey in the middle. Knox told of how when A. C. went to his first prom he just barely saved up enough to rent a tuxedo but discovered at the last minute he didn't have any colored socks and ended up going in gym socks with laundry marker spots on them. "A. C. int just country," said Knox, "he's downright *rural*," and Luwanna laughed her natural deep laugh and just didn't give a hoot whether her boobies wobbled around or not. She caught Knox looking at her thighs and realized her dress was crawling up toward her hips and was glad she hadn't worn pants like Nadine. The men had a friendly argument over which of them was poorest when they were young and decided to settle it by arm wrestling. A. C. had to come over by Luwanna for this and she thought he looked her over but wasn't sure. The men's arms trembled and bulged and the veins stood out and the matching bulldog tattoos shook and the men grinned and laughed and made joking insults about when are you gonna start trying? through their gritted teeth but neither had won when George the Owner came over and reminded them they weren't in a gym. So they slapped each other on the back and said nice going pardner and bought drinks.

Then there was a lot of throat-clearing and when Lu-

221

wanna swiveled around standing there was a miniature little man, just as cute as could be. He was with a little red-headed boy who was cute too and they must have been sitting out of sight in a booth all this time because whenever someone new came in everybody in the place turned to look and Luwanna was sure she couldn't have missed a midget with a cigar. Luwanna moved down a couple stools to make room and Denzel Ray hopped up but the midget didn't seem to be able to make it. He tried several different approaches, even took a little running start, but he just couldn't make it, it was like he couldn't get any push from his legs. Other men in the bar were looking now and making like they were betting on if he would make it this time or not so Luwanna was sorry for him and offered out her hand. He wouldn't take it and tried one more time and winced a little when he hit the ground and then said fuck it, I got business to attend to and started to leave. Knox and A. C. said something about monkey business and about Venus's arms and winked in that sort of sly way that men do and the little man turned and made an impolite hand gesture at the door. Luwanna wondered if the man had a little girlfriend somewhere who he was going to visit in such a nasty mood. She moved back down a stool next to Denzel Ray who was the batboy and very polite. Knox ordered a ginger ale for the boy and George the Owner's sister or brother or mother or whatever she was gave them all a dirty look. Nadine asked about the midget and A. C. said he's a piece of work, aint he? and explained how the baseball team sort of kept him around for comical relief. Denzel Ray piped up and said he wasn't a clown he was a shortstop and they all laughed because he said it so serious.

The men bought drinks and Nadine decided it was time for some more music and even got up to go to the jukebox herself. Luwanna figured she must be drunk enough so she wasn't nervous anymore and also wanted a chance for everybody to see her walk across the room. Luwanna was the tiniest bit ashamed of herself for laughing with the men when they saw the big sweat marks Nadine had on her rear from sitting on the stool. The first song from the jukebox was some slow ballad by a girl singer that Luwanna couldn't catch the words to but she and Knox and A. C. and Nadine got up and danced and Luwanna wondered if her bottom was sweaty too but she really didn't care. Dancing was nice even though Knox was a little shorter than her and kind of clumsy. She thought he kissed her neck at one point but wasn't sure. Knox tipped over someone's drink at a table and apologized nicely but when they got back George the Owner said this isn't a square dance barn you know and that Denzel Ray shouldn't be sitting at the bar. So A. C. said I guess we can take a hint can't we pardner? and Knox suggested they all go somewhere else. They were all standing up and ready to leave for this other place the men knew about when Nadine said she was sweating like a colored person and wanted to change back at the motel. The men said it was just fine with them and that maybe Denzel Ray ought to stay here and wait for his father. Luwanna asked if it was a good idea leaving a little boy in a bar and Knox said what the hell it's his birthday. At that Nadine oohed and aahed a little, smiling and showing her teeth that were now all stained with lipstick so that her smile looked like it was painted on her face and she gave Denzel Ray a sticky little peck on the cheek that made him flinch. Luwanna gave him a big hug and caught her own breath coming back off him, a great sweet gust of warm wine and peanuts and she felt the boy nestle his head for a moment in the pillow that her breasts made and when she let him go he was blushing a little and the men were kidding him. Knox bought him another ginger ale and suggested they pick up a bottle of something on the way to the motel. Luwanna got a last glimpse of herself in the mirror as they were leaving and she saw she looked as she always did, some big barnyard animal afraid of being left in the rain, and she was disappointed because she didn't feel that way at all.

The men shucked the paper from the motel glasses and poured drinks. Nadine forgot about changing and turned on the radio and they all danced some more. Luwanna was sure that Knox was kissing her neck this time. They weren't dancing very fast but the room was and when she saw A. C. and

Nadine go by they were against the wall and their feet weren't moving. It looked like they were still dancing that way when the music stopped and the disc jockey came on but they were making sounds like the men had when they arm wrestled. Finally they were apart and Nadine's mouth looked like it was bleeding even though it was only the lipstick and hadn't Luwanna told her a hundred times she used too much? They had more drinks and when A. C. took Nadine to dance again she excused herself saying she had a headache and felt sick and had to lie down and then she shut herself in the bathroom like she always did. At the end of the next song Luwanna found herself in the bedroom with Knox kissing more than her neck. Somehow the door got shut and the lights went off and Knox was telling her she was beautiful and she almost felt that way lying back on the bed. Knox said some other things but they got muffled in her breasts so she listened harder. Outside she heard someone banging on a door and it was A. C. yelling Nadine? Nadine? then some swearing and Luwanna felt good under Knox, kind of numb and tingly at the same time and then A. C.'s voice was just outside their door.

"Knox buddy? Pardner?" he said. "Don't you take all night in there now. Remember, I'm on deck."

8

The night was not nearly over and George the Owner was nervous. It didn't take much to get George nervous and tonight there was more than enough. He could tell right away when the cowboys and the dwarf and the kid walked in that it was going to be bad news. He had nothing against dwarfs that he knew of and the kid was all right as long as he stayed in the booth but cowboys were always trouble. They were almost as bad as the goddam bikers. He said to Dot the minute they came in to keep an eye on the cowboys and while she was at it to watch for the dwarf too. The more he thought about it, the less sure George was about dwarfs. He wondered if they didn't have special bars they were supposed to go to, like the special fag joints he had seen in Miami.

Then a couple of loose ones wandered in, which was always good for business, and George thought maybe things were looking up. But the cowboys roped them right away and all the interest died down. It was all right when they were just pumping drinks into the girls but then they started roughhousing and backslapping and then the four of them got out and danced like they were in the goddam Grange Hall. Plus they had the kid sitting up at the bar which is another black mark with Sheriff if he decides to make an appearance.

So George had to put his foot down and they left which wasn't good for business and made him look like a wet blanket and he got a little more nervous. Then he saw that they left the kid behind which got him even more nervous than he was and it was only nine-thirty. Goddam cowboys were always trouble. The kid said he was waiting for his father and Dot said if those were his friends then his father must be the tattooed man, without even lowering her voice. Dot does not exactly have a way with children thought George and told the kid to sit in the booth till his father came.

The kid's father turned out to be this long drink of water who came in with a red-faced guy who's all hot and bothered about something. Red Face smelled like chemicals, like the chemicals George threw down the conveniences every morning so they wouldn't smell like beer vomit. Goddam bag broke again, and the big one says how he shouldn't of jammed it in so hard. Jammed my ass said Red Face, trust a nigger to sell you a goddam defective bag. George wanted to hang close and hear if the girl got knocked up or not but the place was already swarming and it was only ten o'clock.

Then as if George didn't have enough on his hands, five or six tough-looking little beans come strutting in with their shortsleeve Ban-lon shirts and tight pants and plunk themselves down at the corner booth. Oh Christ, said Dot in that voice of hers that was almost loud enough for the whole room to hear, it's the Marijuana Brass. Dot is not the most tactful woman around thought George as he went to take their round, praying they hadn't heard. George had nothing against beans if they drank a lot which was good for business and if they minded their p's and q's. But they did have their own place down by the gasworks. George thought maybe this bunch might be pickers who were new to town and would appreciate directions as to where their own kind hung out. On the other hand they might have come uptown just to carve some white meat and were waiting for any excuse. So George just took the order for beers all around from the

226

leader while the rest stared at the few women in the room in that scowling way of theirs.

By ten-thirty George was on the verge of a breakdown, his usual reaction to having to hustle his big butt faster than it was meant to be hustled. The greasers were sitting on their beers and scowling, high school kids were trying to get served underage, Dot was being salty with the customers which wasn't good for business and Red Face was grumbling in his whiskey about the good old days before the Lucky Lady turned into a taco stand. Red Face grumbled even louder than Dot and George prayed that the beans didn't habla American. And just for atmosphere some fat old girl was draped over the jukebox feeding it to play the same song over and over and over. Does your moonshine turn to acid, it asked, in the Mason jar at night?

George caught sight of the red-headed kid standing by his father and suddenly remembered he hadn't seen the other one leave with the cowboys. He didn't like it, it made him nervous. The next time he squeezed past Dot he told her to keep her eyes peeled as there was a dwarf loose on the premises. Dot looked at him funny and told him there was sure something loose somewhere, which he didn't appreciate at all. George was mentally counting the years till his retirement when the hump that broke the camel's pecker strolled in.

The spic looked like Rudolph Valentino rose-from-the-grave, sideburns that wouldn't quit and a lime green outfit that any self-respecting pimp wouldn't be caught dead in. He was steering around this blond in a red dress. The red dress seemed intent on creeping up over her little cupcake cheeks. George joined the rest of the bar in watching her sit down. There was a massive insucking of air. You could see through her panties. You could see through her goddam panties. Eat your old hearts out said the little cupcake cheeks as they flashed and then disappeared on the stool. The talk-buzz recovered a little and the beans in the corner signaled for another round to celebrate the victory of their countryman. Dot left through the back and George asked the powers above why the blond had to pick Red Face to sit next to.

227

First Red Face stared into the enormous pile of shiny gold hair that topped her off, stared as if he had lost something in it. Wonder if the roots are black, he grumbled. George stationed himself so he could both hear and be out of the way if trouble started. Sure thing that something's black around here said Red Face, but not really loud enough to pull her attention from herself in the bar mirror. The spic leaned back against the countertop on the other side of her and surveyed the room with a slight smile. One of his hands played with a silver religious medal around his neck and the other rested at the top of the blond girl's thigh.

Red Face took a deep breath and drained his whiskey. George was very nervous. Red Face took another deep breath. There was a time in this town, he said to anyone within a mile radius who might be interested, when they kept the whores down by the gasworks. George groaned and there was another massive insucking of air. The spic and Red Face stared at each other for a long minute. Can it eat through tooth enamel, squealed the box, can it make you lose your sight? Does your moonshine turn to acid in the Mason jar at night?

The spic asked Red Face what he had said and Red Face answered that he was having a private conversation and the spic said he should watch his mouth and Red Face said the day he took advice from any piss-ant of a greaseball was the day he'd ice skate in Hell. George was hustling bottles off the counter and the spic was on the floor with the girl screaming over him and the beans swarming out of the corner into the fight they had been waiting for and it was still only ten of eleven. The high school kids wandered at the edge of the swinging to get credit for being in a brawl without getting hit and the fat girl at the jukebox joined the screaming without turning around to see what the excitement was and the big one tore out a barstool and cleared a path through them all, swinging it in a wide arc with the kid hanging on to his belt with both hands, batting his way to the door where Sheriff and two deputies were blowing whistles and George thought oh shit, another black mark with the law. A little fight, three

228

wild punches and a bloody nose, was fine, was good for business, but when there was greasers and cutting involved it got George nervous.

The police got Red Face untangled from the beans and the spic untangled from his chippie and started checking ID's on the high school kids and just generally weeded out the population of the room. When they left Sheriff said he'd see George Monday morning and that it was a good thing Dot called when she did or somebody'd of been hurt.

Then Dot came in and said how she knew that bitch would cause trouble the minute she laid eyes on her so she took some action while George just sat on his fat ass letting things fall apart. It was true Dot could think fast sometimes but she had a tendency to rub things in which was enough to make anybody nervous.

9

The brown end of the stick again, thought Buzzy. Sheriff tells me to take the boy to his people.

Meanwhile Sheriff is taking the boy's people and slamming them in the joint. Typical for Sheriff.

Buzzy asked the boy if he had a mother.

The boy answered somewheres. Buzzy wondered if he was being sassed.

George the Owner said he come in with a couple cowboys.

The boy said he didn't know where they were at by now.

Buzzy wished Sheriff had just kept the boy with his father, let him sleep in the joint. But Sheriff had said a jail was no place for a little boy, a jail was not a barroom. That was for George's benefit.

"There's Pogo," said the boy. "I think I know where Pogo's at."

Buzzy asked him where and the boy said at the Venus de Milo Arms. Buzzy asked if the boy were being sassy with him but George just shrugged and said that sounded like a good place to start looking.

"They're a regular three-ring circus," said George.

On the way Buzzy spotted three vags and a D&D but decided to wait till he unloaded the boy. Sheriff got his officers playing babysitter. Typical.

"Hi depitty," said Mama Moon making an innocent face, "how *are* you? I know it's not business cause we're *all* paid up so this *must* be a social call. Your friend is a bit too young though. House rules?"

Buzzy hated to be sassed.

"Pogo Burns?" said Mama Moon making a thinking face, "Pogo Burns? I'm sorry, honey, but I just have a *ter*rible memry for names."

But you never forget a cock, thought Buzzy.

"Could you give me inny idee what your ginnleman friend looks like?"

"He smokes cigars," said the boy, "he wears nice shoes. He's kind of short."

"Short?" said Mama Moon. "You don't mean the midget, do you honey?"

"Midget?" said Buzzy.

"Why he's *gone*, now, depitty. We had a little problem?"

"Let's have it," said Buzzy.

"Oh, nothing serious. You know that statue of Cupid on the lawn?"

"Next to the nekkid one."

"That's the Venus de Milo."

"Go on."

"Well, a few of the girls were fooling around, you know how it is depitty, and they sort of took your ginnleman friend's — uh — clothes? All in good fun of course, my girls are not ma*lic*ious at heart."

Girl scouts one and all.

"Well he was — up*set*? when he discovered them missing. Mr. — Burns was it? Mr. Burns did not see the humor in the situation and went tearing about the house with only his shoes on, disturbing our other visitors and making *very* disagreeable threats."

Mama Moon made a shocked face. "He mintioned a *gun*, depitty, but nothing come of that. Don't allow such things inside. House rules? Well part of the problem was he couldn't get back upstairs though I can't imagine why not. They're not at all steep. He thought we had the clothes hidden somewhere up the stairs but he couldn't climb them and wouldn't believe us when we told him they weren't up there. That's when this gun conversation came to light.

"By now the girls were all bunched at the top of the stairs giggling and so were a few of our ginnlemen visitors who had come out to investigate the disturbance. He *did* make quite a sight but all the attention seemed to upset him even more. He couldn't come up and he wouldn't let any of us down. His back was turned and it sounded almost like he was crying but the moment anyone took a step down he'd go on about how he had a gun and would shoot us all, would 'take us all with him' he said. Very un*reas*onable behavior. I don't think he'll be invited back.

"And then when he saw his clothes outside on the Cupid he just flew off the handle."

"His clothes?"

"The girls had dressed the Cupid in them, depitty, they were a perfect fit. All in good fun of course. Well he cursed and cried and referred to this gun again though Lord knows he had no place to hide it on his person and then he made his way out to get his clothes." Mama Moon shrugged. "That's the last I saw of him, depitty."

Buzzy would have like to close the old bitch down years ago but she had an agreement with Sheriff. Trash will be trash thought Buzzy and left with the boy.

On the lawn he noticed a sock dangling from Cupid's notched arrow.

The boy said the bunch of them were operating out of a trailer camp outside of Samson. The Ponce de Leon. Buzzy called in and got the go-ahead to drive him there and put it on the wire about there being an armed and disturbed midget at bay in the area. Buzzy kept the radio open so he could hear all the action he was missing.

Bikers revving up on Dogwood. Lady called in.

Girl screaming on Lochobee. Lady called in.

Punch and Judy on Titus. Probably the Franklyns fighting over her paycheck.

Cockfight broken up behind gasworks. Somebody forgot to clear it with Sheriff.

Girl not home from dance yet. Lady called in.

The people were hot and bored and tired from the week. Husbands and wives clawed at each other, children shot at their mother's boyfriends, high school punks pestered women in front of the movie house. And Buzzy was chauffeuring a trailer brat.

The boy did not seem too worried about his father being in jail. He seemed to enjoy the ride in the police car, checking out the equipment and listening to the radio calls. He told Buzzy it was his birthday. He asked if he could see Buzzy's gun. Buzzy told him a gun was not a toy.

There was a cutting down by the gasworks. Man attacked his wife and his brother.

The van he left the boy at looked like a cathouse on wheels. Brooklyn Bimbos, it said. Show people, he thought, typical.

10

Now and then he would break into a limping trot, his shod foot on the pavement and his bare one in the dust of the shoulder. His eyes had grown accustomed to the dark.

He came to a sign studded with reflectors. PONCE DE LEON TRAILER CAMP. VACANCIES.

It didn't matter to him anymore about getting away. If he did, he did. But he wanted the midget. If the rest of them were there too they would all go together. He was in that far.

A smooth, newly laid blacktop drive disappeared with a twist into the jungle. To the left of it, in the direction of the twist, the trees glowed with light that did not come from the moon. Dred walked silently almost to the bend when the shadowy creepers brightened into sudden color and he heard an engine. Headlights. He hopped off behind some scrub until the lights swept past. Got to use the back door.

He guessed that the road doglegged into the camp, and began to cut through the brush. Prickers attached, stretched, tore and sprang back. Brambles and stump-stubble needled the bottom of his bare foot and branches crackled at his passing. He freed himself into a sort of clearing of chest-high grass, like an African savanna. At the far end of it were the nightlights of the trailer camp. He had them flanked.

Dred stooped so only his head bobbed above the grass, taking long sliding chickenthief steps on the balls of his toes. Once his hand closed around a clump of something cold on one of the grass stalks and it slithered from under his touch. Wings beat over his head as some hunter bird made a scouting dive at him. Bugs tickled and explored his body and he had to swat what felt like a tiny lizard clinging to his neck. The grass whispered about him and then shushed when his bare foot tromped a burr and he almost cried out. The lights of the white people's camp grew. He came to the edge of the clearing. Directly before him was a stinking ditch, maybe six feet across, and a little concrete hut built into the ground. Shithouse. Beyond that he could see the beginnings of the lot, a half-dozen pastel campers, and, parked at the base of a steaming, moth-dappled arclight, an obscene-looking thing that said BROOKLYN BIMBOS BASEBALL CLUB, INC. Got you, peckerwood.

He would duck into the shithouse first, check on any movement in the lot, then creep up in the shadow of the other trailers. The midget would be alone, ready for bed, naked. If he wasn't alone whoever was with him man woman or child would take the trip too. But there wouldn't be, it was a straight line now, straight from Dred to the white man. Nothing could wedge between.

Dred caught his breath and eased himself a little lower into the grass. Someone was coming toward him, making as if to pass right by the shithouse and come into the field. The safety was off, Dred held the gun up under his chin, ready. Whoever it was coming was backlit, shadowed featureless and haloed with arclight. It was a low silhouette, it came forward with a rolling, bent-legged walk. A midget walk. Keep coming baby. Come to Papa. Dred crouched with all his tension focused into the wrist and business finger of his gun hand, crouched as the figure started across the ditch. The features began to take shape. It was stubble-chinned, it was big-lipped and flat-nosed. Arms hanging to its knees, bulging little legs. It was black.

Black and hairy.

The gun ached for release in his hand but he held off. The monkey was wearing a safari jacket and sharp-looking two-tone shoes. It walked to where Dred crouched in the grass and looked up at him with liquid brown eyes. It extended its hand to shake.

"Fuck off monkey!" Dred hissed. "Go way!"

The monkey waited, pink palm held up.

"You get or I'm gonna shoot your ass!"

It waited, stone still, and Dred began to quiver a little. Getting cold out. The monkey looked up at him, patient, unblinking. Dred shifted the gun to his left hand, looked around, and gave the monkey's paw a quick embarrassed pump. Then it smiled at him, two rows of big teeth and gums glowing electric blue in the faint moonlight, and patted him on the knee. It turned and rolled back across the ditch, past the shithouse, and went to one of the pastel campers. It knocked on the door, a crack appeared and it was gone.

There was something in Dred's mind that had to be dealt with. Legs aching? He seemed to have strained every muscle in them running through the muck. No, something else. He was cold and scratched and bug-eaten, crusted with mud and sweat, one arm throbbing with a patch of proud skin from scalding and the other pig-bit, one shoe on and one shoe gone and gofuck if he hadn't finally taken that piss in his pants on the way into the ditch. It was something more than all that, it was something more than even the bwana monkey or killer hogs or old Orison taken with religion, more than the Black Hollow people all upped and vanished or that Bugbear or the whole fucking *place*, the South, more even than the possibility that he'd been run off the road by a ghost-thing, an old nigger in a straw hat driving a mulecart full of watermelons. What was at his mind was something funny, a picture. The picture showed some crazy African crouching mustard yellow in a trailer-camp jungle, creeping in to murder some freak in woman's clothes and a baseball bat, some whiteman pygmy.

It escaped from him slowly at first, snik, snik, snik, squeezed and distorted from the effort of holding it back, but the pressure built up and it wrenched through his throat from the pit of him, his mouth bunching as if to smile and then twisting into a grimace. It was a hyena laugh, loud and high and on the very edge of hysteria. It fed on itself and he dropped to his knees, the gun fell, tears streaming, his chest sucking, hurting from the laugh. It jerked out from him, bringing him forward on his hands, shivered through him in spasms and left him weak. He caught his breath as best he could, coughing out little laughing gasps and scooped up the gun. He wheeled around and stumbled back through the grass, snik-ing again and then giggling and then lifting a long animal hoot as he ran. He slowed briefly once to kick off the remaining heavy shoe, and then crashed back into the trees heading for the road.

When he got back to it, weak and wheezing, his car had been pulled out of the ditch and onto the shoulder. His flashlight found tracks of a wagon wheel. And on the hood of the car there lay a shining green blimp.

The flashlight spot made a target on its side, there was a crack and wet hunks of melon went whipping through the bush.

The radiator would be better at night. Dred stood at the side of the road, wondering which direction he wanted to go.

11

Here's to the winos of Pittsburgh P-A.
They drink Iron City when they have their pay.
If they're on relief then they drink muscatel,
And know it aint death makes a man live in hell.

Pogo's deep voice resounded loudly in the stall. The deep voice that he had trained lower and lower as a boy, forcing it downward till he was hoarse. At least he would not sound like a chipmunk, not sound like a record played too fast like the other ones he had seen. At least he would sound like a man.

The winos of Harlem, that center of sin,
They drink Gallo half-pints and unlabeled gin.
They sleep in the halls every night and they pray
That dope-fiends or rats do not cart them away.

Pogo belted out the Wino's Anthem, the old street song croaked to the tune of Sweet Betsy from Pike. He sat on the can, under the sign the wise-ass Okie had squirted, and took a pull at his bottle of Rebel Yell. A long, sour-faced pull. Had the nerve to call it bourbon. Label ought to have a horse dead from kidney infection on it.

He moved to put the bottle on the floor but the floor rushed up a little fast and he spilled some. Bad hands. Always had bad hands, always. Some shortstop. Fields grounders like he's killing a snake, beating them into the ground and then picking them up. Some sad, bad hands.

The Old Man was the one with the hands. The shortstop. The machinist. The two pictures he ever kept of himself were the shortstop one, the one signed "To The Scrapper, from the Boys," with the Old Man evil-eyeing the camera in his Schenectady Blue Jays' uniform, and the group picture of the guys in his shop where he broke in at the GE. Kept the pictures but lost both the jobs. Good hands and a bad temper, that was the book on the Old Man. Too much pride to take orders from anybody. If there is such a thing as too much pride in a man.

Out West, the Old Man had said, they don't drag you down for that kind of chickenshit. Out West they're still free. The Old Man had never been west of Buffalo, but knew it was different. He went after it.

> Here's to the winos of eastern L.A.
> They drink their cerveza the Mehican way.
> They drink cheap tecquila from rotten maguey.
> The Chicano winos of eastern L.A.

Pogo noticed he was missing a sock and swore. He very carefully reached down to feel his ankle and be sure it wasn't there. He tried not to lean over because when he did the floor started threatening to come up and get him. He very carefully watched his hand float out and wrap tightly around the bottle neck. He drank. To fatherhood.

There were bosses from New York to California. The Old Man went through almost every state in between. He would land a job and see where the chickenshit was coming from and then push it till it boiled over and he was canned. If the boss wasn't around enough then a foreman would do. Pogo and the Old Lady got to know when it had happened by the look on his face when he came in, pissed and pleased and

239

still full of fight. Another kick in the balls, he would say. It was his favorite expression. He believed that everybody, everything was out to cut him down, to chain him up. Everything was an insult challenging him. Including the birth of his only child.

Pogo was another kick in the balls to the Old Man.

Here's to the people who give us their change,
They think if we touch they'll come down with the mange.
We beg and we bully, we cry and we gag
For one quart of joy in a brown paper bag.

Paint thinner does nicely if you're out of luck,
You cut it with grape juice and call it Cold Duck.
Burns holes in your guts but you don't give a fuck,
Erases your memry for one half a buck.

Pogo stood carefully and pulled his pants down, then plopped back on the seat to take a leak. He drank. He pissed. Fill it and tap it at the same time. Never get anywhere that way. It's a losing game, pal. He drank. To childhood. To motherhood.

At first the Irish kids let him hang with them for the novelty, for the prestige of it. It was like having a guy with TB in your bunch, or a guy who had come back from a reformatory. The gang with the midget. He was like a mascot. If they were trespassing down by the wharf and some guinea laughed or made a remark about him, he was an excuse to start a scrap over. To uphold the honor of the gang. But Pogo was a little too sharp for that, too good a dirty, surprising fighter. He knew how to plan things, how to make trouble for others and keep out of it himself, how to use his head for something more than a punching bag. Pretty soon it was the midget's gang. Who, Tommy Flynn? He runs with the midget's gang. Oh yeah, better not mess with him, you'll be up to your ears in it.

When he wasn't with the guys he was studying the street, learning all the angles. Got to learn how to make the bigshots, the bosses, work against themselves, trip over their own feet. You can't go straight at them or you get your skull busted.

He was a regular at Indian Joe's News Room. He read the magazines and watched the action flow through. The players would come over and rub his head for luck. There was a cash register that faced the window at Indian Joe's, an extra one. When the day's number came in Joe would ring it up as a sale, so the nickel bettors could just pass by and see if they hit without cluttering up the place asking. Sometimes one of the horseplayers, one of the head rubbers, who fell into a pot would give a fiver to Pogo. To keep the luck working.

He was out of school as much as he was in and the Old Lady knew all the truancy people by their first names. The Old Lady was one enormous lap, and if she had her way she would have never let Pogo off it. Always with the teachers, with the doctors, with everybody who wanted to drag him down. Take your medicine, Pogo, take your medicine like a big man. She worried herself gray over him but he could do no wrong in her eyes. That kind of love didn't count for much. The Old Lady would have loved a pound of hamburger if she had given birth to it.

The Old Man played the horses once in a while and always lost. Longshots, always with the longshots. Another kick in the balls, he would say when the sheet came in.

If the Old Man saw Pogo at Indian Joe's or on the street he would nod hullo and pass by.

Oh, but the scraps, the times they had. The midget's gang. Pauly Boylan, Slats Minogue, Matt McGinnis, crazy Marty Quill, and leave us not forget the immortal Douchebag O'Donnell. The scraps, the times, the fun they had together. The legends they made of each other.

Here's to the winos who sleep in the park.
Who try to avoid every flatfoot and narc.
Who puke in the pathways, and just for a lark,
Blow faggots for quarters when it's after dark.

Here's to the winos who freeze on the street.
They gladly bequeath us the shoes off their feet.

They won't need their overcoats after they're gone,
If they aint quite dead yet, we help em along.

Pogo saw that he had skinned his knuckles where he had
punched the marble. Typical, pick on something that can't
fight back. And that you can't beat. He heard a cry from
outside, a long crazy animal hoot. He answered it.

Here's to the winos all over the world,
Who out of low dives every evening are hurled.
Who sleep under bridges whenever it rains,
And do what they can to make mush of their brains.

Pogo knew the knuckles should feel pain and tried to sum-
mon some up. When it came it came fast and was not in his
knuckles. A little painkiller, doc. He drank. To maidenhood.

The girls broke it up. The gang life wasn't so appealing.
Pogo either gave them the willies or made them think he was
cute. Like a puppy dog cute. The guys went with girls and
wondered if there was going to be a war.

Pogo went out on his own. Door-to-door peddler, day-old-
fish hawker, bloodsucker loans, nigger insurance, always
with an angle but always in the real world, a real job. Finally
the private dick. Always reaching for what the real world had
to offer, reaching for the top shelf. Pogo Burns was no circus
clown like Warts Moynihan. Warts with his little wife, his
little house, his little furniture like toys that kids play with,
his little life in his little world. Make pretend. That wasn't
living, it was Munchkinland. If something is too high for you,
you climb it, you don't have a copy made to your size. You
got to have some balls.

Balls. Don't stay put, don't sit moping over the hand you
been dealt. Got to reach out for more than you're supposed
to, jump off the lap and go one step beyond the line. That's
how we got to America, and how America got to the Coast.
Reach out and take it. It's how you end up anywhere in life.
It's how you end up in a fucking toilet stall with a bottle of
Southern Horsepiss for company.

FRIDAY

Here's to the wino that I've come to be,
And here's to the vermin that crawl upon me,
The maggots play football, a snake referees,
Half are the real thing and half are D.T.'s.

The legs were hurting now. The legs had always hurt, it was something he lived with. But lately it was spreading, the hips, the spine. It hurt to bend after a game.

Pogo reached under his shirt and pulled it out. It was uncomfortable stuffed in there. He laid it on the floor next to the bottle and stared at it for a while. Faithful companion. One-way ticket. He drank. To a long life.

The Old Man wouldn't join the union. When did I ever need anybody, he asked, to do my fighting for me? What do I need with dues and meetings, with another set of ballbusters to try and boss me? There were threats and a few minor scuffles, but they only made him firmer. He didn't like the way it had just showed up out of the blue and said it was moving in. It hadn't asked him if he wanted it. He wouldn't join it and he had enough time at the shop so they couldn't get him fired.

They found him down by the Bay, left for dead. There was a wrench by him, sticky with blood.

When he was brought home in a chair his head was shaved and there was a plate in his skull. He couldn't talk though you could tell he was awake and thinking. He was paralyzed but for his right hand. The fingers could move a little. His body rejected the plate and it had to be removed. There was a dent left in the right side of his skull, and if you felt it there was nothing over the brain but flesh. It was soft, like a bruise on a hard apple.

Mostly the Old Man scowled and followed them around the room with his eyes. Sometimes he would focus somewhere out in space and his face and right hand would go rigid and you could tell he was remembering something, hating someone. He was pure rage, bottled and bonded.

And the Old Lady had never been happier with him. She puttered around and changed his clothes and cleaned his messes, prattling all the while, telling him little stories and

243

gossip, wiping his chin while she fed him. Eat your food, she would say. Come on, eat your food like a good boy. Sometimes he could manage to spit some back at her. Pogo was working then, and tried to stay away.

One day Pogo was left alone with him. The Old Man caught his eyes and then looked down to his right hand, the one that still worked a little. The fingers were moving like they were writing something. Pogo got a pad and a pencil. The Old Man's fingers wrapped around the pencil and Pogo held the pad steady. He wrote hard and shakily, almost tearing the paper, but you could read it.

Kill me.

There was a gun in the Old Man's closet. On the top shelf under his work clothes, and the Old Lady was afraid to touch it. He had gotten it when the threats from the union people started.

Pogo faced the Old Man with the gun. The Old Man looked him straight in the eye. Not a speck of fear. And Pogo let him down. Another kick in the balls.

The Old Man crushed the pencil in his fingers, the pieces falling away, and tightened his right hand into a fist. So it matched the other one. And they stayed that way from then on, frozen into fists. Those good hands. The Old Man never looked at Pogo again, never looked at him till he left. The Old Man was still alive, in a home somewhere, last Pogo had heard.

If he had had any balls he would have killed the Old Man. He had never had any, never.

He had looked down the hole before, but never jumped.

He'd had the sickness for over forty years and never took the pill.

He'd been on the edge many times, so many times before, but never took the last step.

Once he had bought a bus ticket for a girl and shot an unarmed man. No balls there. He had been ready that time, ready for it to come. If only the other one had had a piece, if only they could have gone out right there in the barroom like men, blasting away in a white heat.

There wasn't a decent life left for a man to reach for. There wasn't a decent death left for a man to face. It was what happened when you reached California and there was no place left to go.

So you hang on, suck the bottom of the glass. There had been that kid in Frisco with most of his face burned off, begging for someone to let him out of it. He was only a kid, didn't know that you can't ask favors. You're born on your own and that's the way you go.

Pogo killed the bottle. The last verse was coming up. He stood and pulled up his pants, zipped his fly, then sat. He stood to flush the toilet and sat again. He picked it up off the floor so he could look down the hole.

Here's to my death, may it hurry its ass,
Straight from the bottle, to hell with a glass.
A newspaper blanket, my fist for a wife,
I'll die in the gutter where I've spent my life.

Take your medicine, Pogo, like a big man.

Saturday

1

The weekend was not going well for Sheriff. He was a man who didn't like waves, a believer in peaceful coexistence, a smoother-out of difficulties. Sheriff's face had all the necessary features but it was hard to say where one began and the other left off. He had no chin, his face melting directly into his wide neck, his neck into his chest and his chest into his large, smooth belly. Sheriff moved as if his only goal in life was to avoid exertion, he composed his face to keep it wrinkle-free. He wore moccasins to work. But these entertainers, these gypsies, were enough to make Sheriff break a sweat.

Sheriff had let the two out this morning on their own recognizance as there was no great public concern over assaulting fruit-pickers in bars. Just as long as no one got hurt. Sheriff told them they would be fined thirty dollars apiece in court Monday morning and if they were smart that was the last he'd see of them.

But it was Saturday morning, Sheriff looking forward to a pleasant day at the carnival locating missing children, and here they were again. Furman Donicker was ranting and raving and just about pissing blood, waving an advertising flier and a contract and the team manager, the one who had started the disturbance in the Lucky Lady, was ranting and raving and pointing out clauses in his copy of the contract while Buzzy was there straining at the leash saying we ought to lock them back up and throw away the key. Buzzy was always one to wake up sleeping dogs. The only one acting sanely was the other barfighter, the big one. The big one stood looking from face to face nodding as if considering each viewpoint and weighing it carefully.

Sheriff looked down at his moccasins, which was his signal to talk, and waited. The arguing died down. "The situation," said Sheriff in his soft, smooth voice, "seems to be a very simple one. Putting aside the small print of the contract, the fact remains that your midget is your star attraction and he has disappeared for the time being. Now I see three alternatives." Sheriff always saw three alternatives to any problem.

"Number one: The midget may return in time for the game, the team will play, and Mr. Donicker will receive his percentage.

"Number two: The midget will remain unaccounted for and there will be no game and nobody will make any money."

"But we arrest them for breaking contract!" said Buzzy and Furman Donicker echoed a damn straight.

"I don't believe that will be necessary. No money has been advanced or tickets sold. Nobody has been hurt. Disappearance of a midget might come under Acts of God in the contract, along with hurricanes and earthquakes."

Neither of the principals of the dispute looked encouraged by the first two alternatives. The team manager had given up on his star attraction and the carnival promoter had given up on his lawsuit.

"The third alternative is that a replacement for the midget or some other suitable attraction agreed upon by both parties be found. I think if you gentlemen would consider yourselves as partners in a business venture rather than competitors in a court of law it would help matters a great deal."

The team manager thought a moment and then said that he had a boy.

"I don't want him to," said the big one. "That's out."

"Boy?" said Furman Donicker, "What boy? What good's a boy gonna do me?"

"He can move just like the midget. We dress him up nobody knows the difference."

The big one shook his head slowly. "I don't want him dressed up. He doesn't need that."

"Listen," said the carnival promoter, "don't try to pawn no boy off on me. My customers smell a rat and I lose my good name."

"I suggest," sighed Sheriff, "we go have a talk with this boy."

On the way from the office to the team's camper van the manager and the big one had an argument. Sheriff listened casually and could tell the big one was backing down, not because he was wrong but because he was an employee. Sheriff felt sorry for him, but it was a difficult situation. Buzzy scooted up and began to bend Sheriff's ear about false advertising and child labor laws. Sheriff had to explain to Buzzy once again about the lesser of two evils and the precedence of order over law in many cases. Buzzy always lost his debates with Sheriff because Buzzy was always wrong.

In the van men were sitting in their underwear. There were two light-haired ones who looked like the morning after the night before and a pimply faced younger one. The boy, a little red-headed kid, was seated on top of a chair and three bases at a card table, playing solitaire.

"This here's Denzel Ray," said the manager.

"I'll believe it when I see it," said the carnival promoter.

Sheriff felt sorry for the boy. He hadn't been the cause of any of the trouble and here he'd have to pay the dues for it, which wasn't fair. But of course fair came second to solving the problem at hand. "Young man," said Sheriff, "we seem to have us a situation here and you're the only person who can help us."

"Do your midget walk," said the manager, "do your walk like Pogo."

The boy asked if Pogo wasn't coming back.

"Pogo done the vanishing act. You got to be our midget."
The boy looked to the big one, who just frowned.
"We got expenses," said the manager. "We got the advance man to pay, the printer to pay, the lot fee to pay, the trailer park to pay, the high school kids to pay, the license to pay, the fines from last night to pay, we got gas to buy if we're gonna make Frostproof by Monday night. We miss that booking and you can kiss it goodbye. That's the whole ball game."

"He don't look like any midget I ever seen," said Furman and Sheriff motioned him to hush.

The boy looked to his father and asked him if he had to do it. If he had to dress up.

"I guess so," said the big one. "Sometimes a man got to swallow his pride a little. There isn't any other way."

The boy said okay and the manager slapped him on the back and said that's the spirit and Sheriff thanked him for being cooperative. The promoter said he still didn't see no midget. So they plopped the boy in front of a mirror and started in with the powder and rouge and lipstick. All the time Sheriff could see the boy was fighting back tears, trying not to cry in front of all those men's faces that crowded around his in the mirror, trying to get through the initiation without ruining his mascara. The manager broke out the midget's bloomer costume and they put it on the boy, the manager saying all the while that it was a perfect fit. They all went outside and the boy put on the midget's baseball spikes which were also a perfect fit and he walked and ran a little just like a midget would until Furman Donicker shrugged and said he guessed that would do.

Some little children had gathered around the camper and were pointing and laughing and Sheriff had Buzzy shoo them away. The other men got dressed for the game.

Sheriff saw bits and pieces of the action during his afternoon rounds. The boy did fine, nobody was suspicious and they seemed to enjoy the show. Sheriff was a little proud of himself for solving everything so smoothly. It was all a matter of compromise, you give a little, the other guy gives a little and there's no big fuss. No one gets hurt. The carnival promoter knew it, the manager knew it, Mama Moon knew it, the fella who ran the labor camp knew it and all of Sheriff's people except Buzzy knew it. You learned to roll with the punches, nothing worth losing your head about.

Besides the heat and the lack of a breeze it was a lovely afternoon for Sheriff. He ate hot dogs and candy apples, had his picture taken with some children on one of the rides, located a wandering five-year-old and steered clear of the kootch show so as not to make the customers nervous. He went back to the ball diamond when the game was finishing up to oversee the crowd.

There was a little fight. Some children were teasing the boy on his way back to the van. He just stared through them for a while but finally took a poke at one of the bigger ones and was pushed down by the rest. A parent complained about the midget striking her child and Sheriff had to smooth things over. He went to the van to check on the boy, who had a little bit of a bloody nose. The boy was almost crying again but holding it back. Sheriff patted him on top of the Shirley Temple wig and said that he was a good little man. The boy was upset because some blood from his nose had splattered down on the midget's spikes.

"Nothing a little polish won't cover," said Sheriff. "He probably won't be needing them again anyhow."

He left the van and strolled through the carnival grounds. A little breeze was up and Sheriff looked forward to an evening helping lost children.

2

Denzel borrowed Pitcher's industrial soap to wash his face in the van sink. The men punched his shoulder and gave him manly pats on the butt for having done a good job and called him a ballsy little guy for being in the fight. They sat in their sweat, speculating on where Pogo had got to, waiting to shower at the trailer camp.

When Denzel flopped on his belly to crawl under the pay-toilet door he saw shoes in the next stall. Wingtips. One of Pogo's ankles was bare in the shoe.

"Pogo?" called Denzel. "You all right?"

Mr. Bob pounded on the door and shouted where the hell you been?

They all waited for him to strut out and flick his cigar butt and ask what all the racket was. He didn't answer. Mr. Bob had nothing but paper money so Denzel crawled under. Pogo's gun was in his lap and the writing behind him, where A. C. had written "King Pogo's Throne" in shaving cream, had been defaced

Sunday

1

By coincidence the preacher had been a sportswriter in Sarasota when he was younger. He peppered his eulogy with baseball phrases.

"Your name is Pogo Burns," he said, "and there is trouble in the late innings of life. You look to the long season ahead and wonder if you can go the distance."

The preacher always worried that his funeral orations depressed people.

The funeral director was worried because he was a worrying man. The midget was being buried in the last child's coffin he had on hand, a lovely alabaster box with ornate carvings and imitation gold handles. He had three drownings yesterday, boys swimming deep in Magnolia Lake on a dare, and then this midget business and it was only Sunday afternoon. It wouldn't do to have to inform grieving parents that there would be nothing available in the proper size till late in the week. The funeral director was also worried because the poor little man had been barefoot this morning when the lid was sealed. One of Emiliano's nine children would no doubt be wearing new shoes today. He made a mental note to find a new assistant.

"The zip is gone from your arm," said the preacher, "the

spring from your legs. You begin to wonder if it might not be time to hang up your spikes."

Sheriff was worried because a crowd was gathering and threatened to mar the peaceful ceremony. Somehow word had gotten around that a midget was being buried and they flocked on the knoll overlooking the site. There was pointing and whispering and a few solemn giggles.

"It's the bottom of the ninth. You've touched all the bases and you're heading Home. Home."

Mr. Bob was worried about making expenses after having to spring for the funeral. He was worried about making the next booking by tomorrow night.

Lewis was worried because finally there was no one left between him and the boy, and he didn't know how to handle it. Just didn't know.

The Okies were the pallbearers because they were most nearly the same height. Lewis held a wreath he had paid for out of his own money. Pitcher scowled into the hole.

"You come into this world with two strikes against you," said the preacher, "and when you leave it all you can hope for is that the men you leave behind will say, 'He was a good teammate.' "

Denzel was worried because he didn't want to leave Pogo there in the ground and because Frostproof seemed like too long a ride to take alone.